An Angel Remembered

A NOVEL BASED ON A TRUE STORY

Rosemary G. Ryan

WESTBOW
PRESS®
A DIVISION OF THOMAS NELSON
& ZONDERVAN

WestBow Press books may be ordered through booksellers or by contacting:

WestBow Press
A Division of Thomas Nelson & Zondervan
1663 Liberty Drive
Bloomington, IN 47403
www.westbowpress.com
1 (866) 928-1240

Because of the dynamic nature of the Internet, any web addresses or
links contained in this book may have changed since publication and
may no longer be valid. The views expressed in this work are solely those
of the author and do not necessarily reflect the views of the publisher,
and the publisher hereby disclaims any responsibility for them.

Any people depicted in stock imagery provided by Thinkstock are models,
and such images are being used for illustrative purposes only.
Certain stock imagery © Thinkstock.

ISBN: 978-1-5127-8613-2 (sc)
ISBN: 978-1-5127-8614-9 (hc)
ISBN: 978-1-5127-8612-5 (e)

Library of Congress Control Number: 2017907283

Print information available on the last page.

WestBow Press rev. date: 6/20/2017

To my BFF, Vinnie DiTrapani. Thank you for
the honor of sharing your life's story.

In memory of:
Richard S. Proctor – the teacher who taught me I could.
And "my honey," Chet Fromoltz – the
husband who knew that I would.

ACKNOWLEDGEMENTS

Patti A. Bengen, author and long-time friend who encouraged me to resume writing sooner rather than later. Thank you, my fellow Capricorn.

Jane Cavolina, professional editor whose knowledge of grammar and punctuation far exceeds mine. Your expertise was invaluable to this novice.

Beverly Pesti-Dillingham, friend and former housemate who consented to reading each revision, and helped me go through thousands of pictures before finding the perfect cover.

Jason Fromoltz, my son and most demanding editor. Thank you for continuously coming to my rescue when technology and stress threatened to take me hostage.

Ryan Fromoltz, my son who was with me on a day-to-day basis during the good times and the worst of times. Thank you for the broad shoulders to lean on.

Kim Gettemeyer, friend and best hair stylist in Henderson, NV. Thank you for being there from the very beginning and listening all the many times I talked about "the story."

Alyson Walzer, Librarian extraordinaire in Florida who proofread and sorted through my jumbled timeline. Thank you for the suggestion of dating the chapters.

PROLOGUE

October 2000 Las Vegas

Her given name was Vincenza. For most of her eighty years she had simply been known as "Vinnie." Without regret or reservation, she had changed her last name from Giamonte to DiTrapani some fifty-seven years earlier during a no-frills, wartime wedding.

The groom had been a dashing young soldier named Leo and the two of them had remained the epitome of a romantic item until his death in February 2000. In her mind, Vinnie had accepted the fact of Leo's illness, but in her heart, there hadn't been enough time for her to prepare for a life without him. Then again, she seriously doubted any amount of time would have proven sufficient.

Vinnie's devout faith now served as her personal lifeline, reassuring her that Leo was, in fact, in Heaven with God and His angels. Her aching heart briefly smiled as she thought of one golden-haired angel in particular. During moments like this, she longed to be with them.

Although Vinnie's inner clock had seemed to stop with her husband's last breath, the planet continued to rotate on its axis and the calendar on her desk informed her that eight months had passed. The elapsed time hadn't lessened her difficulty in facing each new sunrise without him. Worse yet were the lonely and endless nights when she cried herself to sleep clutching the single pillow on which the scent of his cologne lingered.

Leo had been her best friend and anchor, her sweetheart and ardent lover for the better part of her life. Granted, he was now physically gone from that life, but as she was soon to discover, he still had some surprises in store for her.

On this particular Monday morning, at one minute past nine, she was sitting, spine erect, in an apricot reading chair nestled in the corner of her immaculately kept bedroom. There were no social or doctors appointments scheduled for the day, yet she was attired in a red cashmere sweater and fitted charcoal slacks. Her makeup had been subtly applied with a gentle hand. Her lips were lightly lined and shaded with the rosy pink color Leo favored. Every strand of her silvery-white hair was neatly in place, as if not daring to do otherwise.

She had determined today was going to be the day. No more procrastination. She had a specific task to accomplish...a task she had been dreading since the discovery of the large envelope several weeks earlier. The package had been discreetly tucked away in the recesses of her husband's closet.

Garnering her courage, she looked down at the envelope resting on her lap. She reached out and hesitantly ran her right hand across the length of the parcel. She admitted to herself that its questionable contents weighed far more heavily on her mind than physically on her person.

The French glass doors to the patio were fully opened, admitting the pleasant fall-scented air. A calm desert breeze kissed the fronds of the palms, which she noted with pride, had grown far taller than their block-wall enclosure. Vinnie's appreciative gaze took in every miraculous specimen growing from the once arid and barren soil.

Ultimately, her eyes rested upon a statue of the Blessed Virgin Mary presiding over this miniature oasis. Vinnie sighed heavily, instinctively making the Sign of the Cross, wondering if today would be another day, among the many, when she would be compelled to call upon the Holy Mother for inner strength.

Years ago, moving to Las Vegas had been the furthest thing from the DiTrapanis' minds. Southern California was where they had settled early on and built a solid life for their family. Their custom, rambling ranch-style house, a haven for forty years, was filled with a treasure trove of memories...both the good and those too difficult to bear.

The passage of four decades brought change so gradually to their little community that at first it went undetected. It was a seedling blown on an ill wind that germinated, reproduced and steadily overgrew everything in its path. Houses passed from one owner to another owner, who often had less inclination or financial ability to maintain the property. The English language lost its dominance and was relegated to a second-place standing within its native borders. During the early 1990s, a night time noise echoing in the near distance could accurately be attributed to the random discharging of a gun rather than the innocent backfiring of a motor vehicle.

Leo had broached the subject of moving numerous times.

"We can't stop the hands of time," Leo was fond of saying, and he repeated those words once again to his wife. "And unfortunately," he added this time, "you and I, sweetheart, have to face the fact that we're not getting any younger. Sometimes nature or mankind makes it necessary for even an old tree to be uprooted and transplanted in order for it to thrive."

"Well, this old tree," Vinnie retorted, "is going to have to think long and hard before anyone comes near her roots with a shovel."

The decision to leave California came on the heels of their son-in-law's promotion and transfer to southern Nevada. If their two young grandsons were going to be reared in Las Vegas, of all places, they would need family nearby and a trustworthy babysitter or two.

Vinnie and Leo volunteered for the job and in 1993 packed up their possessions, along with their trove of memories, and headed for the city of neon lights.

Now sitting in the solitude of the pastel shades of the bedroom she and Leo had shared, she concentrated again on the package. Leo had never been a man to keep secrets. They had shared everything during their marriage, so why had this particular item been hidden away?

There was a palpable knot of uncertainty in Vinnie's stomach and her arthritic hands shook as she struggled to release the envelope's stubborn metal clasp.

Reaching inside, the first thing her trembling fingers felt was the smoothness of worn leather. Her tactile sense translated the touch directly to her heart. It was Leo's ancient cordovan journal. She pulled the book free from its confines and protectively clutched it to her chest.

From the time Leo had returned from the Second World War and for the thirteen years that followed, she had often seen him take pen in hand to jot down his personal and innermost thoughts on its cream-colored pages. The last time she had seen the journal was March 8, 1959, a date forever branded into their souls.

Even now the motion picture starting to play in her mind was as vivid as the blue and white Madonna outside the patio door. She could clearly see Leo that Sunday in March, seated at the kitchen table, his body statue like, his face carved in grief. Streams of anguished tears flowed downward, burning his pale cheeks. Yes, it was a day she would never forget…could never forget. It was seared into her brain along with her own primal response to the darkness of that day.

On March 8, 1959, with unsuppressed pain and anger, Vinnie turned her back on God, believing, with all the shattered pieces of her heart, that He had willfully forsaken her and her family.

In retaliation, she hastily grabbed any religious item within her reach. Marching to the tune of this totally foreign drummer, she paraded her collection out to the curb and threw everything into the trash. "Good riddance," she shouted as she slammed the lid closed on the receptacle and on her faith.

Now she gingerly set the journal aside, doubting if she possessed the fortitude to read its aged yellow pages today or ever.

Reaching into the envelope for the second time, she audibly gasped at her findings. Every religious picture or object, even the rosary beads blessed by the pope, that she had gathered in rage on that fateful day and abandoned to the trash, had been miraculously preserved.

Leo, her wonderful Leo, wise man that he inherently was, had known her far better than she had known herself. Despite the crushing and bitter pain, he trusted that with the passage of time, her love for God would be resurrected.

Her wrinkled hands caressed the pictures as she held the beloved beads so tightly that the cross made an indentation in her soft palm. She was oblivious to any discomfort. A faraway look drifted in and slowly filled the sapphire eyes that time had clouded with age, and her mind began its long journey from the present into the past.

BOOK I

CHAPTER ONE

October 1942

It was the chill-laden fall of 1942. The United States was heavily engaged on the battlefields of faraway shores. For wives and mothers, it was the beginning of a harrowing nightmare that either began through the postal service in the form of a draft notice, or when eager loved ones came home with the dreaded announcement, "I've enlisted." They all would soon be shipping out for destinations unknown.

Factories that were previously tooled for the manufacturing of consumer goods were converted to produce whatever was needed to sustain the war effort. It was said that the Heinz Company went from "pickles to pursuit planes," a major retooling from the sweet and sour varieties.

The war was affecting the United States from coast to coast, from the quietest small town to the most bustling metropolises. One such place was New York and its industrious borough of Queens. Within its borders a paper plant was converted to defense work and renamed General Aircraft. The specialty of this revamped facility was glider production. These non-engine, light aircraft had become a pivotal part of the war effort and were used to stealthily drop troops, tanks, and supplies behind the hazardous front lines. General

1

Aircraft employees diligently worked twelve-hour shifts around the perpetually ticking clock as production coordinators struggled to keep up with the increasing demands of the war.

The United States' entry into the war after the December 7, 1941, Japanese bombing of Pearl Harbor had taken men from the home and workplace, and the monumental task of taking up the slack fell heavily upon the female population of the nation's forty-eight states. One such young woman, a lifelong resident of Queens, was Vincenza "Vinnie" Giamonte, and she, along with a multitude of other women, willingly donned work pants and came to the aid of their country. She rode the Astoria Boulevard bus daily from her family home in Jackson Heights on the twenty-minute trip to General Aircraft, where she became an integral part of the wartime work force.

Following America's declaration of war, the population of civilian men in New York spiraled downward, gaining momentum in its descent. A large percentage of those remaining were anxiously awaiting their coming of age so they, too, could proudly serve and defend. Others had wanted to enlist but were temporarily dissuaded by parental arguments and maternal pleadings to the contrary. These young men and parents alike knew, in their heart of hearts, that there would be no arguing or room for sentiment when Uncle Sam pounded his fist on their door.

A smaller percentage of the male populace simply waited, knowing that the long arm of the military would inevitably extend its reach and snatch them up by their bootstraps. They had siblings and other family members who had already been shipped overseas and it was only a matter of time before they also would be called upon to lay their lives on the line. One of these young men was Leonard "Leo" DiTrapani, who during this precarious time in his life was also brought by fate to General Aircraft.

The employees of General Aircraft, regardless of gender, were united in their efforts to assist the Allied troops. There was no room for petty differences and personal quirks. Bonded together by a common cause, everyone made an effort to be cordial and productive. They would smile or wave in greeting when passing each other on the production floor, and they gathered in clusters during breaks. The girls made friendships more readily, knowing they would be there for the duration of the war. Some of these relationships would last a lifetime.

Their able-bodied male counterparts, however, were short-term fixtures awaiting orders to pack up and ship out. The ratio of women to men was a staggering twenty to one. Under different circumstances, this would have been a single man's Garden of Eden, but with Uncle Sam hovering like a predatory eagle, their days in paradise were numbered.

CHAPTER TWO

It was the start of yet another workweek, another twelve-hour shift in Queens. Despite the war, spirits in New York were high because their beloved baseball team, the Yankees, would be playing in the upcoming World Series.

It had been overcast for most of the day, the sun playing an elusive game of hide-and-seek. When evening descended, the temperature followed its lead. Leo was relieved to be off the vintage bus that rattled loudly from Manhattan to Queens, protesting its stop-and-go journey. His light jacket did little to protect him from the cold night air.

He had placed his lunch pail and jacket into his assigned locker and was on his way to put his signature on the night's sign-in sheet when he caught sight of something out of the corner of his eye. His attention was initially drawn by the color and tilt of an auburn head in motion. However, it was the very nice package to which that head was attached that caused his steel blue eyes to linger. The shapely figure was contained within a petite frame. Leo wondered if she'd even reach the five-foot-two marker on the measuring tape in his pocket.

Her stride was buoyant and purposeful as she walked across the production floor in the company's new jumpsuit-style uniform. He surmised she was one of the crew newly reassigned to the night shift. Although she looked like she was in her teens, he knew she had to be twenty-one. It was a General Aircraft rule; when a female employee came of age, she was transferred from the day hours to night-time duty. He really didn't give a hoot how young or old she was, because the woman in his line of vision was definitely a looker with a capital "L."

When the plant supervisor shouted in her direction, "Hey, Vinnie, I need you to fill in for Wilma tonight on glider one," Leo was all ears. While he was mentally filing away her name, he got a little surprise. Vinnie turned toward him as though sensing the intensity of his stare. Leo was pleased to discover there was more fire in those baby blues of hers than in the mid-length red hair that bounced with each step.

Normally, Leo considered himself to be a perfect gentleman, and conducted himself accordingly, but here he was caught red-handed, entertaining ideas that were perhaps not quite so gentlemanly. While his freshly shaven face flushed with embarrassment, Leo raised both his hands to wipe the warmth from his cheeks, but it was a futile endeavor. The color and a sappy expression lingered.

Twenty feet away, Vinnie had indeed felt the heat of Leo's stare. When she looked over her right shoulder, she could see a nice looking male holding her in his gaze. He appeared to be in his early twenties, not overly tall, but a respectable five-feet-nine or ten inches. His shoulders were broad and the rest of his physique slim and well proportioned. His thick wavy hair was the color of Caribbean sand and his complexion, without the blush, she determined to be Scandinavian fair.

Vinnie's thoughts drifted to a book she was reading and was dreamily transported to the era of the novel. In her mental wanderings, she cast him in the role of Norse warrior, a hero preparing to save his maiden fair. She, of course, was the maiden.

The foreman shouted again, suddenly bursting her bubble of romantic images. Vinnie gave her head a slight shake to clear them.

She mentally smacked the palm of her hand against her forehead. "Vinnie Giamonte, you're a first class idiot," she chided herself for the foolhardy musings. But on the other hand, she questioned herself, was it really her fault? After all, she hadn't started this! In the blink of an eye, she transferred the annoyance with herself to him, where it properly belonged. How dare he look at her in such a manner! If she wasn't a perfect lady, she reasoned, she might have marched right up to him, gone toe-to-toe, and wiped that smart-aleck grin off his face…a rather handsome face, she unwillingly conceded.

Leo wisely looked away. He wasn't a soldier yet, but he knew when it was a good tactical move to retreat and regroup. An idea was already forming in his head.

It took a week for him to finagle a work assignment near Vinnie. He bribed a co-worker to change jobs with him by offering a coveted gas ration coupon and a portion of his homemade lunch. It was a huge payment considering the economic times, but he would willingly have paid more. He knew that the draft was following closely on his size nine heels, and he had to effectively use whatever time he had left.

When it was Leo's turn to work with her, he found Vinnie perched atop glider two, expertly rip-stitching its wing with the standard twelve-inch needle. Leo started his ascent up the ladder but paused midway, questioning the wisdom of what he was about to do.

"No, there's no better time than the present," he convinced himself, and with a renewed sense of confidence, finished his climb. He did adhere to protocol, yelling up a precautionary warning of his arrival. He would never forgive himself if his sudden appearance caused her to lose her balance or inadvertently stab herself.

At the top of the ladder, Leo unleashed his hundred-watt smile while wisely keeping a safe distance from the formidable needle in Vinnie's hand. He proceeded to introduce himself.

"Hello, lovely lady. My name is Leo DiTrapani and after due consideration I've decided I'm going to marry you and we're going to make beautiful babies together."

Vinnie was so taken aback that her balance on the glider wing faltered but she dug in her heels, refusing to let this Lothario get the better of her. She reined in her composure, adjusted her balance, and purposely extended the stitching needle out in front of her. It pointed in Leo's direction.

"Hello to you too, young man," she replied with a dignity befitting royalty. "My name is Vincenza Giamonte, but my friends and family call me Vinnie. Since you are neither of those two, you can address me by my given name or even better, Miss Giamonte."

Leo opened his mouth but before he could get a word out Vinnie cut him off.

"I don't know what time period is involved in your 'due consideration,' but I can honestly tell you that all I've needed is one minute, sixty little seconds, to decide you're awfully fresh and presumptuous. If you're here to work, I suggest you get to it and make yourself useful instead of flapping your gums and acting like a horse's patoot. And if you're not going to work, please remove yourself from my wing and take that stupid smile with you."

Leo expeditiously busied himself. He hoped the Yankees fared better in their Series against the St. Louis Cardinals than he had done during his first time at bat with Vinnie.

CHAPTER THREE

Leo was smitten and not at all deterred by Vinnie's initial reaction to him or her continued refusal to date him. And although the Yankees hadn't won the World Series, Leo was still in the game. He was overjoyed when the new six-day work schedule gave both him and Vinnie Sundays off.

On Sunday mornings, he rose earlier than usual to attend church. Rather than going to his neighborhood parish, as he had for as long as he could remember, he made the lengthy bus trip to St. Gabriel's in Queens, where a co-worker had told him Vinnie and her family attended Mass. He also learned that she was one of eleven children but the majority were older and had already left the nest.

The first Sunday he sat near the rear of the church, attempting to blend in with the congregation. He kept an eye on the massive front doors, awaiting Vinnie's arrival. And arrive she did, with a large group of people. The Giamontes, when seated, took up an entire pew of the church. He surmised that some were relatives to one degree or another, but keyed in on the couple he was certain were Vinnie's parents. Leo concluded their daughter was the perfect genetic combination of the two handsome individuals.

The second Sunday, he sat closer to the front and to the Giamontes. The more he watched Vinnie's parents, the more certain he was that there was something unique about them in addition, of course, to their being the people who had brought "his" Vinnie into the world. While he should have been listening to the priest, his thoughts tumbled like bingo balls in their cage and he nearly shouted out "bingo" when the last ball fell into place. He realized it was love that he saw. Not only the love of parents for their children, but their mutual love and respect for one another. A wide grin lit up Leo's face. That's exactly what he wanted for Vinnie and himself and nothing and no one was going to stop him.

The third Sunday, at the conclusion of the service, while people gathered outside, Leo approached Vinnie and her family. He extended his hand to her father and introduced himself to both parents. Vinnie was temporarily stunned into silence, but when Leo asked to speak to her father privately, she wanted to smack him upside the head.

Mr. Giamonte obliged the young man by stepping off to the side. "What did you want to speak to me about, Mr. DiTrapani?"

"Well, sir, I'd like to ask your permission to date your daughter."

Mr. Giamonte held back a chuckle. "Apparently, you don't know my daughter very well. She is of the age of consent and if she wanted to date you, we wouldn't be having this conversation. I have heard your name mentioned around our dinner table and not necessarily in the most positive manner. Nonetheless, I find that parenthood provides one with the ability to read between the lines. I may be putting myself out on a limb here, but I'm going to invite you back to our house for coffee. The rest is entirely up to you."

When Vinnie heard from her father that Leo was returning with them to the house, she decided it might be a good idea to walk home with her guest. It would give her the chance to blow off the mounting steam that was about to erupt from her ears. She would have a few choice words for Leo during the short trip and her ears wouldn't be the only ones burning.

When Vinnie announced that she and Leo wouldn't be riding in the car, Vinnie's youngest sister, eleven-year-old Adele, planted herself on the sidewalk between the couple. Leo tousled Adele's strawberry blonde tresses and she smiled up at him with eyes sparkling with mischief.

"I think I might like you," Adele said without reservation. "I know you like my big sister because you asked to talk to my father. Did you ask him for Vinnie's hand in marriage?"

"No," Leo replied with the most serious expression he could muster. "I actually asked if I could marry you but your father said I have to wait at least until you're eighteen years old. So exactly how many years would I be waiting?" Vinnie put her gloved hand to her mouth to hide a snicker.

Adele's blue eyes became as big as saucers. "Well, I'm eleven now so that would be seven years."

"That's an awfully long time," Leo said, sounding disappointed. "By then I might be too old."

"That's true," Adele pondered out loud, "and before you get more serious about me, I think I should let you in on a little secret. When I graduate from high school, I plan to move to Hollywood. I'm a good artist, but I also have a talent for acting. It would be a real shame to let all that talent go to waste. The first thing I'm going to do when I get to California is get an agent. The second thing I'm going to do is change my name. Not that my name isn't perfectly fine, but taking a professional name is something a lot of stars do. I've tossed a few ideas around and decided on Dell Monte. Someday everyone in the country will know that name."

Leo's expression feigned more sadness.

"I'm sorry if that disappoints you, Leo," she said, responding to the look on his face. "Maybe the best idea would be for you to just marry my sister. Then you could grow old together."

"You're quite precocious," Leo told the child now clutching both his and Vinnie's hands.

"Yep, that's what my Mom says, too, and since I know exactly what that means, I'll take it as a compliment. Now since we settled this marriage thing, I need you guys to shake a leg. There's a brownie left from last night that has my name on it. If anyone else gets it first, I promise you'll never hear the end of it."

Leo looked at Vinnie over Adele's head. Her eyes met his and held. Vinnie felt an unfamiliar warmth tingling through her body. No, it hadn't been love at first sight for her. Then again, maybe it had.

CHAPTER FOUR

Late 1942 to June 1943

During the fall and winter months of 1942, while nature hibernated beneath its seasonal blanket, Vinnie and Leo's relationship blossomed as if in a spring awakening. Their co-workers at General Aircraft had dubbed them "the lovers," referring only to the state of their hearts. Their courtship had been wonderfully romantic but chaste. They were both devout in their faith and would not explore their relationship further until the sacrament of marriage.

Sunday, February 20, 1943, was Leo's birthday, and, he had grand plans that didn't include working. "But alas," he mused to himself, "the best laid plans of mice and men." General Aircraft's call for additional employees took precedence over personal matters, and Leo was determined to make the best of it and improvise.

He went to his dresser drawer and removed the black velvet box that had been tucked under his socks two weeks earlier. He slipped the small treasure into his pocket, bounced down the stairs, and grinned like the cat that swallowed the canary during the entire bus ride to work.

Before the start of their shift, Leo motioned excitedly for Vinnie to come to his locker. "I know it's my birthday, but I have a gift for you. Stick out your hand, close your eyes, and keep those baby blues shut."

Vinnie, not one to take orders under any circumstances, gave Leo the benefit of an extended blink of her eyes then watched him remove a tiny box from his pocket. Demonstrating a magician-like sleight of hand, Vinnie became the custodian of the box. Without opening it, she started jumping up and down, then she deftly flipped the cover up with a thumb and stared at the one-quarter carat square-cut diamond twinkling up at her. Her sparkling eyes widened to match the enormous width of her smile. Before Leo could utter a single word, Vinnie freed the diamond from its velvety bed and plunked it on her size four finger. It fit perfectly.

Poor Leo. He simply stood there like a statue as Vinnie threw her arms around his neck and at the top of her lungs, yelled "Yes, yes" to the question he had not been given the chance to ask.

Responding to the sudden commotion, co-workers quickly surrounded the couple. Vinnie held her ring finger aloft, waving it for everyone to see. There were smiling faces all around, some smiling more than others. Small bets had been placed on the Q.T. as to when "the lovers" would become engaged, so money or ration coupons would soon be exchanging hands to cover those wagers.

From February through mid-May, theirs was an idyllic world, but one destined to be shattered. In May 1943, a letter arrived at the DiTrapani residence addressed to Leo. Recognizing the all-too-familiar official packet, Leo's mother, with shaking hands, tore open the envelope. The letter began with the standard "Greetings," which meant another of the DiTrapani boys would become the property of the United States military.

Leo was the third one of her sons the war would be snatching from her arms. The government was taking her children away in birth order. Three down, two to go, she lamented, biting the inside of her cheek. She still had two younger sons, of or nearing draft age, and they would unquestionably be called if the fighting continued. She felt as though her heart had been divided into five chambers and Uncle Sam was removing one section at a time without benefit of anesthesia. She threw the letter to the floor and stomped on it five times with all her might—one time for each of her boys.

CHAPTER FIVE

Vinnie was expecting Leo's arrival when his familiar knock-knock sounded at her front door. What she didn't expect was the grim look on his face when she answered. For weeks she had been aglow with post-engagement elation but now the bloom was about to be stripped from her cheeks. She saw the letter in his hand and knew it was the harbinger of bad news.

Before Leo could cross the threshold, Vinnie said, "Don't beat around the bush, Leo. Tell me exactly how much time we have left."

"The Air Force is giving me thirty days to get my affairs in order and report to MacDill Army Air Base in Tampa, Florida. I'll be there for three months of basic training, which will take me into September. After that, only God and Uncle Sam know for sure."

Vinnie fell into Leo's arms and cried helplessly. The house around them, normally full of chatter, was eerily quiet as though it too had gone into mourning.

When Leo left, Vinnie went straight to her room and locked the door. Overwrought from the intensity of her emotion, she buried her head in a pillow and let the tears flow.

There was a light knock on her bedroom door. "Whoever it is, please go away," Vinnie sniveled, barely lifting her head from the pillow.

"Sorry, no can do, big sister," Adele said, opening the door with the master key she had borrowed from its "secret" place behind the flour in the pantry.

Vinnie looked up. "Please, Adele, I need to be alone right now."

"No, Vinnie, what you need is a plan. I wasn't exactly eavesdropping, but I couldn't help but hear what Leo had to say. I think you should stop crying and find a way to get married before Leo leaves. If you and Leo tie the knot as soon as possible, you can... how do I say this?" Adele wondered aloud.

The flow of tears from Vinnie's eyes ceased as she looked directly at her little sister. "What exactly do you mean?"

"Give me a break, Vinnie. I'd like to remind you that on my last birthday I turned twelve. With age comes wisdom, and I know that babies aren't delivered by storks. Men and women who love one another, and are married by the Church, can do a lot more than kissing. Sometimes that means babies are made and sometimes not, but you have to be married for it to be okay in God's eyes. He decides about the baby part. Besides, if you're Leo's wife, you may be able to meet him in Florida."

A smile alighted Vinnie's face. "Adele, you are absolutely brilliant."

Adele grinned like the proverbial Cheshire cat. "I know, big sister. That's what I keep telling everyone in this family, but nobody listens."

CHAPTER SIX

Dawn the next morning found Vinnie near the steps of St. Gabriel's rectory. She was waiting for Father Silvio, wanting to speak to him before his six o'clock Mass.

She saw the weathered oak door open and heard the priest speaking to his housekeeper.

"Yes, Mrs. Murphy, I promise both you and the good Lord I'll be back from my home visits in time for lunch today."

Father Silvio prudently closed the door before Mrs. Murphy could scold him yet again for yesterday's tardiness and "utterly ruined midday meal that was no longer fit for man nor beast." Today he'd make a genuine effort to watch the clock.

He spotted Vinnie. He was not surprised by her presence. The St. Gabriel grapevine had a direct line to Mrs. Murphy, and the housekeeper felt it was her God-given duty to daily apprise the priest on any happenings within the parish. Today's breakfast was served along with the story of young Leo's draft.

"Good morning, Vincenza," he greeted her with his ever-present warmth. "I anticipated seeing you sometime today. However, I must say I didn't expect you'd be up with the chickens. Why don't you walk with me to the church and tell me what's on your mind."

As they made their way to the side entrance of St. Gabriel's, Vinnie talked non-stop, moving her hands in conjunction with her lips. To any passersby, it would appear she was signing her side of

17

the conversation for the hearing impaired. The crux of the matter seemed simple in theory. She wanted to become Mrs. Leo DiTrapani during the twenty-nine days she and Leo had left.

Father Silvio listened to Vinnie with an attentive ear and compassionate heart. She and Leo were not the first young, head-over-heels in love couple the war had brought to his door, nor would they be the last. He promised to do his best in cutting through the Church's mandatory pre-marriage red tape and, if possible, perform a private ceremony within the chapel.

Vinnie flew home as though her feet had wings. She raced up the stairs and rummaged through her bedroom closet, tossing out unacceptable items as she went. There had to be a garment she could use for a wedding dress.

Adele walked into the room holding two apples. Vinnie was sitting in the middle of the floor surrounded by discarded clothes. "Catch," Adele instructed her sibling, tossing one of the Macintoshes. "You didn't eat anything before leaving the house this morning. I would also like to add that your room looks like a cyclone hit it. What gives?"

"I have nothing to wear," Vinnie groaned. "I mean, nothing suitable for a wedding dress."

"Vinnie, Vinnie," Adele shook her head. "Aside from our mother being a great mom, what other special talent does she have?" They looked at each other and said in unison, "She can make a silk purse out of sow's ear." Their mother was the best seamstress in Queens and a simple wedding dress would take no time at all. "Problem solved," Adele boasted. "And my work here is done, because you made this mess and you'll be cleaning it up by yourself." Adele turned and skipped out of the room. She noisy chumped on her apple as she made her way down the hall.

CHAPTER SEVEN

With all her plans, Vinnie had forgotten one important thing... to consult Leo. He had wanted nothing more in life than to make Vinnie his wife and start on the production of those beautiful babies he had predicted on the glider wing last fall. But stronger than desire, even stronger than love, was the all-encompassing emotion of fear. Fear that if he made Vinnie his young wife, the war wouldn't hesitate to make her his young widow.

No marriage took place in May or June. Leo obstinately made his decision and stuck to it. He would exchange vows with Vinnie if and when he returned from the war and only if that return brought him home whole-bodied and fully functional.

Leo said his good-byes acknowledging in the recesses of his mind, that these might indeed be final farewells. He left New York on a sea of feminine tears. Vinnie was distraught and inconsolable. She locked herself in her bedroom. Knocks on her door went answered. Even Adele refrained from using the master key.

On the west side of Manhattan, another woman sobbed uncontrollably as Leo kissed her good-bye, "Please don't cry, Mom. I promise nothing will happen to me. In fact, all us boys are going be fine and when the war is over, we'll all be together again. The first thing we'll do is make a big batch of wine with dad like we always do, and we'll celebrate our safe return home."

Leo gave his mom one last kiss on the forehead and left. Behind the closed door he couldn't see the woman who had fallen to the floor on her knees, but the echo of her despair followed him hauntingly out the door and into the street.

CHAPTER EIGHT

June to November 1943

Leo and hundreds of other fledglings arrived in Florida for boot camp in June 1943 along with stifling humidity and ravenous bugs. The training was arduous and often discouraging. Ranking superiors commanded and coached their charges through the physical and mental regimentation.

These recruits would officially carry the title and burden of soldier, young men destined to defeat the enemy across land and sea. Yet, most were only boys given guns to participate in a deadly game of war. Some of them would only return home to parents and spouses in sealed wooden boxes.

Each and every one of Leo's days ended in utter fatigue, but at the day's end, he unfailingly wrote Vinnie during his first semester of War 101. During these initial and increasingly lonely months away, Leo's resolve not to marry until he returned home safe and sound was crumbling. Could he bear to leave Vinnie without making the paramount commitment they would both need to get them through the uncertain months ahead?

Following basic training, Leo was among the graduates transferred to Gulfport Field Air Force Base in Mississippi for the next stage of their combat education. Spouses were allowed visitation.

Leo settled in the best he could in Gulfport. By November, his warring heart won the battle against what he thought was good sense. He took his treasured Cross fountain pen, a high school graduation gift from his parents, from its leather case. He set words to paper, apologizing to Vinnie for being such a "mule-headed jerk," unwilling to see the situation as clearly as she had. The simple fact was that he loved her with his entire being and what he wanted most in the world was to belong to her body and soul.

He continued to write, "There's no way I can leave Mississippi now without landing in the stockade for desertion, but if you love and trust me enough to make the trip here, I will pledge the rest of my life and never-ending love to you before God and man."

Leo's letter reached Queens in record time. After ripping the envelope open, Vinnie read Leo's declaration three times. A triumphant smile lit up her face and she threw the letter high in the air. Before the paper had a chance to reach the floor, Vinnie began tossing her clothes into a worn suitcase she had rescued from the basement six months earlier. The last item to be packed was a Giamonte original wedding dress wrapped carefully in white tissue paper.

Vinnie's parents strongly considered putting their parental foot down; letting their daughter leave the nest was one thing, but permitting her to travel unmarried and unchaperoned to a far-off military base was an entirely different matter.

"We might as well save our breath, sweetheart," Vinnie's father sagely conceded as he conferred with his wife. "Our girl is her mother's daughter," he added, trying hard not to release the chuckle lurking within. "We can talk until we're blue in the face and we still won't dissuade her from going to Mississippi."

Vinnie's father accompanied her to the train. Since her birth, he had been the most important man in her life. A talented musician, born to play the trombone, he traveled for most of her childhood years, yet his homecomings were truly magical. He returned like Santa, bearing handfuls of small presents, not costly in dollar and cents, but valuable treasures to the children. After each of his trips, the growing Giamonte family would gather in front of the fireplace, where Papa would entertain them with his grand adventures and amusing stories about the funny and famous people he met.

To Vinnie he had always been a gentle giant, although when she herself grew up, she realized his five feet ten inches was not the towering height it had seemed when she was a child. His hair had once been sandy brown, his caring eyes vivid blue. He'd been raised in Italy, in the small town of Argenta near the Swiss-French border, and came to this country with his young wife, following optimistically in the footsteps of so many before him. Now the gold in his hair had turned to silver, the hue of his eyes was less brilliant, but he was still the first man she had ever loved.

As they stood silently on the platform at Pennsylvania Station, he held Vinnie's suitcase in a viselike grip, contemplating what to say to his daughter. He knew that he had always been the number one man in her life. He was prepared to relinquish that position to Leo, although his heart was filled with fatherly concerns. His daughter had never been away from the family overnight. Now she was leaving the familiar parameters of New York and the security of family to travel alone to a strange place and embark on a new chapter in her life.

"Vincie," as he had called her since she was a baby, "you know your mother and I only want what's best for you and we really do like Leo, but once you get there, how can you be sure he's going to marry you? This is wartime, my dear daughter, and sometimes young men don't keep their promises."

Vinnie was confident in her reply. "Please don't worry, Papa. I may not be musically attuned like others in the family, but I am in tune with both my strengths and weaknesses. I admit I don't know a lot about the world and men in particular, but I do know Leo. He's a good person who believes in God and himself. He's a lot like you, Papa. He's a man of his word and I love him with all my heart. How could I possibly ask for anyone better?"

There was a moment of weighted silence but no need for reply. He looked steadily at his daughter and could see the beginnings of the impish sparkle so very familiar to him. A grin spread over Vinnie's face.

"Besides all that, Papa, Leo knows for sure that if his intentions aren't honorable, he won't have to worry about being wounded overseas. He'll get his lumps right there in Mississippi, and I'll be on the next train headed straight for home." Her father couldn't help but smile proudly. "Now, that's my girl."

CHAPTER NINE

In Mississippi, Leo paced the length of the railroad platform impatiently awaiting Vinnie's arrival. The train from New York was already ten minutes late and nowhere to be seen on the horizon. He kept checking his watch, his nervous system was in overdrive, and he craved a cigarette in the worst way. He was tempted to bum a smoke from a passerby but better judgment prevailed.

Before the draft, smoking hadn't been a habit. It was an occasional thing to do while out with the boys, and he hadn't cared enough to perfect the art of inhaling. Since boot camp, he acknowledged his inclination to light up with more frequency but he was certainly not alone in the crowd. Cigarettes were dished out like candies, and few soldiers passed up the treat. Enlisted men, who seldom or never smoked as civilians, were puffing away their anxiety. To many it became an involuntary function as natural as breathing.

Leo had indulged himself for one last time two days earlier. He had inhaled deeply and sent the smoke streaming out his nostrils. He was well aware his future bride would not appreciate the cigarette odor on his clothes or the residual tobacco taste on his lips.

Vinnie's train pulled into the station at 3:20 PM, twenty minutes late. When she alighted from the fourth car, he saw her nervously searching the crowd. He waved his arms frantically, trying to get her attention. He heard himself saying "Excuse me" numerous times as he maneuvered through a throng of arriving passengers and military personnel. Relief came to Vinnie in the form of an audible sigh when she recognized the uniformed-clad figure sprinting toward her. Without saying a word, he grabbed his fiancée around her diminutive waist, lifted her two feet off the ground, and twirled her in a circle. For him this was Christmas morning, without the tree and tinsel, but with the most perfect gift of all…his bride-to-be.

When he returned Vinnie to solid ground, her face was aglow with love and adoration. Leo was unquestionably a dashing figure in his Air Force regalia. She was overcome with pride that this man belonged to her and only her. Then he removed his hat.

Leo caught Vinnie's quick inhalation of breath when she glimpsed the crop of sandy fuzz replacing the once handsome head of wavy hair. "Don't worry, honey," Leo consoled her. "They told us we can grow it back when the war is over and maybe by that time you'll get used to it." With a flick of the wrist, the hat was put back in place at a rakish angle that accentuated the glint in his eyes.

Leo grasped Vinnie's suitcase in his right hand, her soft gloved hand in his left. They strolled into town, prolonging their time together by stopping for an early dinner of coffee and cheese sandwiches before going to the rooming house that was to be Vinnie's home away from home. The house and its owners, a military family named Heath, came highly recommended by one of the chaplains. They were a devout Catholic family and, as such, made it perfectly clear that they would not permit Leo beyond the downstairs parlor until he and Vinnie exchanged vows.

Mrs. Heath promptly answered Leo's knock. She was a tall, slender woman of middle age. Her thick brown hair was pulled back from her comely face, which belied her stringent attitude.

With all the proper introductions made, Mrs. Heath pointedly looked at her watch. It was nearing 5:00 PM. Leo was summarily dismissed by the missus and somewhat taken aback. "You can call on Miss Giamonte at a decent hour tomorrow morning," Mrs. Heath said in a no-nonsense tone. "But right now, I can see she's tired from her trip and she needs to unpack her belongings and get acquainted with her new accommodations."

The matron of the house declined Leo's offer to take his fiancée's bag up to the second floor and he soon found himself standing, hat in hand, in front of a closed door while Vinnie obediently followed her landlady upstairs. Mrs. Heath opened the bedroom door and showed the young girl in. "I'll give you some time to make yourself comfortable. I'll be downstairs if you need anything," she reassured her new boarder.

Once alone, Vinnie took in her surroundings. The room was larger than she expected, cozy and cheerful. She eyed the double bed covered with the same gold and orange floral fabric that framed the two wide windows. Soon she and Leo would be sharing that very bed. She could feel the intense heat of the flush rising from her neck, spreading across her face and ending at the tips of her pierced ears.

Vinnie pinched herself and refocused her attention on the other furnishings in the room. There was a nice-size dresser, a night-table with a reading lamp, a small round table with two orange-cushioned chairs, and a tiny desk under one window. She decided the side of the bed nearest the light would be hers. She liked to read and there might be some time for reading a book after . . . she had to pinch herself again.

Being a child at heart, she playfully tested the firmness of the mattress by bouncing up and down, but with each bounce, her energy dwindled. The plump, down pillow invited her to "rest your head for just a minute." As soon as her auburn head touched the pillow's white casing, she was out like a light. Vinnie slept peacefully through the night. She smiled in her sleep. She was exactly where God intended her to be.

The next morning at 8:30, hoping it was a "decent hour" in Mrs. Heath's world, Leo walked to the boardinghouse to escort

Vinnie to Sunday Mass. According to Roman Catholic rules, they were not permitted to receive Holy Communion, since Saturday's schedule had not included the prerequisite stop at the confessional. It was a point they would rectify next week. They spent a quiet day together after services; and since the room did not include meals, they lunched on franks and beans before Leo returned Vinnie to the Heath's.

Leo had been granted leave Monday morning so he and Vinnie could obtain their marriage license. Arrangements had already been made with the base chaplain, Peter Healy, for a late-afternoon wedding in six days. For the anxious couple, Sunday could not come fast enough.

When the clock struck 3:00 PM on Sunday, November 21, 1943, Leo stood nervously knocking on the boardinghouse door. Extremely pleased to see the young man was keeping his word to wed, Mrs. Heath greeted Leo with surprising warmth. She allowed him a view of the staircase as he stood in the foyer, absently tossing his dress hat back and forth between fidgeting fingers. Vinnie descended the stairs gracefully, an absolute vision in white. The bride-to-be, attired in the dress her mother had designed and sewn stitch by loving stitch, was a sight to behold. The dress was normal length, simple but elegant, adorned with a jacket edged in lace with matching hat and veil. Vinnie's white low-heeled shoes were polished to perfection and her hands were covered in dainty lace gloves. Leo's eyes misted when the love of his life took his arm. He had never seen a woman more beautiful. He considered himself the luckiest man in the world.

Transportation was something Leo had not been able to arrange, but the base was within easy walking distance of the Heaths. He had wanted to drive his beautiful bride in a fashion befitting the occasion, but it was wartime and concessions had to be made. If anyone looked curiously at the twosome in their finery, as they walked arm in arm down Main Street, Vinnie and Leo never noticed. They only had eyes for each other.

When the prospective bride and groom arrived at the entrance to Chapel Three, Leo's cousin, Tony, Seaman Second Class from the 113th Navel Battalion, opened the door. He had the honor of being the best man and presented Vinnie with a beautiful bridal bouquet of gardenias that Leo had painstakingly chosen himself, remembering it was Vinnie's favorite flower.

The chaplain's mother, visiting for the weekend, served as organist and witness. The ceremony was brief but poignant as Private Leonard DiTrapani of the 633rd and Miss Vincenza Giamonte of Queens, New York, promised to "love, honor and obey ...until death do us part." It was not the best way to conclude a war-time wedding.

An intimate dinner for three followed the service. Tony came along to celebrate and bought the happy couple a non-vintage bottle of champagne as a wedding present. When dinner was over, Tony kissed Vinnie on the cheek and shook Leo's hand, and left the bride and groom outside the restaurant. He gave Leo a sly wink as he said his good-byes, telling the newlyweds with a grin, "Enjoy the rest of your evening." Leo took Vinnie in his arms and kissed her passionately, not concerned in the least by his sudden public display of affection. They both knew what was going to happen next . . . they were going to the movies. It certainly was not the usual way most young couples would choose to spend their wedding night; but after watching Dorothy Lamour and Dick Powell cavorting about the silver screen in *Riding High*, they walked hand-in-hand back to the room, where they consummated a love affair that would transcend a lifetime.

CHAPTER TEN

Late 1943 to Early 1944

In the weeks following the wedding, the newlyweds enjoyed the privacy of their honeymoon quarters. Leo's military duties took on the regular routine of the civilian forty-hour workweek, a concept passed into law five years earlier in the States. He reported to the base bright and early each morning and was welcomed home to Vinnie's open arms at the close of the day.

The spent their evenings secluded in their own Eden, but the stark light of day revealed minuscule weeds poking their unwelcome heads through the surface of their private garden.

The young couple's first and foremost problem was food. While Leo could eat on the base, such privileges didn't extend to spouses. The Heaths proved to be very pleasant people, but the rental agreement was void of meals and kitchen privileges. Providing for the room itself was emptying Leo's already threadbare pockets; and being the consummate gentlemen, he refused to eat dinner at the Mess Hall while Vinnie was left to subsist on fruits and packaged goods stashed in a dresser drawer.

At half past five on the dot daily, they made their evening constitutional to the Five & Diner, (F&D) a local eatery catering to the military populace of the area. It was there they shared the seventy-five cent daily "Air Force Blues Plate Special" consisting of soup, main dish, two vegetables, salad and dessert, "no substitutions allowed."

Drinks were an additional charge so most often water was the beverage of choice. Occasionally, a cup of coffee was offered free of charge.

"It's been sitting here all day," Midge, the consistently effervescent waitress, would tease. "And thicker than our Mississippi mud. If you two don't want it, I'm gonna toss it out back and watch the weeds die a slow and agonizing death."

When finances permitted, Leo treated Vinnie to her favorite libation…a tall iced tea filled to the brim with ice, extra lemon, and two generous measures of sugar.

The second problem occurred with the numerous unfilled hours Vinnie had during the day. She would tidy up their room, and if she saved her pennies and accumulated a grand total of ten cents, she would allow herself a trip to "F&D" for another of their specials…coffee and two donuts. She would leisurely sip her coffee, chat with Midge during lulls in business, and take one tiny bite of her confectionery at a time until only crumbs remained. The second donut was never eaten but wrapped in a paper napkin and saved for the next day's breakfast.

It was a Tuesday morning when she returned from F&D and Mrs. Heath was sitting by the window in the parlor busily knitting a sweater for her husband. "Sit down and keep me company for a spell," the landlady invited. "Do you know how to knit?" she inquired.

"No," Vinnie admitted. "I come from a large family and most of them are talented with their hands to one degree or another. My father is a professional trombone player and one of my older brothers is a pianist. My mother is probably the best seamstress in all of New

York and my youngest sister is a budding artist. I'm the black sheep who's all thumbs."

"Well, let's give it a try," Mrs. Heath proposed. Under her instruction and watchful eye, Vinnie made an admirable attempt for the first fifteen minutes. Knitting should have been a piece of cake for someone who could expertly rib-stitch glider wings. Working for her country had given her tremendous personal satisfaction, but knitting would never cut the mustard. She persevered until Mrs. Heath finally took pity on her.

"I was wondering how much longer you'd sit there pretending to be absorbed in what you're doing."

"Is it that obvious?" Vinnie asked.

"I could fib and say no, but the truth is, I'd have to be blind as a bat not to see what's right in front of my face. It's clear your interests lie elsewhere."

Both ladies started laughing.

"Well then, if you really don't mind, Mrs. Heath, I'll go upstairs and finish writing a letter home."

"I don't mind at all, dear. You go right ahead. I'm sure your family enjoys hearing from you. And if you should ever be bored enough to again try your hand at knitting, you know where to find me."

Vinnie reached the foyer than turned around. "Mrs. Heath," Vinnie called to her.

"Yes, Mrs. DiTrapani?'

"Thank you."

A half hour later, Vinnie was finishing up a letter to Adele. She wanted to thank her for the beautiful wedding present. With pencil and pad, Adele had drawn a resplendent sketch of how she envisioned her sister and Leo on their wedding day. The picture held a place of prominence above the desk, giving Vinnie a feeling of closeness to the baby sister she missed like crazy.

Vinnie had just licked and sealed the envelope when a tap sounded on the door.

"Come in, Mrs. Heath," she responded, the unpleasant taste of glue lingering on her tongue.

"My dear, you have a visitor downstairs. It's Chaplain Healy from the base. I seated him in the parlor."

Vinnie froze and panic replaced the blood rushing through her veins. A collage of vivid scenarios flashed through her brain with the speed of a B-17 bomber. Was Leo mortally wounded on the artillery field, a victim of a freak accident, or he was lying in a hospital bed, having been rushed there after being run over by an out-of-control jeep on his way to Mess Hall?

"There's no need for alarm, so calm yourself," Mrs. Heath instructed. "He's here to talk to you about a job."

Relief replaced fear and excitement took control. Vinnie practically flew down the stairs but skidded to a stop when she reached the foyer. She took a deep cleansing breath and smoothed down the pleats of her brown calf-length skirt. In the most ladylike fashion, she entered the sitting room, graciously greeting her guest.

"How nice to see you again, Chaplain Healy."

"It's also a pleasure to be in your presence again, Mrs. DiTrapani. I can see that married life agrees with you."

Vinnie's face colored with increasing degrees of intensity. Dreamily, she confirmed to herself that marriage and its benefits definitely agreed with her.

Chaplain Healy feigned a cough. He wasn't clairvoyant, but sensed the need to get the conversation back to safer ground. "Let me get to the reason for my stopping by today," he said. "I've spoken with Leo and I'm aware you're still adjusting to life here in Mississippi and you're unsure how to better occupy your time while he's at the base. If you've visited our base store, or PX, as I'm sure you've heard it called, you've probably met Natalie. She's a lovely girl and valued employee. I don't know if the news has reached you yet but Natalie's husband will be shipping out this week, and she's decided to return to her family's home in New England to wait out the war. That leaves her position open.

"The hours are noon until five, Monday through Friday, at a starting salary of thirty-five cents an hour. Would you possibly be interested?"

"Yes, yes," was all Vinnie could stammer. She did the math in her head. Five hours a day, five days a week. She'd be earning a total of eight dollars and seventy-five cents each and every week. Her petite arms did their best to encompass the robust chaplain in a grateful hug. They said their good-byes, each wearing their own smile of satisfaction.

"Thanks be to you, oh Lord," the chaplain said upon taking his leave. "Thank you for letting me be the bearer of good news today." With greater frequency, the war made it necessary for him to make house calls that were far from pleasant in nature. He felt like the grim reaper when he carried word of a soldier's passing to family and friends. Recipients of his news normally clung to him in grief. Today was a delightful departure, to be hugged with jubilation. As he walked from the house, his heart and step were lighter.

Vinnie was scheduled for the prerequisite physical examination at eight the next morning for any civilian working on the base. As soon as she received the physician's stamp of approval, she was to report to supervisor, Myra Bird "Birdie," at the PX.

At noon on Thursday, she rejoined the ranks of the employed.

CHAPTER ELEVEN

January 1944

The coming weeks were spent blissfully as Vinnie and Leo learned more about themselves and each other. Weekday afternoons Vinnie was ensconced in her work at the PX.

Evenings, after F&D, the couple would unwind in the world of make-believe, viewing movies on the large screen of the local cinema or base theater. Saturdays were looked forward to with childlike anticipation; they were double-feature days, two movies for the price of one. One of their favorite films starred Red Skelton in his comedic portrayal of "the Fox" in *Whistling in Brooklyn*. There were tears in their eyes from laughing so hard.

But reality loomed ominously on the horizon, and on January 24, 1944, the carpet of contentment was pulled out from under them. News had come down through official channels in the predawn hours.

A notice was posted ordering all members of the 633rd to report to the Briefing Room at 0900 hours. When Leo entered the room, he could feel the electricity bouncing off the stark walls. No one was seated. The men had assembled in small groups and were engaged in animated conversation. Excitement, apprehension and the musky scent of testosterone permeated the air.

When their commanding officer entered, all talk abruptly ceased and squad members scrambled to be seated. The room was unnaturally quiet.

The commander broke the silence as he stood at the podium looking at the attentive faces before him. "Well, gentlemen, as you most likely assume, our time has come. At 1500 hours on Wednesday, just two days from now, we'll be shipping out to England to join the Allied Forces in northwestern Europe. Our specific orders are currently under wraps, but we'll be further briefed upon arrival. Remember, this is what you've been trained for. The boys over there are counting on us and it's up to the 633rd to do our country proud. Schedules are posted for the remainder of our base time. Dismissed."

Only whispers could be heard among the men. Everyone had known this day was inevitable but few were prepared for the intensity of its reality. Leo felt like he'd been kicked in the stomach by a mule.

When Vinnie reported to work that day, uneasiness hung in the air like a brewing Mississippi storm. "Oh, dear Lord," she mumbled. She'd experienced this phenomenon before. It happened whenever another group of men was being transferred to the active war roster. She was going to ask her friend Annie which squad was leaving. But Annie, normally the first one to greet her each day, averted doleful brown eyes. Vinnie knew.

Within seconds, she experienced difficulty getting air into her lungs. It was what she had dreaded since coming south. She didn't recognize the shrill voice that made its way out of her mouth.

"Annie Rosen, you get your skinny behind over here this instant and tell me what's going on." Annie inched forward, with tears threatening to break free. She forced out the words, "The 633rd is up next."

Vinnie's heart began to pound. The depth of emotion scared her, as did the level of physical pain. She was sure she was having a heart attack. "Oh, dear God, please don't let me die yet," she pleaded. "I haven't had a chance to say good-bye to Leo."

Supervisor Birdie made her way to Vinnie and instructed her to "go to the ladies room and splash some cold water on your face. You're here until five, so you're going to have to pull yourself together."

Vinnie did as she was told, but Birdie's attitude sparked her anger. Why wasn't the woman being more empathetic?

Truth be told, Birdie had been through this many times before. She had learned a woman feeling anger was easier to deal with than one shedding tears. If she responded to the amount of sympathy she felt, all three of the ladies present would be huddled together, bawling their eyes out for the rest of the day.

Vinnie made it through the remainder of her shift. Whenever tears started to fall, Birdie responded like a drill sergeant, assigning her another specific task. Vinnie's upper lip curled into a snarl repeatedly in response to her supervisor's orders, but Birdie's tactics were successful in stemming the waterworks.

At five that evening, Leo met his wife at the PX. He didn't have to see the mask of grimness covering Vinnie's face to ascertain that word of his departure had, indeed, reached the base store. She threw herself into Leo's arms and latched on to him with the force of a professional wrestler.

As the two stood there, arms and bodies intertwined, they had no concept of time. Like a spring downpour, the tears came in torrents but neither one of them uttered a word...until an undefinable noise ruptured the uneasy silence. Leo stood back and held Vinnie at arm's length. A thunderous cacophony of hiccups escaped her downcast mouth as her nervous diaphragm spasmed.

Leo's lips parted in an infinitesimal smile that widened to a full-blown grin. Laughter settled in his red-rimmed eyes, transforming their color into a mischievous shade of blue. Leo stifled the next hiccup with a zealous kiss on his wife's pale lips. Vinnie didn't find her predicament amusing in the slightest and she stared daggers into his eyes, but alas, with Leo's charm, she was soon disarmed.

A reluctant smile hinted at the corners of her mouth. "Okay, two can play this game," she said to herself. "I can give 'em as good as I get 'em." She grabbed Leo by his collar and planted a big one right on his kisser. The stunned expression of her husband's face was priceless. They looked at one another and then burst into laughter. The laughter's gay refrain temporarily dispersed the shadowing clouds of gloom. Hand tightly gripped in hand, they began walking the short distance to F&D.

CHAPTER TWELVE

Dinner at the diner that evening was solemn. Vinnie unconsciously chewed the small bites of chicken she had taken but had difficulty swallowing. She finally gave up and pushed the plate away. Midge, who waited on them, knew better than to ask if there was something wrong. Having worked near the air base since the onset of the war, she was all too familiar with the look that haunted Vinnie and Leo's eyes.

That night and the night that followed, the room on the second floor of the Heath's was the arena where the couple's emotions were laid bare. If and when sleep came, it found the two spooned together without an inch of space between them. Even when Vinnie's soft breathing told Leo she had finally fallen asleep, he would feel a stray tear falling from her closed eyes onto his cradling arm.

It was agreed that on "D-Day" (the day of Leo's departure), Vinnie would report to work as usual. Under the circumstances, they thought it best to keep things on the most even keel possible. So in the early morning of that day, Leo bid his farewells to the Heaths. Vinnie was sound asleep, having only an hour earlier succumbed to her body's physical demand for rest. Leo could see the dark circles under her puffy eyes and did not have the heart to wake her. Instead, he walked to the desk and reached for a piece of writing paper.

With his fountain pen and a hand unsteadied by the myriad of feelings cascading through his system, he jotted down a brief note then returned to his wife. He carefully sat on the edge of the bed for a time just watching her sleep.

"I love you, Mrs. DiTrapani," he whispered gently, brushing the auburn hair from her face. "You're the best thing that's ever happened to me. Pray that when this war is over, I'll be able to come home to you in one piece. If God allows me to return and spend the rest of my life with you, I will never ask for more." He made the Sign of the Cross then brushed her still lips with a parting kiss.

When Vinnie awoke, her hand reached out, feeling only the cool emptiness of Leo's side of the bed. The heat from her husband's reclining body had dissipated hours early. She was not surprised.

She found the note he had left on the pillow. As she read it, her eyes blurred with moisture. "With all that I am or will ever be, I will love you through eternity." She pressed the note to her heart and the floodgates opened.

Just before 2:00 PM, Leo came to her at the PX. It was time for him to go. He was accompanied by Chaplain Healy, who was present in both an official and personal capacity to lend support. People in the PX discreetly looked away as the young couple clung hopelessly to one another. The war had touched all those present and there was no end in sight.

It wasn't long before the chaplain said, "Leo, my son, it's time to go." Leo cupped his wife's face and tried to kiss away the tears streaking her flawless skin.

"I'll be back as soon as I possibly can," Leo promised his wife, his voice fracturing with emotion. He took a deep breath and tried to swallow the huge lump in his throat. "I love you…with all my heart and soul."

Leo had to pry Vinnie's arms from his body. He physically handed her over to the chaplain and stoically walked through the door, knowing full well that one glance back would transform him into a one hundred and seventy-pound statue, incapable of ever moving again.

Dazed and leaning on Chaplain Healy's extended arm, with an unsteady gait Vinnie walked back to the boardinghouse.

The chaplain tapped twice and turned the knob of the unlocked door. Mrs. Heath quickly appeared in the foyer. The two looked at each other over their ward's downcast head and Mrs. Heath nodded. With her compassionate heart on her sleeve, she opened her arms and Vinnie was transferred to her care.

Chaplain Healy quietly closed the door, his responsibilities weighing heavily on his chest. He prayed for this particular day to end and for the fortitude to see it through. He headed east, making his way to another house where another woman waited. Some days it was difficult to work for both God and the Air Force. At the next home, it was his duty to represent both his employers, as he informed a pregnant wife that her husband wouldn't be returning home.

Back at the Heaths, the lady of the house assisted Vinnie up the stairs and tucked her into bed. She promised to be back in "two shakes of a lamb's tail" with a cup of strong tea, which she intended to lace with a therapeutic dose of brandy.

Sleep never came to Vinnie that night. As she prayed, she realized for the first time she was not unique in her sorrow and she certainly wasn't alone. Throughout the country, a sisterhood of wives of all ages, religions, and ethnic backgrounds were shedding tears of loneliness and sorrow while their husbands dutifully served their country. She may not have been able to hold onto Leo, but the one thing she could hold onto, with both hands, was her faith. She prayed for all of them until the sun rose.

CHAPTER THIRTEEN

On the 28th of January, the Heaths chaperoned Vinnie to the train station and watched as she boarded the railway car that would carry her home to New York. Saying their good-byes had been difficult for the ladies. They had formed a bond during Vinnie's short residence and when they hugged each other in a final embrace, Mrs. Heath felt as though she were seeing off her own daughter.

"You take care of yourself, young lady," she instructed Vinnie in a voice husky with mixed emotions. Part of her was sad to see her charge leaving. The other part of her was glad the girl was returning to the bosom of her own loving and supportive family.

"Remember to always trust in God and His infinite wisdom. You and Leo will be in our daily prayers and we'll ask our Lord to keep you both safe."

Vinnie located an empty seat away from the other passengers. She didn't feel up to making idle chitchat with strangers. She had sent a Western Union wire ahead to Queens, hopeful the telegram announcing her return had reached her parents.

So when the northbound train finally pulled into Pennsylvania Station, she wasn't sure if her father would be waiting for her. She stepped down from the car gripping her battered suitcase.

She didn't see him at first. Her eyes scanned the people crowding the platform and her expression became one of disappointment. She carefully searched the sea of faces one last time before heading to a bus that could take her home. But then she recognized his familiar walk, gray overcoat, and black fedora coming toward her. "Oh, Papa," she shouted, running to meet him halfway. She dropped her suitcase and ran into his arms.

When Vinnie walked into the house in Jackson Heights, the aroma of her mother's cooking welcomed her home. She made a dash for the kitchen, where her mother was standing in front of the stove, stirring and taste-testing a simmering pot of sauce.

Mrs. Giamonte surprisingly didn't rush to her daughter. Instead, she held out the wooden spoon offering her a sample taste, a tradition since the girl was in diapers. For Vinnie, it was as if time had stood still in the house on 94th Street. For the first time in days, she felt the tension draining. Some things were as they should be. This was her haven, comfortable and safe. It felt wonderful to be home.

Vinnie's mother wasted no time in taking in every inch of her returning child. She observed that her daughter was thinner, but that could easily be remedied. With a few hearty home-cooked meals and freshly baked bread topped with a dollop of rationed butter, she would fill out nicely.

As a mother, Mrs. Giamonte couldn't help noticing the sense of loss and sadness in her daughter's expressive eyes, but there was also something decidedly different shining through. It was something only another female would notice. Mrs. Giamonte smiled inwardly. The young girl who had left Queens a few months earlier had returned home a woman.

Correspondence between Vinnie and her husband crisscrossed the Atlantic Ocean on wings of faith and love. Leo's daily letters to his wife were a priority he listed along with eating, sleeping, and staying alive. It was the one constant in his life and it kept his connection to home a reality rather than a fading memory. Each day Vinnie waited by the front door for the afternoon mail delivery. Some days the smiling postman handed her two letters that had managed to arrive at the same time. Other days, the mail carrier sadly shook his head. "I'm sorry, Miss Vinnie, there's no letter today." He hated disappointing her. He preferred the days when she practically tore the mail from his hands.

On those days, after grabbing any correspondence from Leo, she would run up to her room and absorb every word printed. Later she would read parts of the letter aloud to Adele, who would lie on the bed and sigh, "I hope someday a man will love me as much as Leo loves you."

When it was time to go downstairs to help with dinner, Vinnie would reluctantly fold the letter neatly back in its envelope and gently place it in a blue box she tied with a white satin ribbon saved from her bridal bouquet.

Following the evening meal, Vinnie gladly helped clear the table and shared the chore of doing the dishes with her mother while Adele attended to homework or sketched them as they worked. They daily alternated washing and drying and it became a special bonding time for mother and daughter.

As Vinnie looked at her mother, she couldn't help but notice the waves of gray washing over the once vibrant brown hair, and the deepening creases around the knowledgeable hazel eyes. Her olive skin, a trait from a Castilian ancestor, had aged but still held the remnants of its youthful beauty.

Vinnie had deep admiration for her mother. An immigrant from Italy, she came to this country a young bride and had given birth to twelve children. One had died as a toddler. Presently, only three children remained at home. The rest were off on their own, either married or pursuing other dreams. From the time she came to America, she had helped supplement the family income by working as a seamstress, capitalizing on her natural sense of style and ability to create a beautiful garment from mere pieces of fabric. What she lacked in formal education, she made up with natural intelligence and grace. She was warm, humorous and kind of heart. In her, Vinnie not only had a parent she loved dearly, but a role model and best friend.

With the dishes put away, Vinnie would kiss her mother and father good night and retire to her room, where she wrote Leo each night without fail. She would tell him of her entire day from sunrise to sunset. It didn't matter if the day's events were interesting or trivial. She was sharing her day, her life, with him.

On Saturday and Sunday mornings, Vinnie and her father scoured the New York papers for news of the war. Sometimes he tried to get to the newspaper first to scan the articles to see if there was perhaps something Vinnie shouldn't read. Of course, she caught on to what he was doing the first time a page was missing.

"I'm not a child anymore, Papa. I'm a married woman concerned with what's happening to my husband three thousand miles away. If it were up to me, I'd be fighting on the battle field shoulder to shoulder with him."

Mr. Giamonte wisely swallowed the retort on the tip of his tongue. He knew his daughter all too well and frequently silence was the better part of valor. He held the paper up to his face to hide his widening grin. "Such independent females nowadays," he thought to himself. "What is this world coming to? Well, at least she's Leo's problem now, or will be when he gets home. I'd better say a few extra Hail Marys that this crazy war ends soon."

CHAPTER FOURTEEN

March 1944 to 1945

Vinnie cherished her time with the family, but mentally and financially she needed to go back to work. She found herself with too many empty hours along with an empty purse. As a deployed serviceman's wife, she was entitled to a $50 monthly allotment from Uncle Sam, but she wanted to save as much of that as she could so they would have the beginnings of a nest egg when Leo came home from the war.

She didn't have the heart to return to her old job at General Aircraft. Although the building on Astoria Boulevard held pleasant memories of her and Leo's first meeting and their early days together, returning there would be a constant reminder of what was then and could not be now.

Vinnie's determined search for employment ended with a position at American Time in Manhattan. As its name indicated, this Fifth Avenue firm's specialty was time clocks, watches, and timing components. Each employee was trained in the wiring, soldering, and calibration of numerous devices.

Vinnie was extremely pleased with her new position. It offered diversity, challenge, and a view of Rockefeller Center. In the winter she could watch skaters, eighteen stories below, exhibiting their varying degrees of talent as they glided or stumbled around the world-famous rink.

Noontime was her welcomed break. At the stroke of twelve each day, she made the transition from mild-mannered employee to a woman on a mission. She gobbled her lunch, barely taking the time necessary to swallow, or ate as she briskly walked across Fifth Avenue to St. Patrick's Cathedral between 50th and 51st Streets.

She came to the magnificent cathedral for solace and to pray. She would kneel before the Pieta, the statue of Mary cradling the lifeless body of her son after his Crucifixion. She hoped with all her heart that the Blessed Virgin would hear and answer her prayers. She asked the Madonna for Leo's safe return, as well as the countless others sent overseas.

For the young couple, weeks slowly turned into months and passing months into a year. The often-turned pages of Vinnie's calendar soon read 1945. While Leo's unit moved from England to France, fierce battles continued across the European continent and in the mighty Pacific. America's casualties numbered around two hundred thousand. Whenever Vinnie came home and there wasn't a letter from Leo, she automatically feared the worst.

On April 12, 1945, Americans mourned the loss of its thirty-second president, Franklin Delano Roosevelt, a man who served as commander in chief of the United States for a historic period of twelve years. As his successor, Vice President Harry S. Truman was sworn in to the country's highest office. Not only had Truman inherited the White House, he inherited the war as well. Fortunately, clouds of hope dotted the horizon.

Turmoil simmered into a steady boil within Deutschland's Third Reich. Many in the government's hierarchy questioned Hitler's military ability. More so, they seriously questioned his mental stability. The German people were weary and prayed for some semblance of their old life.

Short of food, supplies, and morale, German military defenses began to crumble like dominos. The Soviet Union had breached Germany's eastern border and battled its way across the Fatherland until triumphantly occupying one third of the country. On the west flank, Allied troops bravely fought for possession, one mile at a time, until they cordoned off the city of Berlin.

For perhaps the first time since his rise to supremacy, Adolf Hitler was forced to face reality. His power and time as Fuhrer were coming to a crippling end. On April 30, in his bunker, some twenty-five feet below ground, he made the final decision of his command. He put a gun to his head and pulled the trigger.

Eight days later, on May 8, Germany unconditionally surrendered to the Allied Forces and the day was labeled VE Day, for Victory in Europe. Europeans and Americans openly rejoiced in their home-town streets but the battle still raged on in the Pacific.

It wasn't until July 26, 1945 that Truman, Churchill, and Chiang Kai-shek, leaders of the three major world powers (the U.S., England, and China) issued a statement containing an ultimatum for Japan to surrender. Despite the triumvirate's dire warning of the consequences of non-compliance, Japan refused.

In response, on August 6, a trio of B-29s took off from North Field Airbase in the West Pacific. Their destination and primary target was Hiroshima, Japan. Some six hours later, the lead plane, christened the *Enola Gay*, opened its bay doors and dropped an atomic bomb code-named "Little Boy" on its industrial and military target. Its blast was equivalent to 13 kilotons of TNT.

Three days after the first bombing, the U.S. B-29 Superfortress *Bockscar* released the nuclear bomb "Fat Man" over Nagasaki. Its detonation reached beyond 21 kilotons of TNT. On the fourteenth day of August 1945, with its country in ruins, Japan capitulated.

Its formal surrender came on September 2, aboard the USS *Missouri* in the bay of Tokyo. September 2, or VJ Day Victory in Japan meant the end of the Second World War. All over the globe, friends and strangers embraced one another with unrestrained joyousness, and many danced in the streets.

When the official end of war documents were signed, Leo's division was camped on the outskirts of Paris. Word trickled in that the war was over. By nightfall, the encampment was awash with the amazing news. Shouts of elation echoed from every sector. Backs were slapped, arms punched, and faces kissed in jubilation. They would soon be going back home.

CHAPTER FIFTEEN

Fall 1945

Three weeks after Japan's surrender, Leo's battalion boarded the train from Paris to the port city of LeHarve. There they would embark the destroyer, the USS *Ericsson*, one of the newly commissioned vessels to transport troops home. Once on board, Leo and his fellow soldiers, lined the decks. They gleefully waved their farewells to France, many tossing their hats in the air.

Local newspapers in New York, New Jersey, and Connecticut printed the pending arrival of each military ship bringing American troops back to the tristate area. Under the name of the ship was listed the branch of service and squadrons it carried. Daily Vinnie scoured the columns of the *New York Times* hoping and praying for word of Leo's return.

On the Wednesday evening of October 3, after dinner and dishes, Vinnie checked the newspaper for word of Leo's arrival. When she saw his division, the 86th Airborne, scheduled for return on the *Ericsson* on Tuesday, October 9, her eyes sparkled like brilliant sapphires. She circled the information then ran screaming through the house.

"Papa, Mama, Leo's coming home. He's really, really coming home. Papa, papa, please come with me to meet Leo's ship," she pleaded, shoving the paper in front of his face. He read the article, relieved to the core that the dream of Leo's homecoming had turned into a reality.

But his daughter read the uncertainty in his eyes as he considered her request. There would be throngs of people waiting while hundreds of soldiers exited the ship; and they had heard that once the men came off the ship, they were required to report to Fort Dix in New Jersey. She would only have a few minutes with Leo, at best, and that was only if she could actually find him.

Vinnie paused, catching her breath. "Papa, you know I'm going . . . with or without you." He did, indeed, know that she would. Against his better judgment, he consented. Tuesday morning when the carrier arrived, they would venture into the fray at the harbor.

On October 9, Leo was among the multitude crowded on the deck of the *Ericsson,* drinking in the view of New York Harbor. When his eyes caught sight of the Statue of Liberty, tears trickled down his checks. Lady Liberty was a sight for sore eyes and the most beautiful woman Leo had seen in two years.

It was both a time of celebration and reflection for all aboard. During their tours of duty, each one of these men had come face to face with the grim reaper as it extinguished life all around them and stole their innocence and youth.

Some had visible scars. Others bore a burden of guilt, not understanding why God had chosen to spare them, in particular, and not the squad mate or friend less than a foot away. They were the men who had held the dying in their arms while life ebbed from broken and battered bodies. They were survivors who carried their scars on the inside, hidden from view.

The three-hundred-and forty-eight foot-destroyer docked without effort. Once on American soil, the soldiers would be directed to buses assigned to transport them to Fort Dix to be processed out. It was a long disembarkation, but a number of the men somehow managed to find family and friends among the mob of people energetically waving American flags and handkerchiefs.

As Leo walked down the gangplank, the rational part of his brain reasoned that his wife would not be there waiting. It was far wiser for her to be safely at home and not in this mass of humanity. But his heart had its own agenda and wanted her there. He searched the crowd for her face…the face he had only seen in his dreams for two long and lonely years.

With his duffle bag slung over his shoulder, he pushed his way through the crowd toward the waiting buses. With each step he scanned the sea of faces, but his wife's was not among them. When he reached the designated transport, he did not go inside. While others boarded, he waited outside the door, until the driver finally yelled to him, "Hey, buddy, I ain't got all day. There's one seat left on this heap and it's got your name on it. It's a long way to Fort Dix if you're planning on hoofing it."

Leo reluctantly turned to board, but his peripheral vision caught a flash of red coming in at close range. He recognized the windblown auburn curls escaping the red kerchief that had loosened in the breeze as she zeroed in on him. He had less than thirty seconds before impact. He braced himself as she exploded into his arms. Without saying a word, she covered his face with kisses and their tears of joy commingled.

The men on the bus hooted and hollered.

"Ain't youse guys ever seen a pretty girl before," the driver shouted above the din.

"Sure, we have but it's been so long we're just enjoying the view," someone piped up from the rear.

The driver felt a tug at his heart, but he could only give the couple a few minutes together. "Hey, buddy," he again addressed

Leo, "I hate to be a party pooper, but I gotta get youse back to Dix before they send the MP's out lookin' for us."

The idea of going AWOL was extremely appealing but Leo knew the military police would find him sooner rather than later and he didn't relish spending his homecoming in prison.

He gently removed his wife's arms from their locked position around his neck. His eyes bored into hers. "Honey, listen to me. They've already told us we'd have a temporary leave in two days and I give you my solemn word that I'll be home as soon as humanly possible."

He gave her one last toe-curling kiss that held the infinite promise of things to come.

Their second day at Fort Dix, the returning soldiers were granted their well-earned thirty-day leave. Through a friend of a friend, Leo sent word to Vinnie that he would be coming home as promised. He hitched a ride with a few guys headed for New York, but before they got to the Lincoln Tunnel, a tire blew on the old Ford. As the driver maneuvered to the side of the road, expletives wafted through the car's open windows. Without a jack in the trunk, getting home was going to take a little longer than expected.

Meanwhile, Vinnie was impatiently counting the minutes until Leo's arrival in Jackson Heights. She had been alternating between sitting on the front steps of number 2518 and standing on her tiptoes attempting to get a full view of 94th Street. The minutes ticked away, but she stubbornly remained at her station, not wanting to miss the car pulling up.

She rehearsed all the things she wanted to say to him, but when the rusted black Ford finally pulled to the curb and Leo squeezed out of the backseat, all coherent thoughts evaporated. Leo only had a split second to toss his duffle bag to the ground before Vinnie threw herself into his arms. Leo was amazed they both remained in an upright position. She wrapped her arms and legs around him and locked her lips to his.

Mrs. Giamonte stood inside the front door, wanting to give the couple a private moment. As tears welled in her eyes, she surprised herself by laughing out loud. Leo had survived the war, but she didn't know if he'd survive his homecoming.

Her husband came to stand next to her, putting his arm tenderly around her. She leaned her head on his shoulder and sighed. "Look at those two. Isn't it wonderful to be young and so in love?" He smiled warmly. "It's not so bad being old and still so in love either, *il mio amore*," he said softly, his lips reaching down to caress hers.

Leaning into her husband's embrace, she looked up at the heavens and whispered, "Thank you." They had so much to be grateful for.

Chapter Sixteen

Vinnie and Leo's reunion far surpassed the anticipation and dreams of two anxious years apart. Vinnie's room became their hideaway, where they shared countless hours whispering and laughing as only those at the dawn of love can do. They cuddled under the blankets, trying to be quiet and often failing as they shared the overflowing emotions and intimacy the war had denied them.

It was more or less a formality when Leo reported back to the base in New Jersey at the end of his thirty-day leave. When the ink was dry on his discharge papers, he was free to settle into the blessed normalcy of everyday life.

But for Leo and the thousands of young men returning home, there were no employers waiting with open arms and ready job offers. When the war ended, so did the need for the vast defense industry that had sustained the nation's economy. The majority of defense plants were closed or reconverted in the months after VJ day. .

At Fort Dix Leo had been offered the option of becoming a reservist, a position touted by the government as a means to supplement civilian-life income with a steady, though minimal, monthly check and limited physical participation. For many it seemed the natural progression from their former military status, and any source of guaranteed income was foolish to refuse.

The requirements for a reservist were fairly simple. One: they would be expected to report to a local base one weekend a month. Two: They would spend two weeks every summer at a base designated by command. Three: In the event of another war, they were being held "in reserve" and would be called to duty.

In the fall of 1945 America had started its journey down the road to recovery. Civilians across the country and those in power in Washington, D.C., firmly believed the United States would never again send its youth to battle on foreign soil. Becoming a reservist seemed both logical and practical. Leo and hundreds of others eagerly signed on the dotted line.

After Leo's last two days at Fort Dix, he returned to the house shouting and waving his discharge papers triumphantly. Vinnie hurried to meet him when she heard the commotion.

"Welcome home, honey. Thank God this time it's for good." Her tone grew more serious when she continued, "You belong to us now and not Uncle Sam."

She quickly realized the word "us" had slipped from her mouth and the seriousness of her expression changed into something mischievous. Leo caught the change instantly. His wife stood in front of him resembling a child who was privy to a secret and couldn't wait to spill the beans.

Before he could say a word, Vinnie's alabaster face contorted. She cupped both her hands to her mouth and ran for the stairs. Leo, his heart rate quickening, followed in her wake. He discovered the bathroom door thrown wide open and his wife kneeling on the linoleum floor, her arms encircling the white porcelain commode, retching. He ran to the top of the staircase yelling for his mother-in-law.

When Mrs. Giamonte reached the bathroom, Leo was on his knees next to Vinnie, carefully holding her hair away from her face. His own face was etched with questions and mounting fear.

Mrs. Giamonte simply patted Leo on the shoulder and informed him, "Your wife will be find…in a few months." His panic increased when he heard "a few months," and it reflected in his frightened eyes. His mother-in-law gave him a reassuring smile. "Leo, she is not the first woman since Eve to be afflicted with morning sickness."

Leo's body froze but a dumb look occupied his face. It took several long seconds for the light of comprehension to dawn. When it did, he grinned like an idiot, a certifiable one. His beautiful, wonderful wife was expecting a baby, their very first baby. Elated tears spilled from the corners of his now smiling eyes. He kissed Vinnie on the top of her bowed head and jumped up to embrace his mother-in-law.

When Vinnie could finally catch a breath, she looked up at the happy duo. "Hey, you two, remember me? I'm the one who's pregnant and the only one with her head in the bowl. Could you stop hugging long enough to help me up?" Leo lifted Vinnie to her feet and planted a big kiss on her still wet lips. Mrs. Giamonte turned to leave with an amused look on her face. Leo was definitely a man in love, and a brave one to boot.

The young couple couldn't have been happier. After the first three months, Vinnie's morning (noon, and night) sickness abated, and although her body retained its normal slimness, her expanding tummy proudly announced the baby growing within.

God continued to bless them as Leo struggled to find employment in the limited post-war market. His earlier training as a Linotype operator and his proficiency in that field, combined with his natural determination, landed him a coveted position with a local magazine in Ozone Park. Only Leo and one other person out of the three hundred applicants were hired.

Vinnie blossomed in her mother-to-be state. She was a loving wife and the picture of domesticity. She took pleasure in tidying their personal nest on the second floor and in helping her parents around the house until the latter stages of pregnancy. By then, it seemed like her protruding stomach arrived at all destinations well in advance of the rest of her. Her once tiny feet swelled to the size of footballs and even walking became a chore. Her siblings were put to work as "cranes" to pull her up from the couch or chair.

Vinnie wondered how on earth her mother had gone through this a dozen times. Since her father had frequently been on the road, pregnant or not her mother had taken care of the house and her children. Without a word of complaint, she met her family's needs and continued to work from home.

Perhaps it got easier after the first one, but there was no way Vinnie would consider doing this repeatedly. In her eyes, women like her mom deserved a medal of the highest honor.

In the early hours of July 18, Vinnie went into labor. By the time Leo got her to Boulevard Hospital, the contractions were coming every seven minutes and Vinnie's face became a canvas of pain each time another spasm ripped through her.

The attendant at the desk pointed to a wheelchair several feet away. "Mrs. DiTrapani, please have a seat until we're ready for you."

Between contractions, Leo managed to get his wife seated as instructed, but he felt totally helpless. He lightly stroked his wife's cheek.

"Honey, I wish to God that I could go through this for you."

Vinnie didn't hesitate to reply. "Leo, right now I wish to God, with every fiber of my being, you could too!" She grabbed his hand with superhuman strength as another pain began its assault and peaked.

A girl with dark hair, dressed in nurse whites, cheerfully approached the expectant parents. "It's time we took the little mother to her room so we can have our baby."

Vinnie released her grip on Leo's partially paralyzed hand and was seriously tempted to grab the perky nurse by the throat. She wanted to shout, "First of all, kiddo, you don't look like you're old enough to be out of high school. Secondly, there is no WE having this baby, only ME, and me isn't exactly smiling right now." Luckily for the nurse, another debilitating contraction short circuited the words that hadn't yet traveled to Vinnie's lips.

The young nurse, totally unawares, continued in her bubbly tone, "Are we ready to go?" but didn't wait for a reply. She simply commandeered the wheelchair, and pushed Vinnie down the long white hallway while humming a merry little tune.

Leo knew his wife all too well and had seen the firestorm brewing in her eyes when she was wheeled off. "If looks could kill," Leo thought, "that poor little nurse would end up needing a hospital bed of her own."

As the morning turned into afternoon, Leo anxiously paced the white-and-black tiled hospital floors. For the first time in three years, he yearned to have a Camel cigarette between his lips, but settled for his fifth cup of some liquidized sludge the hospital passed off as coffee. With cup in hand, he continued walking back and forth.

For Vinnie the minutes felt like hours, and now she could barely catch her breath as the rapid waves of transition engulfed her. When a tide of pain ebbed, her thoughts drifted temporarily taking her away from the labor room.

Her throat and lips were parched and her russet locks clung to her throbbing head in wet clumps. She wished Leo was there to wipe her brow with a cool wet cloth and give her a sip of…iced tea. Ah yes, that's exactly what she wanted…a tall glass of iced tea overflowing with ice and two heaping teaspoons of sugar. Vinnie's craving and mental meanderings momentarily transported her back in time to their newlywed days in Mississippi.

As soon as she could garner the strength, she was going to get up and go to F&D, where Midge would pour her that drink and would listen attentively to her when she complained about these terrible pains in her stomach. Maybe Midge would know what to do.

An impatient voice calling "Mrs. DiTrapani" broke through her reverie. She was annoyed by the intrusion and reluctantly returned to the delivery room. She soon recognized the voice of her doctor, ordering her to push.

With the next contraction, Vinnie leaned forward and pushed with all her might. "Just one more push," the doctor fibbed. Three arduous pushes later, Vinnie's tears of pain turned into tears of relief and joy as a perfectly rounded head made its debut followed by a pair of diminutive shoulders and tiny legs. At 3:00 PM on Thursday, July 18, 1946, a beautiful seven-pound baby girl came into the world. Her wide eyes were outlined by long dark lashes and her precious head was adorned with a halo of damp golden ringlets.

Vinnie's heart pounded with an all-encompassing love she deemed heaven-sent, a love with no strings except those binding this child to her heart forever. She longed to hold her baby, but the crotchety delivery nurse whisked the newborn away, sternly reminding the new mother that "we must follow the rules, young lady, and you'll see your baby soon enough."

The new mother was too exhausted to argue, but she fell asleep with a few choice words, definitely unladylike in nature, dangling on the tip of her tongue.

It wasn't until an hour later that Leo got his first look at his child through the nursery window. He had to remind himself to breathe as he gazed upon the quiet bundle wrapped in pink. His daughter looked so tiny and fragile, but when the nurse picked up the sleeping newborn, the baby let loose an indignant wail that rocked the walls of the nursery. Leo's face beamed broadly. "That's my daughter and she's already expressing her opinion. I wonder who she takes after!"

CHAPTER SEVENTEEN

August 1946

On the fourth Sunday after her birth, their daughter, outfitted from head to toe in garments sewn or knitted by both her grandmothers, was christened with the name Lenora. The DiTrapani and Giamonte families proudly gathered around the baptismal font at St. Gabriel's as Father Silvio bathed the infant's uncovered satin curls in holy water.

The good Father had performed countless baptisms, but was decidedly taken with this one child. He readily acknowledged her beauty, except it wasn't her physical appearance that emotionally stirred him. Rather it was the way in which her hazel eyes seemed to bore into his and the way she appeared to be listening and comprehending his Latin words. He had never before seen such serene intensity on a tiny infant's face. He found himself at a loss, not exactly sure of what he was witnessing but aware that he should consider himself and those around him blessed.

Following Lenora's christening, the family of three settled into a life they would temporarily share with Vinnie's parents. Leo was working hard and struggling to put a few dollars away out of every paycheck so he and Vinnie could perhaps, in the not so distant future, get a small place of their own.

It was something he and his wife often discussed and it was a dream that could blossom into reality for many young couples due to the foresight of two visionary men. Previously, in June 1944, President Roosevelt had signed legislation informally labeled the "GI Bill of Rights." This law would provide for the education and job training of those returning from a war still in progress. But a unique proviso of the bill was the low-interest, zero-down-payment home loans that would be made available to servicemen through the Veterans' Administration. Such low-cost loans would enable millions of city apartment dwellers, and families forced to share lodging with others, to move into suburban areas and achieve the new American dream of home ownership.

But homes were yet to be built and an entrepreneur named William Levitt would fill the need. Prior to the war, Levitt & Sons built mostly upscale housing on New York's Long Island, but in 1945, they devised a plan to revolutionize the home construction industry.

The Levitts had purchased seven square miles of potato farms close to the existing town of Hicksville. This suburban area was their proposed site of mass-produced, low-cost housing, a novel concept but one direly needed to provide housing for the post-war population. Incredibly houses could be built in a matter of days and sold for just under $8,000.

Roosevelt and Levitt gave Leo, and others like him, a chance for the future. In the meantime, however, Leo insisted on paying room and board to his in-laws. He wanted to contribute his fair share and explained, in no uncertain terms, to Vinnie and her parents that he didn't expect any free rides on life's highway. The Giamontes, on the other hand, were more than glad to share their residence, but wisely knew a young family starting out needed the privacy only a place of their own could provide.

With their voices somewhat hushed, they discussed the situation one evening behind the closed door of the bedroom they had shared for thirty years. "I know they should have a place of their own," Mrs. Giamonte confessed. "But I do so enjoy having them here. It brings such happiness to my heart to see our daughter with her own little girl. Do you think I'm being selfish?"

Her husband learned over and patted the hand that had remained soft to his touch through the decades. "If that were the case, my dear, we'd both be guilty. I've grown quite attached to that little one. I can't put my finger on it, but there is something unique about Lenora. I can see it in those sparkling hazel eyes of hers, which, I might add, she inherited from her beautiful maternal grandmother. It's almost as though she knows something that we adults couldn't possibly comprehend. On the other hand, perhaps I'm just being a silly old man. Don't pay any attention to my rambling."

She snuggled closer to her husband. "You're certainly not old, Mr. Giamonte, and I might let you prove it. As for your being silly, I'll have to give you my opinion on that later." She ardently kissed the man she had loved since she was fifteen years old, then reached over and turned out the light.

CHAPTER EIGHTEEN

During their breakfast discussion the next morning, while Mr. Giamonte drank his steaming espresso and Mrs. Giamonte diced fresh garden tomatoes and onions for an omelet, they decided the best thing to do to keep their daughter and her family in close proximity, yet still afford them some degree of privacy, was to build an extension onto the rear of their existing abode.

The property lot was certainly deep enough to nicely accommodate the expansion and the addition would serve to enhance the financial value of the home. Finding a reputable construction company would not be a problem since Mrs. Giamonte's first cousin, Carmine "the carpenter," owned and operated Cione's Construction in the Ozone Park area. They knew the job would be professionally sound and, with the family discount, wouldn't cost the proverbial arm and a leg.

The work on the apartment began at the end of September. Carmine started with his regular- size crew, but when word spread that Mrs. Giamonte was cooking meals for the workmen, stories of her delicious home-made pastas and mouth-watering parmigianas encouraged others to volunteer their services. As a result, there was a steady stream of construction men on the premises from sunrise to sunset.

The basic structure was completed before the worst of winter weather set in and the apartment itself was ready just before

Christmas. Everyone was enormously pleased with the outstanding job. Thanks to Mrs. Giamonte's cooking and the influx of workers it seduced, the job had incredibly come in under budget.

Cousin Carmine, as the construction company's owner, had only one complaint. His crew had increased in size...not so much in the number of employees, but in the waistlines of those who worked on the Giamonte house. Some of the men had tears in their eyes when the job was finished. If only their wives could cook "like Mrs. G.," they would willingly go to church every Sunday and give thanks.

With the apartment structurally complete, there still remained the sizable task of furnishing the four rooms. Leo's salary had increased to $28 a week and he continued to receive his monthly stipend from the military as a reservist, but there was no possible way he could stretch his take-home dollars to provide the items required to set up their new home.

Mrs. Giamonte and Mrs. DiTrapani, Sr., contacted family members, requesting usable furniture, fabric, and household odds and ends...anything that would aid their mutual endeavor. Others whose talents could be utilized refurbishing, refinishing, or upholstering were put on stand-by to assist as needed. Under the direction of the matriarchs, the families worked tirelessly, crafting or donating all the essentials for the new apartment down to the toilet paper in the bathroom.

What could have ended up a major hodgepodge of odds and ends resulted in a transformation of once-bare rooms into something homey and welcoming. But it was Lenora's bedroom that provided the icing on the cake. Her Aunt Adele had designed the room, inspired by the child herself. The room was a vision of blue sky and cumulus clouds. Among the billowing white puffs, there floated angelic cherubs, their yellow-gold wings captured in various stages of flight. As a finishing touch, the crucifix given to Lenora and blessed by Father Silvio during her Christening ceremony was hung with loving care above the door.

Vinnie and Leo were thrilled beyond words and grateful beyond measure when they got their first look at the completed apartment. When they entered Lenora's room, Vinnie viewed the artistic creation in silent awe. Leo, also temporarily deprived of words, was the first to recover, regaining both the use of his tongue and his humor.

"I believe this may be the first time in the family's history that any of us can remember my wife being at a total loss for words. I suggest that each and every one present make a note of the time and date of the monumental event."

Vinnie playfully shot her elbow in the direction of Leo's unprotected ribs, but he gently grabbed the extended arm and pulled her into a bear hug. His eyes misted in gratitude.

On Sunday, December 14, 1947, the official housewarming for the finished project took place in the Giamonte's main house. The apartment was more than adequate for the family of three, but a much larger space was needed to provide for a proper family celebration. Everyone visited the new addition, nodding their heads in approval and uttering oohs and aahs as they entered Lenora's room.

Father Silvio, a jovial expression on his wizened face, attended the party and blessed the new home. The Roman Catholic priest always liked interacting with his parishioners, but took special delight in visiting the Giamontes, particularly when a full course meal was involved. Whenever he was asked how he enjoyed his dinner, Father Silvio would pat his contented stomach and say, "Heavenly, just heavenly."

As the party was winding down and many of the family had left, Leo politely excused himself and his wife. He took her hand in his and led her to the rear apartment. Although they were no longer newlyweds, Leo insisted on ceremoniously carrying Vinnie across the threshold and enthusiastically kissed her warm, waiting lips under the Christmas mistletoe hung by Adele in the small entryway.

With Lenora tucked in for the night and sound asleep in the main house, Leo's spirited blue eyes twinkled. Maybe it was too soon to start contemplating having another baby, but thinking had nothing to do with the activity on his agenda for the night.

.

CHAPTER NINETEEN

Late 1947 to July 1948

It wasn't long before Vinnie and Leo did get around to planning that second child. Vinnie didn't conceive as quickly as she had when Leo returned from the war, but her husband had things under control.

"It's a tough job," he would laughingly complain. "But I'm up to the task. When my wife, my current commanding officer, gives me 'that certain look,' like any soldier worth his stripes, I'm ready to report for duty."

Once the couple was successful, Vinnie was again beset by the maladies of early pregnancy. She soon tired of spending a significant portion of her day on the bathroom floor and decided to keep a "PB" (puke bucket) close at hand. The bucket, and little Lenora, now seventeen months of age, were Vinnie's two constant companions.

In the morning, Vinnie attempted to make breakfast for Leo and Lenora while she nibbled on some salted crackers and tried to keep those down. After Leo left for work, she bathed and dressed her daughter and tidied up around the apartment. At 10:30 AM she turned on her radio and listened to Arthur Godfrey while she and Lenora played in the living room.

Noon was scheduled nap time for mother and daughter, but they didn't necessarily sleep. Vinnie liked to put a Frankie Laine or Dinah Shore record on their Victrola and recline on the sofa, swollen feet elevated...the "PB" within easy reach.

Lenora would sit contentedly with her favorite blanket and fluffy pillow on the brown-patterned rug in the middle of the room. She'd coo with her baby doll, hum to the music playing or engage in some game of her own making.

Sometimes when Vinnie's queasy stomach rebelled during their quiet time, Lenora would abandon whatever game or thoughts her creative mind was engaged in, get up, and purposely toddle to her mother. She would pick up the damp facecloth her mother kept next to the couch and lightly wipe her mother's lips, as she had often seen her father do. Then she would learn over and gingerly place a kiss on her mother's stomach.

Whenever Lenora did that, Vinnie would look at her beautiful daughter and tears would come to her emotional eyes.

"Daddy and I are so lucky to have you, sweetheart. You're our little angel sent from Heaven."

A smile would come to Lenora's tiny lips then spread across her cherub face like the sun's rays coming over the horizon. The glowing smile radiated all the way down to her half-pint heart that pumped with pure joy.

When the time came for the new baby to be born, Leo hurriedly took Lenora next door, where she would stay with her grandparents. Returning to the apartment, he attempted to whisk his wife off to the hospital, but she stubbornly refused.

"There's absolutely no sense in rushing, Leo," she firmly stated. "At least I know what to expect this time around and if I have to be in pain, I'd rather go through it in the privacy of my own home. Believe me, it's certainly a lot better than lying in an antiseptic-smelling hospital bed with some crusty old nurse saying, 'There, there, dear.

It's not really that bad.' Anyone who could say that obviously has never been horizontal on a hard delivery table struggling to push the equivalent of a seven-pound watermelon out the spout of a garden hose. That really gets my dander up, Leo, and you know how I am when someone pushes me over the edge."

Leo turned away for a second and rolled his eyes. He did, in fact, know how testy she could become. With a frustrated sign of resignation, he gave in. "Okay, sweetheart, you win, but we're only going to stay a little while longer."

With all his good intentions, Leo was no help to his wife whatsoever. When he sat, he constantly fidgeted, and when he stood, he relentlessly paced. He offered Vinnie his hand to squeeze when another sizeable contraction made its ascent but all the color drained from his taut face. He looked as white and rigid as a freshly starched sheet hung out to dry.

When the pain ebbed, Vinnie struggled to catch her breath. "Leo, I think we'd better get to the hospital as soon as possible… you look as though you're going to need the doctor a lot sooner than I will."

At noon, on Wednesday, July 28, 1948, their eight-pound son Leonard loudly announced his entrance into the world. His tiny head was covered with golden down, his delicate eyelashes so light in color they were nearly invisible. Still prone on the delivery table, Vinnie's face glowed with serene satisfaction. "God has given us another beautiful baby. Oh, my Leo will be so proud."

When Leo arrived at the nursery, his expectant eyes searched for the bassinet labeled DiTrapani and excitedly motioned to the attendant, pointing to the baby and then back to himself. The nurse promptly held up the sleeping bundle. As he gazed upon his son, Leo swore he could feel his chest expanding to accommodate the growing size of his heart.

"Thank you, God," he whispered. "You have given me more than any one man has the right to ask. I may not have a lot of money, but you have made me a very rich man."

One week later, when the couple brought the baby home from the hospital and introduced him to his big sister, for Lenora it was love at first sight. She thought the baby was one of her birthday presents, even though he arrived much too late for her party.

Lenora had turned two on July 18, but acted more like five or six according to her parents and grandparents. She gave the new baby her undivided attention and watched over her little brother as though personally appointed to be his guardian angel.

"My baby," she would say and kiss his tiny hands. Leonard would rapidly kick his short legs and squeal in delight. The love was undeniably mutual.

BOOK II

CHAPTER ONE

July 1950

Both Lenora and Leonard had birthdays to celebrate in July and their parents decided to combine the festivities. A party would take place at the main house with an open invitation to family and friends.

A triple-layer rectangular cake was baked and decorated for the occasion. One side of the confectionary was golden vanilla topped with four candles for the birthday girl. The other side was rich chocolate with two candles for the birthday boy. Two additional candles were placed squarely in the middle of the swirling peaks of pearl white frosting. One was for good luck and the other for good measure.

The children blew out the eight candles with some assistance from their doting Aunt Adele, who was standing behind them with her steady beau, Mike. Before anyone could cut the cake, a beaming Adele asked for everyone's attention. She displayed her ring finger, dramatically sweeping it from right to left. The adorned finger sported a lustrous quarter-carat diamond within a fourteen-carat gold setting.

"Mike asked me to marry him when I graduate and I've accepted," she announced, her face radiant with happiness. She and Mike looked at each other with adoration and officially sealed their pact with a lip lock. A round of applause and congratulations followed. Adele caught Vinnie's eye. They knowingly winked at each other. Not one but two of the Giamonte girls were destined to be lucky in love.

Under normal circumstances, the dual birthdays and engagement would have been a time for jubilation, but the tranquil life the DiTranpanis shared in Queens, and the lives of many others across the country, were about to change. A few weeks earlier, on June 23, President Harry S. Truman announced that the United States, as part of a United Nations resolution, was doing the unthinkable: it was again sending its troops to fight on foreign soil.

The status of Leo and his fellow reservists was changed to "active" overnight. The group they had joined in 1945 and considered a safe haven would now be returning them to the battlefield. Americans would be defending South Korea's 38th Parallel against hostilities from the North, but the U.S., for all intent and purposes, referred to this political hotbed as a police action rather than a war.

Vinnie had been extremely upset, but kept it bottled up until the birthday party was over. It was then she allowed her temper free range as she ranted to Leo about the Asian crisis and the United States' questionable intervention.

"This country is still recovering from a major war. We had no choice but to go into combat when the Japanese brazenly crossed the Pacific Ocean and attacked Pearl Harbor.

"And when we learned of all the inhumane atrocities committed in Europe, at the hand of that lunatic and his fanatics, I was proud the United States had been there to help. But what in Heaven's name are we doing in Korea, of all places? Does calling it hostilities or a police action make our men any less dead when they're on the receiving end of a bullet?"

Leo shook his head. "Honey, I couldn't agree with you more, but I don't know what to tell you."

He certainly didn't have the answers. He was an average man who loved his family and the Almighty. The future was not in his humble hands but in those of God and country.

The directive from the Air Force arrived the day after their conversation and Vinnie's already sour mood fermented. Her husband was ordered to report to Barksdale Air Force Base in Louisiana in seven days' time. The primary question of his deployment was left hanging in the air.

During the next seven days, the precariousness of their situation was sorely testing Vinnie's faith. She was vocal to an extreme. She continued to rant and rave about the "idiotic" powers-that-be in Washington, D.C., but some of that anger was threatening to spill over onto an even higher authority. Had God brought Leo home physically unscathed five years ago only to take him away again… perhaps permanently this time?

Mrs. Giamonte, witnessing her daughter's distress and unsure of how to help, asked Father Silvio to place the young Mrs. DiTrapani on his list of house calls.

When Vinnie went to answer the firm knock on the apartment door, she wasn't at all surprised to see the priest standing on her doorstep, and Father Silvio wasn't a bit surprised when Vinnie, who only hours before had stoically watched her husband drive away, burst into tears. He knew this was going to be a tough one; but he also knew Vinnie was one tough cookie and God would see her through, despite her daunting personal doubts.

With Father Silvio's encouragement, in the coming days Vinnie forced herself to focus on the only bright spot in this situation. This time around, Leo's rank had its privileges. She and the children would be permitted to join him in Louisiana with their choice of on-base or leasable off-base housing facilities. The four of them would be together until Leo was shipped out.

Vinnie prepared the children, telling them that at the end of August, they'd be "going on an exciting adventure to a place called Louisiana and a new house where Daddy waited for them." She started packing up their personal possessions. The Air Force assumed responsibility for transporting their furniture and numerous boxes, which would soon be neatly stacked on the dark oak floors throughout the four rooms.

Late evenings and early mornings found Vinnie kneeling at the side of their full-size bed. She would reluctantly glance at Leo's unused portion of the bed… it looked sadly pristine. Twice a day she prayed for her family, asking God for the strength to face whatever lay ahead. She thought she was finally gaining a grip on her emotions when she was hit by an unexpected curve ball thrown from left field… a throw initiated by her own mother.

For several days, Mrs. Giamonte had looked pensive. There was obviously something weighing on her mind, but Vinnie was too distracted with her own problems to broach the subject. The last thing she wanted was to open another can of worms.

"Vinnie, honey, we need to talk," her mother finally said as she poured them both another cup of coffee at the Giamonte's kitchen table. Vinnie knew those words were never a good sign, no matter who the speaker.

"I don't know how to put this so I'm just going to come out and say it." There was a slight pause while she inhaled, then expelled the words. "Papa and I have been thinking about selling the house and moving out to California."

Vinnie's jaw dropped and no air entered or exited her lungs.

"We only have Adele and Robert at home in this oversized house," Mrs. Giamonte hastily continued, "and when Adele graduates high school, she and Mike will be getting married.

"You know we're not as young as we used to be and it's getting harder each year to maintain the house and the garden. Of course, your brother and sister help as much as they can, but they're only kids, with school studies and busy social lives.

"And it's the winter months that concern me the most. Your father is of an age when he shouldn't be out shoveling snow from the sidewalks and driveway. And even if he tells me he's simply going out to supervise the kids, I know it's only a matter of minutes before he grabs a shovel and digs in. The weather in southern California would be so much better for him, and we'd have your two brothers nearby."

Vinnie had yet to utter a word, but the distress in her eyes was evident. California wasn't on the other side of the world, but it was on the other side of the country.

"Oh, honey, please don't look so upset," Mrs. Giamonte pleaded. Our moving won't affect your living arrangements," she hurriedly tried to reassure her.

"I'm sure you remember Mrs. Spinelli, the elderly lady who lives a block over and rents out rooms. Well, she has a grown grandson with three children. He wants to be closer to his grandmother and his wife is expecting another baby in six months. They've outgrown the house they own in New Jersey and are looking in our neighborhood for something larger.

"They've already made us a more than decent offer and we'd be foolish not to at least consider it. And since for the time being you'll be living in Louisiana, and the apartment will be vacant, the Spinellis made a suggestion I think you'll find agreeable. They plan to rent out the apartment on a month-to-month basis. This way, when you're ready to come home they can make it available to you again. They also promised not to increase the rent beyond what you're already paying."

The fog engulfing Vinnie finally lifted.

"I'm sorry, Mama. I didn't mean to rain on your parade," Vinnie responded most apologetically. "It's just, everything's happening at one time. The thought of you and Papa leaving this house where we all grew up will take a little getting used to. I'm afraid my motives for wanting you to stay here are purely selfish. But I do want you and Papa to take life easier and the West Coast seems a good place to do it, especially since Joey and Charlie are so happy out there.

"As far as Leo and I go, we're at the mercy of the war. I'm not planning on crossing any bridge until I'm standing one foot in front of it."

Vinnie got up to leave and hugged her mother. "You know how much I love you and Papa. You've done a terrific job of raising your children and it's definitely time you thought of yourselves. Whatever you decide is fine by me."

CHAPTER TWO

August 1950

With the apartment's contents packed and ready to go, Vinnie and the children moved into the main house with her parents. Leonora and Leonard excitedly watched from the bay window while the movers loaded the mammoth truck parked at the front curb. Their furniture and personal belongings would arrive in Louisiana within a week and hopefully provide a degree of familiarity when they stepped into their new surroundings.

Their last morning in Queens dawned gray and dismal, perfectly matching Vinnie's mood. Huge raindrops pelted the sturdy windows and thunder rumbled in the distance. The children pulled the bedcovers over their heads and Lenora giggled. When she turned, she saw her little brother looking uneasy and vigorously sucking his thumb.

"Are you afraid?" she asked in a whisper.

He nodded his head affirmatively, his mouth still holding the tiny thumb captive.

"There's nothing to be afraid of Leonard. Grandma told me it's only God's angels bowling up in Heaven. It's a game they play with a black ball and bunch of white pins. The angel rolls the ball and tries to knock down the pins, kinda like Grandpa does when he's playing bocce in the park. When an angel knocks down all the pins, it makes that big noise up in the sky and the head angel yells stee-rike."

When the next crack of thunder boomed, laughter bubbled from Leonard's mouth. The thumb was set free and he clapped his chubby hands. "Yeah, all down...tree-ike."

By the time breakfast was finished and the dishes put away, the rain had stopped but the sun refused to come out of hiding. It was almost time to leave for the train station.

"You two stay here with Grandma," Vinnie instructed the children. "I need to check the apartment one more time to make sure we haven't left anything behind."

She made one last trip, fully aware the structure was stripped bare, but wanting to say one final good-bye. After opening the front door, she hesitated in the tiny entryway and listened to the silence. The empty rooms were unnaturally quiet. When she managed to take several steps into the living room, her footfalls sounded foreign on the wooden floors. Vinnie realized there was more missing from the apartment than simply the furnishings. Gone were the sounds of her children's laughter and the merriment of family gatherings. Her somber eyes took in the unadorned walls and barren floors, but her heart returned to happier times.

She reminisced about their well-attended housewarming... Leo so gallantly carrying her over the threshold...their kiss under the mistletoe in anticipation of their first evening alone in their new home...then nineteen months later proudly bringing Leonard home from the hospital to his elated big sister. She vividly recalled last Christmas Eve, when the children were so excited they got stomachaches and couldn't sleep.

Her pleasant stroll down memory lane was interrupted by the sound of the teenager next door gunning his hot rod's engine. She glanced at her watch. It was time to go.

When she closed the door for the last time, she knew, full well she was also closing the door on a significant chapter of her life.

Chapter Three

It was with solemn resignation Vinnie boarded the train to Shreveport, Louisiana, holding tightly to the hands of her children. As they seated themselves on the train, she summoned her strength and feigned a smile of reassurance.

"This is the beginning of the grand adventure we talked about. Our journey aboard this big train will take us to parts of our great country you've only heard about in the stories Daddy and I read to you. From these very windows, you'll have a bird's-eye view and be able to see things totally different from New York.

"When we arrive in Louisiana, Daddy's going to meet us at the station to take us to our new house, that's right around the corner from where Daddy works."

The children listened with rapture and squirmed in their seats with delight. Vinnie's forced smile remained in place, but her brow creased with worry as she contemplated their future.

Leonora, perceptive beyond her years, put her tiny hand on her mother's shoulder.

"You don't have to worry, Mommy. We're not alone. Remember Father Silvio told us God is always with us if He's in our hearts? Well, God is in my heart right now and I'm taking Him all the way to Louise and Anna's."

Leo, in the meantime, felt an overwhelming emptiness without his wife and children. He busied himself during his off-time hours by preparing for his family's arrival in the South. In accordance with his wife's wishes, he rented a house off base. The kitchen was the first room Leo painted. It had been a generic white and needed a little pizzazz. Now, with its new buttercup yellow walls and contrasting white woodwork, it looked cheerful and inviting.

It was a single-story, side-by-side, attached two-family dwelling within a complex that housed military personnel. Each of the units contained a kitchen, living room, two bedrooms, and bath. There was a main entrance in front and a rear door leading to an open field out back. Clotheslines were strung in the backyards from one end of the compound to the other. On windy days it looked as though the freshly laundered clothes were patriotically saluting the nearby base.

Leo, thinking of Vinnie's displeasure with the move, decided to surprise her by splurging on something dandy that had long been on her wish list. It may have been second hand, but the reconditioned washing machine would serve its purpose in more ways than one. Leo meticulously polished the white finish of the Maytag until it gleamed. The finishing touch was a gigantic red bow fastened decoratively to the wringer.

When Leo met his family at the train, the hollowness he had been feeling inside was replaced with joy. It was a warm reunion of kisses, hugs, and "I've missed yous." The children were tired but excited, and talked non-stop about their train trip on the drive to their new home.

When Vinnie and the two children stepped over the threshold of their residence, it was instantly comforting to be surrounded by the familiarity of their personal belongings and furniture. Vinnie hugged Leo tightly.

In the security of her husband's arms, she felt as though she were awaking from a bad dream. She realized she had wasted far too much of life's precious time worrying and not enough time appreciating each new day and its gifts granted by her Creator. She definitely owed Him an apology.

Vinnie extended her arms for a group hug. As long as she, her husband, and two children were together, they were divinely blessed. It didn't matter whether they were in the state of New York, Louisiana, or far-off Timbuktu. Wherever they were together, they were home.

CHAPTER FOUR

Adjusting to their circumstances and surroundings, the DiTrapanis settled into their adopted community of off-base housing with other families of career military personnel and reservists forced to uproot because of the war. They were all in the same boat, hoping to stay the course and remain afloat.

The Steeles were the family in the adjoining unit; Major Robert Steele, his wife, Betty, and their son, Bobby. Robert Steele was born and raised in Boston, Massachusetts, where his affluent family rubbed elbows with the Kennedys. Maturing handsomely during his years of service to his country, Major Steele was the epitome of an officer and a gentleman.

His face was angular and distinguished. His six-foot-four presence was authoritative, his physique rock solid like his inner being. He opted to keep his prematurely gray hair cropped short which added to the image he outwardly projected.

Under full, gray brows, his intelligent, dark brown eyes were commanding or reassuring as circumstances warranted, but his family and friends knew that under the decorated military uniform there was a marshmallow lining.

Betty was a model-slim five foot ten, but possessed a few appealing curves where they counted most. She wore her Celtic red hair pulled back and clipped at the nape of her neck, where a few unruly locks inevitably escaped the clasp. It was a simple and undemanding style that suited her heart-shaped face. Her sparkling emerald eyes were consistently warm and devoid of makeup. When you got up close, you could see the tiny freckles dotting the bridge of her perfect nose, gifts, her paternal grandfather used to tell her, from "the little people" in his Irish homeland many miles across the sea. Betty's ancestors had made the voyage across the Atlantic Ocean and settled in the southern portion of the United States, and she spoke with the mellifluousness of that region. It was a family joke that the twang in her speech escalated in direct proportion to her emotions. Robert often teased her, saying that in the excitement of some moments, he actually needed an interpreter to understand what his wife was saying.

Bobby was a miniature, dark-haired version of his dad. His already long legs made him appear taller and older than his four years. He had his mother's endearing smile and smattering of freckles.

Vinnie found needed consolation in her close friendship with the Steeles, and refuge in her faith, frequently visiting the church on weekdays to pray. She and Betty, along with the other wives, had been sitting on pins and needles waiting for their husbands' final orders. Would they be sent overseas, their lives in jeopardy or remain safely stateside?

It was a Tuesday morning when Vinnie heard a loud knock at her door. She rushed through the house and swung the door open to find Betty winded and babbling.

"Our prayas have been answered," Betty repeated three times as she grabbed Vinnie's hands and pulled her down the stoop. She then started jumping up and down. "Our men are staying heah," she shouted mid jump. Comprehension took a moment to dawn, but Vinnie's elation became evident as Betty led her in a ceremonial ring around the Rosie.

Vinnie's face flushed with excitement then slight embarrassment. She hoped no passerby would take notice of their antics. If they did, they would surely send for "the men in the white coats" and they'd be confined in straitjackets as they were rushed off to the nearest mental asylum. Nevertheless, Betty's gaiety was contagious and Vinnie gave in thinking, "Why not?" Life was good, very good, in their Louisiana community…but would not remain so indefinitely.

CHAPTER FIVE

August 1951

It was a typical Monday morning in the small military community. The date was August 6, 1951. The men had reported to work at the base and the women were home tending to their children and the endless list of daily household chores.

The weather this day was far from typical. The sun was optimistically casting its luminous rays through fluffy clouds high in the cerulean sky. The light breeze that fluttered in from the east was void of the usual summer heat and humidity.

Vinnie, after putting the second load of wash through the wringer of her Maytag and hanging it out to dry on her portion of the backyard clothesline, decided to take a well-deserved break with the children. A little relaxation, fresh air, and sunshine would do them all some good.

Betty Steele, also out taking advantage of the delightful weather, waved in greeting. "How y'all doing on this fabulous day?" She came over to join them, with Bobby in tow. He was two years older than Leonard but the two of them had been inseparable playmates since the first day they met.

Lenora sometimes joined the boys in games of her choosing, but she viewed all young males as basically silly creatures (her brother, whom she adored, occasionally included). Being a big sister, she opted for the role of mother hen, keeping an eye on Leonard and Bobby's shenanigans from a safe distance. That's what she and her doll would do today.

Bobby had just gotten his first two-wheeler bicycle for his fifth birthday from his grandparents in Boston. It was custom-made with a low-speed motor, something totally unique. Major Steele had disconnected the motorized mechanism until his son was a little older. Bobby couldn't wait to show Leonard his prized possession. He brought the shiny red bike out front and demonstrated his ability to balance the gleaming apparatus without adult assistance. Leonard, amazed at what his friend could do, trotted up and down the sidewalk beside him. He thought Bobby was the cat's pajamas and was having the grandest time. Laughter excitedly bubbled from his chubby frame and his eyes sparkled with innocent delight in the early afternoon sun.

Abruptly, the sounds of merriment ceased, causing Vinnie and Betty to instantaneously look in the boys' direction. They saw their sons awkwardly sprawled on the ground. Leonard's little sandals were still flying in the air. What had at first appeared to be an ordinary misadventure for the two small boys soon turned into a nightmare. Leonard had somehow lost his balance and tripped into the bike, toppling it and the two boys over. Bobby was visibly shaken, but physically unharmed. Leonard wasn't as lucky.

Vinnie frantically ran to her son's side to find blood gushing from the youngster's head. The boy was breathing, but wasn't making a sound. A detached spoke from the bike's front wheel laid besides him, its jagged edge crimsoned with blood.

Betty looked at her neighbor's ghastly white face and locked onto Vinnie's frantic eyes. Betty's heart felt like a sledgehammer pounding against her rib cage and her emotions threatened to render her useless. She feared that Vinnie herself might be going into shock, and both mother and son were now solely dependent upon her. She briefly closed her eyes and begged God for strength.

"Vinnie," Betty said again, lightly shaking her friend's shoulder. "You've got to get a grip on yourself for Leonard's sake. I'm goin' to leave you alone with him for only one minute. Don't move him. Comfort him in anyway ya can, but don't lift his head. Stay put until I get back."

On legs the consistency of Jell-O, Betty forced one foot in front of the other as she raced into her house. She grabbed an armful of clean white towels and dashed back to the front walk. As Vinnie continued to hold Leonard's lithe body in her lap, Betty struggled to carefully wrap the towels around the child's fragile head to absorb the continuous flow of blood.

The accident, however, did not go unnoticed. From her unobstructed view two doors down and across the street, Ada Goldberg had witnessed the two boys falling. She dropped the garden hose with which she had been watering her postage-stamp size lawn and propelled her Rubenesque body forward with a speed that belied its size.

"*Gott in Himmel* (God in Heaven)," she exclaimed when her startled gray eyes surveyed the scene of the accident up close. She did an immediate about-face and marched double-time back to her house. There she placed an emergency call to her husband, Colonel Benjamin Goldberg, at the base, apprising him of the situation and stating in no uncertain terms that Leo be notified of the accident, without delay, and relieved of duty in order to meet his wife at the base hospital.

The call completed, Mrs. Goldberg wasted no time in returning to the bloodstained sidewalk. As soon as the other two women left, she would hose down the walkway and wash away the grim remnants.

As befitting an officer's wife, Mrs. Goldberg was used to taking charge, but she also knew when to advance with caution. Barking out orders right then would risk pushing the two overwrought women over the edge.

Mrs. Goldberg's words were calmly but firmly spoken. "Betty, you're going to bring your car out to the street, stay behind the wheel, and leave the motor running. I'll help Vinnie and Leonard into the front seat. As soon as the door is closed, I want you to drive directly to the base hospital."

Betty nodded silently, but her eyes sought Lenora and Bobby, who had been temporarily remanded to the front stoop with stern orders from Mrs. Goldberg "not to move an inch." The two small figures sat obediently huddled on the steps, frightened out of their wits and barely daring to breath.

"Don't worry about the other *kinder* (children)," Mrs. Goldberg said in a softer tone. "I'll look after them. With her next breath, her tone changed back to one of urgency. "Betty, time is of the essence. Get moving."

Betty got behind the wheel of her faded blue 1938 Desoto, an eighteenth birthday gift from her parents, slammed the shifter of the old coupe into reverse, and backed the protesting vehicle into the street. Mrs. Goldberg, outwardly composed except for the slight trembling of her hands, carefully maneuvered her two charges into the passenger seat.

"You poor *shayner boychik* (darling boy)," she whispered under her breath as she closed the car door. With her two passengers positioned for flight, Betty popped the clutch, launching the car in the direction of base. Her right foot pressed down heavily on the gas pedal, her slender fingers perspiring profusely as she fiercely gripped the steering wheel, her mind and heart willing the ancient six-cylinder to go faster.

Vinnie sat next to Betty in a trancelike state with her swaddled son held close to her heart. She crooned soothing sounds as she rocked ever so gently back and forth. She didn't want to think... didn't want to feel. All she could do was pray to the Lord above and hope with all her heart and soul that He was listening.

CHAPTER SIX

When Leo received news of his son's accident from his commanding officer, he bolted from the artillery range and raced blindly in the direction of the hospital. His feet intermittently refused to cooperate. Several times he stumbled but willed his body to remain upright.

Upon reaching the hospital doors, he nearly collided with an empty gurney being pushed by two men from the emergency unit.

"The kid's not here yet," one of the men said to him, correctly guessing that Leo was the anticipated arrival's father.

Leo backed up, allowing the stretcher to pass, then stopped dead in his tracks. His upper body swayed until it found purchase against the building. His right side was in stitches from the prolonged run and his breathing and pulse rates were off the charts. He had but a minute to take a cleansing breath before the DeSoto sped into the drive and screeched to a stop.

The medic and his assistant hastened to the car with the gurney, swung open the unlocked passenger door, and attempted to take Leonard from his mother's arms, but Vinnie refused to hand over the precious bundle in her lap.

"Look, lady," the attendant said to the woman protectively holding onto the child. "Time is important here and the kid don't have it to waste while you and me play a game of tug of war." In a rush of fresh tears, Vinnie's shaking arms released their hold on her son. Her eyes became so blurred that she could hardly make out

Leo's face when his hand reached into the car for her. Together they followed on the heels of the medics, but they were detained once inside.

Despite their persistent and loud protests, the couple was shown to a small waiting area where they were asked to remain and stay calm while the emergency team assessed the situation. Calm, however, was not an option for the distraught parents.

Except for the outside sounds filtering into the waiting area, the room was uncomfortably quiet. The couple, as if programmed to do so, took turns pacing the faded carpet. As they paced, their lips moved wordlessly. They were lost in their own thoughts, praying that their son would be all right.

Betty had parked the car after the emergency team had taken Leonard. She crossed the parking lot and entered the hospital alone. There she remained in the background, unnaturally subdued. She didn't know whether her presence would be a comfort to or an intrusion on her friends. Reverently she bowed her head, asking God for guidance.

"Dear Lord, ah don't want to intrude on their personal grief, but Ah feel ah'm a part of this and mah heart is grievin, too. Mah feet seem glued to this verra spot, not lettin' me take a step either forward or back. Holy Father, please let your gentle hand guide me in the right direction."

Betty raised her head, slowly opening eyelids she hadn't realized were clinched shut. She had to blink several times before her vision cleared, but in the seconds that followed, it was in her mind's eye that she could see the clearest. She vividly recalled the image of two frightened children huddled together on the front steps of the house and understood exactly where God wanted her to be.

She swallowed, reclaiming the voice in her dry throat, and approached the DiTrapanis.

"Ah don't know what to say to y'all," she said emotion weighing down each word. "Ah feel personally responsible for Leonard's accident. If it wasn't for mah comin' over and that awful bicycle, none of this would have happened."

"Oh, Betty, please don't say that," Vinnie countered emphatically. "It was an accident. No one is to blame."

The two women stepped toward one another then embraced, holding each other in the warmth of understanding. When the two woman separated, Betty was the first to break the ensuing silence.

"Vinnie, Leo is here with y'all and the two of ya have each other to lean on. Ah honestly think Ah'd be more useful at home attendin' to Lenora and Bobby. Even though Ah'm an adult, Ah'm havin' trouble copin' so Ah'm certain the children are frightened and confused by what happened. Ah'll pick them up from Mrs. Goldberg's and bring em back to mah house. Ah'll do my verra best to reassure them and answer any questions they may have."

Vinnie and Leo both nodded in agreement. Betty quickly hugged each of them. She didn't know what else to say. She wished some profound words of comfort or wisdom would miraculously emerge from her quivering lips but none were forthcoming. She valiantly reined in emotions, she turned and left, her courage taking her only as far as the hospital parking lot.

Betty pulled open the driver's door of the DeSoto and slid behind the wheel. Her right hand started to shake as she struggled to place the key in the ignition. A torrent of tears obscured her vision and the keys noisily fell to the floor. The emotions she had been so stoically holding inside fought for their freedom and she surrendered to their demand. She laid her head on the steering wheel and wept.

CHAPTER SEVEN

In the meanwhile, for those present in the emergency room, one look at the doctors' stone faces as they examined the closely shaven left side of the child's head told the severity of the situation. As professionals, they only had bits and pieces of informative relative to the child's accident, but were determined to place the pertinent pieces of the puzzle together.

They concurred that due to some inexplicable cause, the bicycle spoke jettisoned like a missile from the wheel, piercing the child's skull and penetrating the left temporal lobe. Rather than anchoring itself inside the brain, the spoke forcefully exited the same way it went in. They weren't sure whether this was good or bad or a combination of both. Not having to remove the spoke surgically was a positive. On the negative side, it was likely that upon its exit, the spoke took microscopic bone and brain tissue with it.

There was only one fact of which they were certain. The depth of the puncture and its collateral damage were presently undeterminable. There were intense discussions among the physicians but little debate. The team wisely conceded that the trauma to the left temporal lobe of one so young was beyond their scope. With their limited facilities, treating this child would not be possible. The unanimous decision was made to airlift Leonard to Brooke Army Hospital in San Antonio, Texas, immediately. Urgent calls were placed for an aero-medical transport, but none would be available until the following morning, when a Texas-bound aircraft from the northeast could be diverted to Barksdale.

The staff looked at each other, seeing who among them would volunteer to speak to the patient's parents. Several pairs of eyes landed on Dr. Glacken.

"I guess I'm volunteering," the usually jovial physician said. Fifteen minutes later, at a pace far slower than his normal gait, Dr. Glacken walked from his office to the waiting room to break the news to the fretting parents. A vein pulsated on the right side of the fifty-five-year-old doctor's bald pate. He absently ran his hand along the gray fringe still clinging to the sides of his scalp.

He couldn't remember a time when healing and medicine weren't a part of his life. He truly loved his profession and was grateful when the miracles of medicine (or those of a higher power) let him be the bearer of good news. Today, there was no miracle or good news to bestow on waiting family members. It was on days like this when he fleetingly wondered if perhaps he should have gone into the family business and been a plumber like his father.

CHAPTER EIGHT

Betty had remained in the hospital parking lot until she was able to get her emotions under control. Finally summoning a reserve of inner strength, she put the car in gear and drove the short distance to her house. She parked the car then walked across the deserted street to Mrs. Goldberg's. The absence of the normal daily activity on the block added to the surreal feeling engulfing her.

When she reached Mrs. Goldberg's door, Bobby and Lenora bolted toward her, throwing their short arms around her long slender legs and asking, in high-pitched voices of worry, about Leonard and how soon he would be coming home.

"We'll all have lots of time to talk at our house," Betty assured them. "Right now, we're goin' to thank Mrs. Goldberg for lookin' after us and go back to the house and maybe eat a little somethin'."

When they turned, a watchful Mrs. Goldberg was behind them. "Thank you, Mrs. Goldberg," Lenora and Bobby said in respectful unison.

"Oh, you're quite welcome, *bubelehs* (sweethearts)," Mrs. Goldberg replied with warm sincerity in her smile. "You know the colonel and I are pleased as punch to have you here any time. Betty, dear, I need to see you a moment."

Betty followed Mrs. Goldberg into the spit-and-polished kitchen, where she was handed a bag containing Leonard's little sandals. Looking in the bag, the color drained from Betty's face. She swallowed hard, trying to dislodge the lump forming in her throat.

Mrs. Goldberg, delaying any discussion of the contents of the bag, asked in hushed tones, "How is our little Leonard doing?"

Betty despondently shrugged, her body slouching forward.

"When Ah left the building, he was still bein' examined by the doctors and no one had come out yet to talkta Vinnie and Leo. Ah felt terribly guilty about leaving em at the hospital; but they do all have each other, and Ah think the children may need me more here. Mrs. Goldberg nodded her head in grandmotherly affirmation. She didn't inquire further, but instead conveyed to Betty what had transpired during her absence.

"When your car first pulled away, the children looked so forlorn. They stayed seated on the stoop and didn't budge....such *shayner kindlach* (beautiful children), those two. Normally I try to mind my own business. The colonel gets unreasonably upset when I'm a nosey *yenta* (busybody) like my mother.

"But I'm afraid I may have overstepped my bounds earlier. I felt it necessary to tell Bobby and Lenora that everything was going to be fine and dandy and little Leonard would soon be as right as rain. I don't know whether they believed me or not, but the rigidness in their bodies eased a bit so I took that as a good sign.

"I must admit, they both looked at me as though I was totally *meshugeneh* (crazy) when I picked up that dreadful bicycle and asked them to do me a huge favor by walking the two-wheeler into your backyard. Uncertainty was written all over those sweet faces, but good manners prevailed and Bobby *schlepped* (dragged) the bike next door with Lenora trailing one step behind.

"As soon as their backs were to me, I moved with a speed I didn't think physically possible considering my rather, ah, ample figure. I took the garden hose and cleaned the sidewalk in front of the house so that you or Vinnie shouldn't have to deal with such unpleasantness.

"I was picking up Leonard's sandals from the side of the curb when I saw the children returning. I shoved the sandals behind my back, but knew I wasn't fooling them for a moment. Such smart *kinder* (children), your Bobby and Lenora. But I plowed ahead with a smile plastered on my face like everything was just hunky-dory and suggested we go to my house for some chocolate chip cookies and milk. They politely agreed, but it was terribly obvious their little minds were elsewhere. They hardly ate a bite." Mrs. Goldberg dabbed at her glistening eyes.

CHAPTER NINE

Leaving Mrs. Goldberg, Betty escorted the children back to her house. Returning to the comfort of her kitchen, she slipped a floral-printed apron over her pink cotton dress. She then instructed the children to take turns washing up in the bathroom while she readied the cast iron skillet for grilling cheese sandwiches. Bobby again took the lead in doing what was asked. With his head downcast, he was also the first to return to the kitchen. He was bravely fighting back tears, but losing the battle.

He tugged on his mother's apron as Betty flipped over a cheese sandwich. "Mommy, do you think it's kinda my fault Leonard fell? I only wanata show him my new bike and we was having so much fun. I didn't mean for him to get hurt and I feel awful bad inside." His tiny voice quavered "I'm never going to ride that stupid thing ever again," he said and he fell into his mother's arms.

It was a terrible weight to be carried on such small shoulders. Betty knelt down on the kitchen floor and did her best to explain.

"Of course it wasn't your fault, sugar. It was an accident and sometimes bad things just happen. It wasn't your fault, or Leonard's or anyone else's," she said, attempting to convince herself as well as her son. She hugged Bobby close, then carefully wiped his tear-stained face with her apron.

Throughout lunch Betty kept a close watch on the children. Bobby's eyes retained their red puffiness from earlier, but he looked considerably better. Those courageous little shoulders were not sagging quite so much. Lenora, on the other hand, hardly touched her plate, even though grilled cheese was her favorite.

"May I please be excused, Mrs. Steele?" she asked meekly. "My tummy really isn't very hungry this afternoon."

"Of course, honey. Why don't y'all go on inside and play."

Hugging the doll that she had carried with her through the course of the morning, Lenora left the room.

After washing the dishes and tidying up the kitchen, Betty checked on the children. Bobby was in his room strategically positioning his toy soldiers to do battle against the North Koreans.

Lenora was in the living room. She had taken a washcloth from Betty's laundry basket and wrapped it around her doll's head. "Don't worry, my little baby. The doctors are going to fix your head and make it all better. Lenora's right here and I promise I'll ask God to take special care of you." When Betty overhead this, she felt her heart tremble. She was afraid it would break in two.

At the hospital, it was late afternoon before Leonard was comfortably situated in a private room. There was no way in Heaven or Hades that Leo was going to leave the hospital and the staff didn't argue. The Air Force had granted him an emergency leave and his only thoughts were of his son. Vinnie, after some verbal arm twisting, was persuaded to go home, check on Lenora, and prepare for the next day's trip to San Antonio.

When Vinnie arrived at the Steele's, she found Lenora napping on the sofa, her head resting on Betty's lap. Betty put her index finger to her lips, motioning Vinnie not to say anything. She eased Lenora's head onto a comfy pillow and walked to the kitchen, where she automatically put the kettle on for tea. Vinnie had followed but had not yet spoken. When Betty turned, she saw tears of grief and the shadow of fear in her friend's eyes.

Vinnie's voice erupted with emotion, her words and pain spewing forth.

"The doctors said there's a serious injury to one of the lobes in his brain. They've managed to slow the bleeding, but they're not equipped to deal with this kind of injury particularly in a child.

"They've called all over the country asking for a military hospital plane to fly him to an army hospital in San Antonio that has more experience dealing with catastrophic injuries. Oh, Betty, his eyes are open and he can talk, when prompted, but he's lying there so pale and listless. He reminds me of a little rag doll with the stuffing knocked out of it. Why would God let something like this happen to such a small innocent boy?"

Betty didn't have an answer but compassionately put her arms around her dear friend and held her tightly.

A short time later Lenora awoke. She heard low voices coming from the kitchen and followed their sound. The women, now seated at the table, were sullen but more composed, barely sipping their tepid tea.

Wiping the sleep from her eyes, the first words out of Lenora's mouth were "Mommy, where's Leonard?"

Vinnie did her best to explain a precarious situation she didn't fully comprehend herself. "Leonard is going to be absolutely fine," she said recalling Mrs. Goldberg's often-used phrase, "from your mouth to God's ears," and for perhaps the first time she understood its true meaning.

"Since he's such an exceptional little boy," Vinnie continued, "the doctors are going to send him to a very special hospital in a city called San Antonio in the state of Texas. An Army plane is making a special trip here to pick him up.

"You know how Leonard and Bobby like to play soldiers," she said to her daughter. "Well, the plane that's stopping for your brother is carrying real soldiers coming home from Korea who also need those doctors in San Antonio. Because Leonard is so little, they're letting Mommy and Daddy go with him, and even though you're special, too, no other children are allowed on the plane."

As always, Lenora's precocious mind appeared to dissect and analyze her mother's words.

"I hope they're letting other mommies and daddies on the plane, too. Grandma DiTrapani told me that when her sons were soldiers, they were only boys. I'm sure if one of them was hurt and going on a plane like Leonard, she would want to go, too." Vinnie's heart smiled and felt a smidgen lighter. Lenora, her sweet Lenora, always had that effect on her.

The little girl remained with the Steeles while Vinnie went back to her house to prepare for the next day's journey and gather a few things for her daughter, since Lenora would be staying with the Steeles while they made the trip to San Antonio. Betty had immediately volunteered to take care of her. "Bobby can bunk in with us and Lenora is more than welcome to have his room."

Vinnie haphazardly threw items into their old leather suitcase, hoping it would hold together for one more trip. She moved through the house like a robot, mindlessly doing chores without any assistance from her rattled brain. She took out the vacuum and cleaned the already dust-free floors. She needlessly tided the neat-as-a-pin house. The only time she was cognizant of her actions was when she looked heavenward to pray.

An hour later, Vinnie found herself standing at her front door, suitcase at her side and a paper sack containing some of Lenora's things in her arms. "I guess I'm ready to get back to the hospital... or as ready as I'm ever going to be." She, like her husband, would be spending the night in a chair beside their son.

Vinnie returned to the Steeles and handed the bag to Betty. "This should hold her for a couple of days, but here's the key if you need anything else from the house."

"Mommy," Lenora said, "you look like you need a really big hug."

Vinnie wrapped her daughter in a tight embrace, afraid to let go. She knew her child would be safe and well cared for, but leaving Lenora behind was tearing at her conscience as well as her heart.

"I know you'll be a good girl for Mrs. Steele. Please do whatever she says. Remember that Daddy and I love you with all our hearts… and so does Leonard."

Holding fast to her mother, Lenora responded, "I love you all, too, a whole bunch.

And Mommy, when I say my prayers tonight, I'll ask God to do something special for Leonard."

As the hours passed, Betty grew weary and longed for this tumultuous day to come to an end. It felt like days since Leonard's accident rather than hours. It was quite late when she tucked Bobby in for the night and listened while he said his prayers. When she went to say goodnight to Lenora, they both knelt beside the single bed surrounded by trucks and toy soldiers. They folded their hands in prayer and Lenora began.

"Now I lay me down to sleep. I pray the Lord my soul to keep. If I should die before I wake, I pray the Lord my soul to take." Betty concluded with "amen" but Lenora said, "I don't mean to be impolite, Mrs. Steele, but I'm not finished yet."

Looking upward, Lenora spoke with a small but purposeful voice. "Dear God, I know you're really busy up there in Heaven, but I have a big favor to ask you...the biggest ever. Leonard hurt his head real bad today and I was going to ask you to throw him a special kiss from Heaven to help make it okay, but I have another, even more better idea.

"Tomorrow, Mommy and Daddy are going to take Leonard to Texas on an Army plane. It's one with soldiers coming home from that place where all the fighting is. If you have time, could you please take your plane to Texas to make sure everything is okay? Mommy said Sand Aunt Tony isn't too far from here, but I don't really know how far it is from Heaven. And if you're too busy to go, I'll understand; but maybe you could just send one of your angels. Since they can fly by themselves, you won't have to worry about them using your plane. Amen. P.S. I love you and Leonard does, too!"

Betty couldn't say a word. She didn't know whether to laugh or cry. She rose unsteadily from her knees and kissed Lenora atop her flaxen head then took her leave in silence.

CHAPTER ELEVEN

During Tuesday's early hours, the hustle and bustle on the tarmac was apparent. The drab olive C-47 with its red medical insignia descended gracefully, gliding onto the runway and taxiing into the hub of activity. It was a much smaller plane than what the family had envisioned as a hospital aircraft, but the purpose of the plane was of far greater importance than its size.

An ambulance delivered the youngster to the idling plane. His stretcher was expeditiously carried through the double cargo doors into the craft, where the mobile bed was slid into receptor brackets and securely locked in place for the flight. There were three beds on each side of the plane. Critically wounded combat soldiers occupied the other five bunks.

Vinnie and Leo struggled to avert their eyes from the wounded as they made their way to the forward cabin. It was a heart-wrenching sight and a grim reminder of the realities of war. Truth be told, two of these young soldiers were hovering on the brink of death, one was missing his right arm and leg, and the last young man had his flesh singed to the bone. They were heavily sedated to make them as comfortable as possible and vigilantly monitored by a military nurse. She prided herself on being a consummate professional, but even that couldn't keep the cold tendrils of reality from tugging at her heart. For a few of her patients, San Antonio would be the final destination in life's journey.

Vinnie and Leo took their places in the unyielding seats. The plane was not designed for the comfort of its infrequent seated passengers. Few words were exchanged between the couple during the two-and-a-half hour flight. They were both lost in their own restless thoughts, but their hands remained tightly locked together... each the other's lifeline.

* * * *

Upon awakening at the Steeles later Tuesday morning, Lenora was energetic and cheerful. She ate everything on her plate and asked for seconds. Betty was somewhat concerned about the drastic change. She wasn't an expert in child psychiatry but she was a mother possessing that special "mom radar" that detects when something is amiss.

"Lenora, y'all seem to be feelin' much betta today."

"Oh, yes, Mrs. Steele," Lenora cheerily replied.

Betty carefully continued. "Ah'm verra happy to see ya doin' betta but Ah thought perhaps we should go to church and light a candle to pray for your li'l brother."

Lenora's response almost knocked Betty off her low-heeled shoes. "If it would make you feel better, Mrs. Steele, we can go say a prayer for Leonard, but God told me He's very much aware of what happened to my brother and He has the matter in His capable hands. I'm not supposed to worry my pretty little head about it anymore."

Lenora paused thoughtfully for a moment. "Gee, I hope God told Mommy and Daddy not to worry, too.

CHAPTER TWELVE

When the C-47 landed on the runway in San Antonio, Vinnie could see six ambulances waiting, their drivers prepared to rush the planes' occupants to Brooke Army Hospital. She and Leo tried to wait patiently during the transfer, but found their reserve of patience had run dry.

When at last Leonard was placed in the ambulance, Leo leaped in after him and sat next to his son, forgetting the wife he left standing outside.

"Leo," she had to call twice.

He looked in the direction of the voice that was penetrating his mental haze. The fog lifted.

"Sorry," he said to her sheepishly while rising and extending his hand to assist her inside. When the doors of the vehicle were closed, the ambulance turned on its siren and flashing red light and sped away.

At the hospital, Vinnie and Leo were asked to be seated and unobtrusive while Leonard was examined, admitted, and eventually placed in a hospital crib. Leo did his customary pacing and, at some point, stopped checking his watch. A nurse was kind enough to bring them coffee, but while they were grateful for the gesture, the beverage went untouched.

Vinnie engaged in silent prayer, but her thoughts wandered and settled in the vague lands of "if onlys and what-ifs." If only I hadn't taken the children outside yesterday; if only I had made Leonard put on his shoes instead of his favorite sandals, if only I had watched him every single second, if only...then perhaps none of this would have happened. Then came the "what-ifs." What if they can't help him? What if there is damage to his brain? What if my baby dies?

It was nearing 4:00 PM when another nurse entered the waiting area and took Vinnie and Leo into their son's room. Leonard's eyes were open. He was awake but groggy. A tall, stocky doctor stood beside the heavily padded crib, his size making the room and child appear all the smaller. He extended his huge right hand to Leo.

"Hello, I'm Dr. Hart, and I'll be overseeing your son's case." Seated in a chair off to the side was a woman dressed in a white uniform. Looking in her direction, the doctor made the proper introduction.

"This is Mrs. Hastings. She'll be your son's private nurse. Part of her job will be to see that our instructions are followed to the letter. That may be difficult for you, but to do otherwise could result in dire consequences for your son. It's imperative that you do not lift your son out of the crib, and you cannot hug him. You can lean over the railing and touch his hands or feet, but you must be extremely careful not to come in contact with any part of his head."

Vinnie and Leo faces tightened with apprehension and their eyes filled with questions.

Duly noting the couple's distress, the doctor continued. "I'll attempt to describe the present situation in the simplest terms I can.

"From the exterior of his skull, we can readily see where the spoke went in, but it's what we can't see, inside the temporal lobe, that concerns us the most. The x-rays confirm that the puncture made by the spoke caused a V-shaped indentation. The bottom of that V is dangerously close to the brain and," the doctor hesitated a fraction of a second. Leo took that opportunity to jump in.

"And what, doctor?' he demanded through taut lips.

"And the best case scenario will be for the sides of the V to remain stable while the bottom lifts of its own accord. If it does, we're hoping your son will be out the woods."

"And if it doesn't?" Vinnie raised her voice, momentarily forgetting her son was in earshot.

"That's something we'll have to deal with if and when the time comes, but our first course of action will be to keep the boy comfortable and inactive.

"Several tests still need to be run, but most important, we will continue to monitor what's going on near the brain. I want you to know that we don't expect things to change overnight, but time could be our ally. It may seem too simplistic in theory, but we have to take a wait-and-see approach.

"In the interim, should you have any questions, Mrs. Hasting will be privy to whatever we know." With that said, he again shook Leo's hand, nodded sympathetically at Vinnie and left the room to continue his rounds.

"I don't like that big man," they heard from a small voice in the crib. Vinnie and Leo's full attention was redirected to their son. The child's face showed his uneasiness with his new surroundings.

"Leonard, sweetheart, Dr. Hart is here to help make you all better just like Dr. Stephens back home," Vinnie tried to explain, but Leonard wasn't listening and attempted to sit up.

"Honey, you have to lie down and go night-night," Vinnie coaxed soothingly wanting her son to rest.

"No, I want a story first," the little tyke demanded despite his tranquilized sleepiness. "Lenora always tells me Oz." It was the story Lenora told her brother over and over again.

"I'm sorry, sweetie. Lenora isn't here right now, but I'll tell you the story if you'd like."

"Yes, Mommy, I'd really like that. Tell me please."

When Vinnie finished her rendition of the tale, the child put up his index finger, indicating one more time. Vinnie smiled and began yet again. Leonard was soon sound asleep.

The couple had asked for permission to remain with their son overnight, but were told their request would have to go through official hospital channels. The hospital did make the rare exception of letting them stay beyond visiting hours that first evening.

At 7:00 PM, Mrs. Hastings glanced at her watch then looked at the couple. "I'm confident Leonard will sleep through the rest of the night; and be assured, he won't be left unattended. I heard your son mention Lenora. If she's a sibling, she won't be allowed entry. Children are not permitted to visit patients."

Vinnie and Leo wanted to protest, but the nurse didn't give them the opportunity.

"And perhaps now would be the perfect time for you to leave," Mrs. Hasting added.

Vinnie and Leo took her words as a request rather than a suggestion. It had been a long day that needed to come to an end. Tomorrow would be a new day to choose their battles.

CHAPTER THIRTEEN

When Vinnie and Leo left Leonard's room, they were both physically and mentally exhausted and had neither a destination nor sleeping accommodations. With their suitcase in Leo's hand, they trudged to the nurse's desk asking if anyone knew where they could get a room. The two nurses on duty negatively shook their white-capped heads.

Leo's eyes reflected his weary frustration and Vinnie's filled with tears--until she sensed a calming presence in the room. She looked up to see a young, dark-haired officer with the most mesmerizing blue eyes she had ever encountered. There were flecks of gold surrounding his pupils and his understanding orbs were warmly fixed on her face as he stood tall in his captain's uniform. Vinnie's pulse began to race.

"Excuse me," the handsome gentlemen said, approaching the couple. I apologize for my intrusion but I couldn't help overhearing your inquiry."

He smiled radiantly. "First of all, let me introduce myself," he said, extending his right hand first to Leo then to Vinnie. "My name is Gabe, and as of today, I've been assigned temporary duty here at Brooke. Although I'm not a doctor, I am what some people would call a patient's liaison. My responsibilities often vary, but my current assignment is to assist the critical patients placed under my guidance."

Neither Vinnie nor Leo uttered a sound so the captain continued. "It's apparent that you're having a bit of a problem, and I may be able to offer assistance. It just so happens, I'm well acquainted with a very respectable boardinghouse that's within walking distance of the hospital. If you'd like to take a seat and wait while I check on someone, I'd be happy to show you the way."

Relief flooded the couple's faces. "Thank you, thank you, Captain," Leo said, zealously pumping the young man's hand.

Within the half hour, Captain Gabe graciously escorted the appreciative couple to the home of the O'Malleys, which would become their home for the foreseeable future. With a grateful hug from Vinnie and a firm handshake of gratitude from Leo, the captain walked away with a satisfied smile on his face and a bounce in his step. He turned back once, saluted the couple, and faded into the growing darkness. Under the glow of the street lamp, Leo noticed Vinnie's face flush but he couldn't see inside where her heart and stomach fluttered simultaneously.

Leo poised his hand to knock, but the door flew open before his knuckles could make contact. A stout woman, her gray tresses curled tightly with bobby pins, wiped her flour-coated hands on a disheveled apron and beamed in welcome. Also welcoming was the fragrant aroma of freshly baked bread.

"Ah, yourselves must be Mr. and Mrs. DiTrapani, wouldn't you now? We've been expectin' you. Meself, I'm your landlady, Mrs. O'Malley. Don't stand there, dearies…come in, come in."

The couple stood awkwardly in the small entryway while Mrs. O'Malley prattled on, barely pausing to take a breath. "Me husband, his Lordship himself, is in the livin' room, on me best sofa no less, sawin' wood to beat McNamara's band.

"It will certainly be no trouble at all, at all to have you stayin' here with us while lookin' after your lad at the hospital. Tis a terrible thing to happen to such a little tyke and yourselves now lookin' dead on your feet. You'll be wantin' me to show you to your room, won't you now?"

Vinnie and Leo looked at one another quizzically. Had they missed something important here? It stood to reason, the captain may have phoned Mrs. O'Malley, but reasoning and Mrs. O'Malley didn't appear to go hand in hand. It was more likely that Mrs. O'Malley had direct radio-wave communications from her metal hair clips to the hospital's grapevine, or she was completely off her rocker. They easily read each other's thoughts. Perhaps it would be wiser to turn around and make a hasty retreat, but where would they go?

The bewildered couple gave in to sheer exhaustion, and throwing caution to the wind, agreed to stay at least the night. They hesitantly followed the eccentric matron up the stairs to their nicely appointed room at the head of the landing, where she bid them a pleasant good night.

Leo hurriedly closed the door, locked it, and put his ear against it in case Mrs. O'Malley was still on the other side. When he assumed the coast was clear, he turned to Vinnie. "What in the world just happened here?"

"I haven't got the faintest idea," his wife answered. "But to tell you the truth, at this point I'm too pooped to worry."

They both kicked off their shoes and collapsed onto the inviting double bed. When they landed, their mutual sighs of relief bounced off the beige walls. Vinnie glanced to her side and saw that on the small night table next to the bed there were two glasses of iced tea, overflowing with ice, accompanied by a plate of aromatic soda bread slathered with home-churned butter.

She nudged Leo with her elbow and his tired eyes followed her bewildered gaze. With his last reserve of strength, he managed to lift himself into a sitting position. He mentally reflected one second... two at the most.

"Honey, I honestly don't remember the last time any food has passed these lips and this is one time I'm not going to look a gift horse in the mouth. I'm going to take the first bite, but listen to me carefully. If I should suddenly keel over, leave me wherever my body lands. Make a beeline for the front door and get yourself as far away from here as you can!"

CHAPTER FOURTEEN

Wednesday morning, August 8, the vibrant Texas sun rose over the horizon, spreading its golden warmth over the city of San Antonio. Dawn's first rays crept in through a slight part in the curtains of the second-story bedroom where Vinnie and Leo had spent the night. The new day found the couple sprawled atop a white chenille bedspread fully dressed in their rumpled traveling clothes from the day before.

The previous night's fatigue had engulfed the pair, immersing them into a dead-man's sleep. Now, in the early hours of the day, Vinnie's breathing was soft and even. Leo was awake, theoretically, his addled brain functioning on auxiliary power. He procrastinated, putting off the daunting task of opening his eyes. He yawned widely and stretched his aching body. One red-rimmed eye voluntarily popped open, followed by its mate. Leo stared at his unfamiliar surroundings.

"Where in the world am I?" he asked on a rush of breath. He forced himself to focus and bam, reality hit him like a runaway freight train.

He and his wife were stranded in the wide-open spaces of Texas, where his three-year-old son was hospitalized in a facility designed for critical cases...with no prognosis positive, or otherwise. The staff consisted of highly skilled professionals, so Leo felt safe in allowing himself to trust the hospital personnel to attend to his son's medical needs. What concerned him even more, though, was the youngster's emotional well-being. The doctors and nurses were total strangers. Several dramatic scenarios played through Leo's fertile imagination, causing him to shudder and the hair on his arms to rise. He vividly imaged his pint-sized son curled in a protective ball, quivering in his hospital crib. Tears born of fear and confusion trickled from the child's innocent eyes. Leo could see the bed starting to shake. "The doctor can stuff his orders," Leo bellowed. He physically reached out to pick up the boy. The only thing his hands held was air.

Leo blinked and the scene inside his head changed to an equally disturbing one. Leonard was standing on his tiptoes, his blonde head fully draped with bloody gauze, peering over the confining bars of his crib. He was trying desperately to climb over the railing. Leo could hear his plaintive cries, as he called for him and Lenora.

"Lenora," Leo said in a soft breath. He shook his head, mentally berating himself. "What kind of father am I to have forgotten my daughter?"

Granted, Lenora was mature beyond her years, but in actuality she was a mere five years old. She was umpteen miles away in Louisiana, separated by extenuating circumstances from her brother and parents, who themselves were in a strange city, residing in a stranger's house, not knowing literally or figuratively which end was up.

Leo's rare temper surfaced. It did a slow burn and erupted into volatile flames. He wanted to slam his fist into the nearest wall, but settled for pummeling the goose down pillow that had lain beneath his head. His precise motions mirrored those of professional boxer Jersey Joe Walcott in the ring.

When his opponent was down for the count, Leo looked at the battered pillow, reflecting with guilt upon his actions.

"I'm sorry, God. I don't know what came over me. In my heart, I know we're all your children and you wouldn't burden us with more that we can bear, but I'm really having a problem with this. In your infinite wisdom, I hope you'll understand my anger wasn't directed at you. You are all knowing and I'm but a simple man, adrift on an uncertain sea. You are my rock and anchor. Please don't hold my human failings against me or my family."

Leo's disruptive movements coaxed Vinnie from the depths of sleep. She groggily sat up and pushed her shapely legs over the side of the bed.

"Leo, I had the oddest dream," she confided to her husband. "There was a terrible tornado back in Louisiana. It appeared out of nowhere and looked like a giant Hoover vacuum. I was sucked up like a piece of dust. Inside everything was whirling around me. I was surrounded by bright red bicycles, endless clotheslines of white towels, and hundreds of sad-faced rag dolls. I reached out for one of the dolls. It looked so much like Leonard. I held it close to my chest and tried to protect him, but before I knew it, the vacuum spit me out into the clouds and I was alone."

"Okay," interjected Leo, "I think I know where this is going, but feel free to continue."

"Well, thank you," Vinnie said with minor irritation, but took up where she left off. "So rather than falling like one hundred pounds of dead weight, my body simply floated to the earth. Once on solid ground, I gave myself the once-over. I wiggled my fingers and toes. All essential parts remained attached and functioning."

"At least that's a good thing," added Leo, a slight smile forming on his lips.

"Yes, but when I landed," Vinnie added, "I expected to be in Texas. Instead I had ventured into the land of Oz. There I was, dressed in a silly pinafore, with an audience of happy-go-lucky leprechauns tending to giant shamrocks growing in the open fields."

Leo's smile widened. Vinnie ignored him.

"I introduced myself and did my best to explain my predicament. I told them it was terribly important that I return home to my little boy, who had fallen and badly hurt his head. The spokesman for the group told me they sympathized with my situation but they were merely stewards of the land and were unable to help me. Nevertheless, they did know of someone who could possibly help. I would have to travel to the great Emerald City to consult with the even greater wizard of Oz. He was the only one with the power to send me back to Leonard. Oddly, the wizard's name was O'Malley."

"But, of course," Leo interrupted with a rolling of his eyes.

"Leo, no more comments from the peanut gallery," Vinnie retorted, "or I promise you this story is going to get even longer."

Leo made a hand motion to zip his lips then gestured for his wife to continue.

"As I was about to say, when I asked them for directions, they chuckled and told me to follow the yellow brick road. I thanked them and was off to see the wizard. That's when I woke up."

Vinnie's puffy eyes surveyed their room. "I dearly wish all this too was a figment of my imagination." Frowning, she sighed, "I guess we're not in Louisiana anymore, Leo."

"No, we're not, my dear, and I'm sorry if I made light of your dream, but time's a-wastin'. I think we should get up and get moving."

Freshly dressed and properly groomed, Vinnie and Leo eagerly arrived at the hospital, but were taken aback when they were stopped by a guard in the lobby.

"Can I help you?" a man in uniform asked.

"No," Vinnie politely responded. "We're the DiTrapanis and we're going up to see our son."

"Sorry, ma'am, your son is not permitted any visitors," the young man replied.

"We're not visitors," Leo added, his tone laced with annoyance. The couple kept walking, but the guard blocked their path.

"What is going on here?" Leo demanded. Vinnie and Leo's eyes met, sharing an expression of confusion. It took but a moment for that confusion to be replaced by bone-chilling fear. Had their baby taken a turn for the worse during the night? Was his tiny body now lying on a cold slab in the hospital's morgue?

Vinnie was on the brink of hysteria and Leo's heart had plummeted to the pit of his stomach. He swallowed hard, hoping his voice wouldn't shake.

"I want to see the person in charge of this hospital immediately," Leo demanded.

As if in response to his demand, a statuesque middle-aged woman in business attire came striding authoritatively toward the distressed couple. The woman was assaulted by their loud questions and stretched emotions.

"Please, Mr. and Mrs. DiTrapani, I need you both to calm down. I'm Mrs. Hart. My husband is in charge of your child's medical care and I can assure you both your son is in stable condition. He was monitored continuously throughout the night. He had a quiet and uneventful evening and that's exactly what we hoped for. He is scheduled for tests today, but you'll be able to visit him during our regular visiting hours, which are one to five."

"But we wanted, at least, for one of us to be able to stay with him," Vinnie pleaded.

"That's something else I wanted to discuss with you," Mrs. Hart continued. "Our administrator has asked me to tell you that he has given considerable thought to your request to remain in your son's room around the clock. Unfortunately, although dealing with a patient so young, is a somewhat unique experience for us, the administrator regrets that he must decline your request. He has responsibilities to the facility and staff and he would be putting the hospital in an untenable and possibly negligent position if he went against the governing rules."

Vinnie stepped forward, stretching herself to her full height of five feet two inches. Her spine was ramrod straight. She addressed the woman defiantly.

"I don't give two hoots about your rules and regulations. I want to see my son now, Mrs. Hart." Her tone and her stance made it clear she was spoiling for a fight. She was taken aback when the imposing woman declined her challenge.

Mrs. Hart's facial features softened and her professional demeanor lost its rigidness. "I'm terribly sorry, Mrs. DiTrapani. My husband and I were never fortunate enough to be blessed with children of our own, so I won't pretend to know the extent of what you're going through. However, it doesn't take a medical professional to recognize the tremendous strain you and your husband are under, so please listen to me for a minute.

"When this ghastly accident happened, you wisely made the decision to make the journey here for us to help your son. That's precisely what we plan to do, but we're going to require your complete cooperation and utmost patience for whatever time he is in our care. It's important that you let us do our job.

"Remember, your little boy is in our excellent hands and I'm sure he'll be extremely eager to see you at one o'clock."

With the wind blown out of her sails, Vinnie tearfully gave in, taking out the rosary beads she had been fingering in her pocket. She made the sign of the Trinity and kissed the miniature crucifix.

Mrs. Hart leaned in closer. "Hold tight to your faith, Mrs. DiTrapani. I've been privileged to witness a number of miracles in my career. Always keep one thought in mind. With God all things are possible."

Chapter Fifteen

Vinnie and Leo slowly walked from the hospital a little after nine that morning feeling disheartened after their conversation with Mrs. Hart. To make matters worse, the rising San Antonio air temperature and humidity assaulted the pair. Despite his sullen mood and the beads of perspiration forming on his forehead, Leo did his best to appear optimistic.

"Look, honey. We have to face the fact that the head honcho of this hospital isn't going to budge about us staying with Leonard. And maybe Mrs. Hart was right in saying we brought the little guy here for a reason and it's best to let them do their job. We're forgetting that while we may be powerless here, God isn't. Let's agree to put this in His hands and go on."

Vinnie nodded in agreement. "You're a wise man, Leo DiTrapani. That's one of the many reasons I love you." She took Leo's hand in hers and they continued walking.

They had gone only a few yards when Leo made a suggestion accompanied by an artful wink. "Since I'm so wise, I think the next thing we should do is get something into our stomachs. If you paid me, I couldn't tell you the last time I had a decent meal, and my empty belly is rumbling."

Vinnie grinned. "I'm relieved to hear you say that. I thought it was my stomach making all that racket."

A half mile down the road they came to Café Miguel. The interior of the establishment was cozy, with colorful booths, but afforded minimal relief from the humidity. The burnt orange stucco ceiling had three fans that fought to circulate the muggy air, but it was a losing battle. Behind the counter, blades of a large floor oscillator rotated feverishly within the partitioned kitchen domain of the Mexican owner, Miguel, who also served as the short-order cook.

As soon as they were seated, a brunette waitress with a welcoming expression hurried to their table. "What can I get you folks?" she asked, pulling an order paid from her apron pocket.

"Ice water," they answered in unison. "Lots of ice and keep it coming," Leo added.

The server glanced over her shoulder, glimpsed her portly boss expertly flipping hot cakes on the griddle, then turned back to the couple and lowered her voice.

"I'm sorry, folks, but if you're not gonna order anything else, Miguel will charge you for the water."

Leo chuckled. "Don't fret, young lady, we're on the brink of starvation and require sustenance. Leo saw the shadow of sadness tinge the waitress's dark-lashed eyes. She wasn't sure if he was teasing or they were actually down on their luck.

He graced the waitress with one of his hundred-watt smiles. "Peggy," he addressed the waitress, spying her name tag, "I'm sorry if I'm not coming across the proper way. We're not destitute, but we are a long way from home and, more than likely, you'll be seeing a lot of us in the days ahead. I'd like to make the proper introductions. This lovely lady sitting across from me is my wife, Vinnie, and my name is Leo. I'm in the Air Force in Louisiana and we're both here in San Antonio because our son is being treated at Brooke."

Peggy's expression turned to one of bafflement. "Excuse me if I seem even more confused, but there's no way you two are old enough to have a son wounded in Korea."

Leo's smile increased several watts. "No, indeedy, we're not. Our son is, in fact, only three years old. He was transported to Brooke because of an accident back home." Leo swallowed hard and continued. "A bike spoke went into his head and our local base hospital couldn't handle it. As a result, the three of us were flown here to Texas."

Peggy cringed. "Oh, my goodness! What a horrible thing to have to go through!" she exclaimed. "My husband is also in the service and we have a little boy ourselves. I can't even begin to image going through something like this."

Her empathetic brown eyes sought out Vinnie's and the two women formed an instant maternal bond, but the process was interrupted by Miguel.

"Chica," he yelled to Peggy. "In case you forget, weez got other customers."

"Yea, yea Miguel. Hold your Mexican horses. I'll be right there."

"Sorry, guys," she said to Vinnie and Leo, "but duty calls. I'll be right back with your water and plenty of ice."

True to her word, Peggy was back in a few minutes with four glasses, two for each of them. The couple drank greedily until their thirst was quenched. Only then did they pause to order eggs ranchero, wheat toast, and despite the heat, coffee.

The Mexican brew proved bold and welcome. When they finished their meal, Leo asked Peggy to extend his compliments to the chef. Nowhere in New York or Louisiana had he tasted eggs like that. "Tell your boss he's a magician in the kitchen," Leo instructed.

"If it's all the same to you, I'll simply tell him you enjoyed the meal. Miguel is a nice guy, but give him a swelled head and there will be no working with him."

"I'll leave that entirely up to you," Leo said with another one of his winks.

With their hunger and caffeine cravings sated, Leo reached for his wallet to pay the bill and leave a substantial tip. As he did so, Vinnie noted a look of uneasiness on his face.

"What's wrong, Leo?" she questioned.

"Sorry, honey. I was thinking about our money situation. We have to pay for our room and food while we're here. Cash on hand may become a problem."

"If worse comes to worst, we can ask my parents to wire money and we'll pay them back down the road." As soon as the words were out of her mouth, Vinnie's face fell. She felt like she'd been struck by a bolt of lightning...her parents. Her countenance paled to a chalky white. "Oh, Leo, my parents! In all the excitement, I forgot to call or wire them. They have no idea what's happened to Leonard."

After Leo paid the bill, he asked Peggy to convert several dollar bills into change for the outside pay phone. Leo decided a personal call was in order rather than sending a wire. He held the door open for his wife and they walked the few feet to the phone booth. Leo handed Vinnie the coins and she picked up the receiver. She dropped in the first coin and dialed the local operator. She then asked to be connected to a long distance operator. Feeding more coins into their respective slots, she was finally connected to her parent's exchange in Pacoima, California.

It took six rings before her mother picked up the static-laden line. When Vinnie heard her mother's voice, her own faltered. "Mama, it's, it's Vinnie."

"Honey, is everything alright? Are the children okay?"

"I'm not really sure how to answer that, Mama. Lenora is fine. She is staying with the Steeles, the next-door neighbors I wrote you about, but Leonard is another story. He had an accident, a very serious accident, on Monday, and there's damage to his head. They tell us he's in stable condition, but the Barksdale base hospital had him airlifted to Brooke Army Hospital in San Antonio. That's where I'm calling you from now."

"Sweetheart, your father and I are on our way. Give me a number where I can reach you."

"I'm sorry, Mama but we're renting a room from the O'Malleys and I'm not certain they even have a telephone. When I get back to the house, I'll ask Mrs. O'Malley and call you as soon as I can. If you need to reach us in the meanwhile, I would think you can leave word for us at the hospital."

"That's fine, dear. Either way, it will take me a little time to get our things together. Vincenza, listen to me, please. Keep calm, because if you get yourself in a state, you won't be helping the baby. I'll say the rosary for Leonard as many times as I can before we get there."

"Thank you. I love you, Mama."

"I love you, too, my darling girl. God willing, we'll be there as soon as possible."

Fifteen minutes later, Mrs. Giamonte was struck by what she considered divine inspiration. She then called the long distance operator asking to be connected to the Steeles residence in Louisiana. Betty heard the three-ring chime of the telephone indicating a call coming in for the Steele residence.

"Hello," Betty said, but only heard the harsh crackling of the line. "Hello".

Over the noise, the nasal voice of an operator replied, "Long distance calling. Will you accept the call?"

"Yes, yes," Betty replied, assuming it was Vinnie calling with some good news from Texas. "Thank goodness you called, Vinnie. We've been so worried about Leonard."

But the voice on the other end of the line did not belong to her friend.

"Hello, Mrs. Steele," the caller said in greeting. The voice wasn't even familiar. "I'm sorry to disappoint you, but this is not Vincenza. This is her mother, Mrs. Giamonte. I understand Lenora is staying with you while her family is in Texas. I have a proposition for you."

CHAPTER SIXTEEN

Vinnie and Leo walked at a fast pace back to the O'Malleys. A key to the front door had been left on the night table in their room. When they entered the house, looking wilted from the increasing temperature, Mrs. O'Malley and her feather duster were busily attacking invisible dust bunnies.

"Well, it's obvious yourselves are having a devil of time copin' with our heat. Go on into the kitchen and sit down at the table, why don't you. There's freshly brewed tea coolin' itself in the ice box."

Mrs. O'Malley joined them at the kitchen table. "The mister hisself is out and hopefully keepin' out of trouble at the hospital. He's a 'jack of all trades' as you say here in the States. He's got hisself a job at Brooke fixin' and cleanin' things, don't you know."

No, they didn't know. Vinnie and Leo looked at one another. That certainly answered a lot of questions. "So that's how you knew so much about us," Vinnie said, her relief reflected in her voice. "Last night we were a little concerned about that."

"Ah," replied Mrs. O'Malley, the light slowly dawning. "And yourselves must have been thinkin' me a mind reader or totally daft. No, dearies. I'm not fey like me Grandma Bridgette or a few drams short of a pint like some of me other relations, but that's not how I knew about yourselves."

With a faint blush on her checks, Mrs. O'Malley went on. "It was that handsome Captain Gabe, with those beguilin' eyes of his, who came knockin' on our door early yesterday morin'. He sat at this very table tellin' the mister and meself about what happened to your lad sayin' you'd be needin' a decent place to stay."

Vinnie and Leo again looked at each other questioningly. Leo shrugged, "Honey, at this point your guess is as good as mine."

"Now if you'll be excusin' me, I have to get back to me chores," the landlady said, whimsically still thinking about Captain Gabe's visit.

"Yes, of course, Vinnie said, "but before you do, I have one quick question."

"Well, go ahead and spit it out, dearie," the missus urged.

"We called my mother in California from the pay phone in front of Miguel's. She asked for your number here, but I couldn't say for certain that you have telephone service. If you do, may I give the number to her?"

"No problem, at all, at all," Mrs. O'Malley was saying as she scribbled the number on a piece of paper. The couple thanked her and headed for the front door.

"Now, there's no sense in yourselves makin' an extra trip out in this heat if ya don't have to. Just use the phone in the livin' room and we'll settle up the cost later."

Mrs. O'Malley made a show of leading them to the phone. She picked up the black receiver and heard voices already engaged in conversation on the party line.

"Mrs. Garcia," she interrupted, "would you kindly be gettiin' off the line now. The missus here has to make an important call to her ma in California…Well, I'm very sorry that Mrs. Perez's poor daughter's been in labor for twenty-four hours but yakkin' on the phone isn't gonna make the baby come any faster. I'm givin' you to the count of three to get off the line before I get me Irish up…And the same to yourself, Mrs. Garcia."

A deafening bang echoed as the line disconnected. Mrs. O'Malley handed the phone triumphantly to Vinnie. "Go right ahead, dearie. Make your call."

Chapter Seventeen

Back at the hospital, it was a routine working day for Mr. O'Malley. He liked his job at Brooke. It got him out of the house and kept him busy. After finishing the hearty lunch his wife had packed for him, he entered the confines of the hospital basement.

"Perhaps tis but the calm before the storm," he said aloud to himself when he unlocked the door.

"Tis a rare afternoon, indeed, when the powers that be put no demands on me time." He was the only person in the lower recesses of the medical facility, and he embraced the solitude as if it were a long-lost friend.

Mr. O'Malley was happiest when he was busy. His mother had taught him that idle hands were the devil's playthings, and since he was inclined to agree, he chose to tackle the often-neglected task of maintenance on the back-up generator.

"There's no time like the present, me love, for us to renew our acquaintance," he said to the machine, with a trace of affection. He gave the object a reassuring pat and positioned his ample posterior on the edge of a sturdy wooden stool. With his arthritic knees positioned inches from the generator, he leaned his well-padded torso forward, enabling his hands the freedom to gently probe and explore.

As his mind and spirit relaxed, he was not surprised to find his vocal cords voluntarily engaged in a hardy rendition of his beloved "Danny Boy." He was half way into the solo when he sensed the surrounding gray concrete walls were not his only audience. He cautiously glanced upward, surprised, but not unduly alarmed, to find a uniformed-clad figure standing in front of him.

Mr. O'Malley took off the spectacles his aging eyes needed for close-up work and rubbed the bridge of his nose with a calloused thumb and forefinger. His unexpected guest's striking blues eyes danced with amusement at the residue of grease left on the Irishman's nose.

"Well, if it isn't Cap'n Gabe hisself," Mr. O'Malley said.

"Guilty as charged," the officer smiled and extracted a perfectly folded handkerchief from his uniform pocket and handed the linen square to his elder. The captain's smile broadened across his serene face as he waited for Mr. O'Malley to wipe the spot on his nose before speaking again.

"I selfishly didn't want to interrupt," the young man admitted with a touch of awe in his voice. "You're the finest Irish tenor my appreciative ears have had the pleasure of hearing on this side of the Atlantic."

'Well, thank you kindly, Cap'n. Me pipes have gotten a little rusty o'er the years, but didn't me Ma always tell me she could hear the angels in Heaven weeping whenever I sang that song? But now I guess me ears must be startin' to go as well as the old vocal cords. I apologize for not hearin' ya come in. I seldom get unexpected company down here and would never be anticipatin' a gentlemen such as yourself to be payin' me a visit in the basement. I'd get up and shake your hand, lad, but me legs are stiff and I wouldn't want to be responsible for messin' up that spotless uniform you're wearin'."

"No, on the contrary," the captain reassured him. "It's I who should apologize to you, sir. I have to admit that I'm frequently guilty of appearing out of the blue. It's a habit I developed over the years that people often find disconcerting.

"However, there is a special reason for my visit. I find myself in need of your assistance Friday, as well as the use of the hospital's station wagon, to insure that all goes according what I have planned."

"Okay, Cap'n," Mr. O'Malley said. "Let's hear this here plan of yours."

"Well, first of all, Mr. and Mrs. DiTrapani are expecting guests, but unbeknownst to them, there will be five people landing at the airport the day after tomorrow on two different flights. The anticipated arrivals from California are, as we know, Mrs. DiTrapani's parents, the Giamontes, and when their plane lands, I'd like you to drive them straight to your house.

"Now, even though Mrs. Giamonte will probably insist, there are to be no detours to the hospital. The family matriarch will undoubtedly provide a convincing argument to the contrary, which is perfectly understandable since she's extremely nervous about her grandson and is anxious to see him with her own eyes.

"But I'm depending on you to draw on your innate charm and ingenuity to persuade her that going to your house straightaway would be the most sensible course. Stress the point that it will give her the chance to freshen up after her flight and also provide an opportunity to get her emotions under control. You may also mention that your dear wife has made special preparations and refreshments will have been laid out for their punctual arrival. If that fails to sway her, you have my permission to throw in a little guilt.

"Tell her you're a dutiful husband who would like to keep his happy home, and you wouldn't want to take personal responsibility for upsetting the missus when she's gone to so much trouble."

"Well, I certainly wouldn't be a liar, now would I?" Mr. O'Malley added with a conspiratorial wink. The captain paused for a moment and grinned in confirmation.

"Now then," he said, returning to the matter at hand, "our other three guests are coming in from Louisiana. They will be a very pleasant and welcome surprise for the DiTrapanis. Their daughter, Lenora, and her two escorts should be brought directly to the hospital. And in fair warning, be prepared for the little miss. She takes after her grandmother."

"That sounds all well and good, Capt'n but with all due respect to your position, I can't be just takin' off on me own with the hospital's vehicle without goin' through the proper channels."

The captain's amused eyes matched his widening grin. "And right you are, Mr. O'Malley," he replied with a chuckle. "Although I've been known to bend the rules slightly, when the occasion warrants, I'm a firm believer in adhering to the rules of higher authority. So when you go upstairs, you'll find your work schedule for Friday properly amended and the wagon's keys waiting for you in the office."

Mr. O'Malley nodded his balding heard. "And speakin' of a higher authority, Capt'n, have you spoken to my missus with regard to this little matter?"

"But, of course, sir," the captain confirmed. "Earlier this morning, I had the pleasure of personally speaking with your charming wife and at this very moment she's happily preparing rooms for your guests and humming a merry tune while she goes about her work."

"I guess I can't be arguin', can I now?" Mr. O'Malley said sagely.

"My good sir," Gabe continued, "I can only reiterate what the missus has been telling you since the day you married her-- you're a wise man, indeed, Mr. O'Malley."

The Irishman returned his glasses to their proper place intending to reply, but when he looked up, his visitor was gone.

CHAPTER EIGHTEEN

Friday was scheduled on a precise timetable. Mr. O'Malley was not surprised in the least that his work roster allotted him the time to make the two trips to the airport.

If all went according to plan, Vinnie and Leo would be leaving the house at noon. That would give them time to stop at Cafe Miguel's for a combination breakfast and lunch and still arrive at the hospital before visiting hours.

Allowing for a large measure of resourcefulness on Mr. O'Malley's part, the Giamontes would be delivered to the house, without incident, during Vinnie and Leo's absence. Then Mr. O'Malley would have the task of putting the wagon's pedal to the metal to meet the second plane.

Fortunately, all went off like clockwork, and when Mr. O'Malley delivered Betty and the children to the hospital ten minutes before visiting hours, he let out a loud sigh of relief.

When the doors opened admitting Lenora first, Vinnie and Leo stood motionless in the hospital's lobby as if their feet were riveted to the floor. Their astounded eyes fixed on what they both believed to be an apparition. Coming through the door was an angelic female with hair of gold and beaming, long-lashed eyes. The blonde ponytail, fastened neatly with pink ribbon, bounced to and fro as the petite figure dashed to her parents. Her movements were so swift her Mary Janes barely touched the floor.

Vinnie, a step in front of Leo, was the first to feel the warmth of Lenora's outstretched arms. She kneeled to receive a flurry of butterfly kisses. Leo quickly stepped forward, crouching down so his arms could encircle the two most important women in his life. All extraneous sounds ceased as if the world, too, was observing the poignancy of the moment. But the silence was short-lived, as an excited Lenora bombarded her parents with a verbal barrage.

"Mommy, Daddy! I missed you so much. I got to fly on a really big plane and Mr. O'Malley picked us up at the airport. He talks kinda funny – not ha ha funny but funny different. So I asked him if that's how people in Texas talk. He told me that people born in the Lone Star State, that's Texas, would sound peculiar to my sensitive ears. And his 'liltin voice' was special because he was born on an Emerald Island where he kissed some kind of bologna stone."

"Oh, really," her father interjected.

"Yes, really," Lenora said seriously and proceeded. "So I told Mr. O'Malley I knew a lot about the Emerald City, but I really didn't like bologna and I would never ever kiss a dirty old stone. That's almost as yucky as kissing a boy."

Changing figurative horses in mid-stream, Lenora paused, took in half a breath, swallowed daintily, and rambled on while her parents inwardly groaned.

"Grandma and Grandpa are at the O'Malleys. The missus is getting them settled in and Mr. O'Malley will bring them to see Leonard in a little while. The most important thing is both Grandma and I are here and we'll take care of everything. You don't have to worry any more, Mommy. Now I'd like to see my brother, please."

"Lenora, sweetheart, you're coming here has been the best surprise your father and I could ever have. We missed you terribly, but you need to slow down those runaway horses of yours."

"Mommy, you're always telling me that," Lenora responded disarmingly, with a purely impish grin.

Leo teasingly tugged on her ponytail. "Whoa, horsey. There's a speed limit in this here hospital," he said, poorly imitating a Texan drawl.

In return, Leo received a giggled "Oh, Daddy" from his daughter.

Vinnie simply shook her auburn head, rolled her laughing blue eyes, and reminded herself that blessings come in a variety of packages. It was then she noticed for the first time that they were not alone. Two familiar figures were waiting patiently off to the side. The nicely dressed woman was standing posture-perfect, the top of her red head covered with a fashionable white summer hat. In the crook of her left arm was a coordinating purse and her right hand rested lightly on the shoulder of a young boy.

The boy's stance betrayed his discomfort at being attired in his Sunday best and having to witness so much emotion. His lanky body learned forward, both hands plunged deeply into his pants' pockets. His downcast eyes focused on his Buster Brown shoes as his right foot repeatedly moved as if he were kicking at an imaginary stone.

Betty tapped Bobby's slouched shoulder then pulled him into a reassuring hug. He looked up at her and then toward the DiTrapani's. His freckled face flushed to a vivid pink, but his small mouth turned upward. It was a moment of poignancy, as mother and son shared something deeper than identical grins.

Betty's grin blossomed into a full-fledged smile as she and Bobby walked forward to join the DiTrapanis.

"Well, goodness gracious. Isn't this the prettiest picture, seein' y'all together?" she commented, reaching out to pat Vinnie's arm with her white-gloved hand. "Now Vinnie, I know your mind must be bustin' with questions, so before you explode, let me tell you what happened.

"Your sweet momma called me all the way from California to ask about the possibility of us bringing Lenora here to Texas. I told her it might be possible, but it was a big undertaking and while

Lenora's presence might be a comfort to y'all, additional visitors would more than likely be a hindrance rather than a help.

"Your momma reassured me in that soothing voice of hers that the good Lord had whispered in her ear that this ordeal with Leonard may last longer than anyone anticipated. God put it in her heart to take Lenora to California to stay with them for the duration.

"When Robert came home for dinner that night, the four of us discussed it as a family. We agreed that Bobby and I would fly with Lenora to San Antonio and if you had reservations at all about her going to California, we'd simply take her back with us. So I tossed a few things into a suitcase for the three of us…and here we are."

Grateful tears formed in Vinnie's eyes and she managed an affirmative and heartfelt smile.

CHAPTER NINETEEN

Lenora saw her opportunity and tugged on her mother's dress, "If you and Mrs. Steele are done talking, can Bobby and I go see my brother now?"

The adults looked at one another. No one wanted to be the bearer of bad news. How could they possibly explain to an independent and strong willed five year-old that medical center ordinances prohibited children, escorted or otherwise, from venturing into the patient wards?

"I'm so sorry, sweetie," Vinnie said as she knelt down again so she could be eye-to-eye with her daughter. "This hospital doesn't allow children to visit the people here who are sick. I know you're terribly disappointed, but you're old enough to understand that we must obey the rules."

Lenora stood contemplatively, placing her left arm across her stomach and positioning her right elbow upon the extended arm. Her right index finger reached up and rested lightly on her chin, as she tilted her flaxen head slightly to the side.

"But who made the rules, Mommy? I don't think God would have. Some of the people here aren't sick at all, just hurt real bad because they were sent far away to fight. They're special people and isn't Brooke supposed to be a hospital for special people and isn't the hospital supposed to do its very bestest to make people feel better?" She paused for a split second to take a breath then continued.

"I'm sure seeing children, their own little boys and girls, would really make the men here feel a hundred times better--maybe even two hundred times better."

Lenora then lowered her voice.

"My heart kinda hurts inside because I know there are lots of soldiers here. Some of them are daddies...but there's an angel waiting to take them to Heaven. It would be really nice if their children could see them one last time and kiss them good bye."

The adults stood dumbfounded. No one could think of an appropriate response, but they were saved by the sudden approach of Mrs. Hart.

When Mrs. Hart reached the small gathering, she did not waste valuable time with pleasantries but instead came directly to the point.

"It's come to my attention that a number of friends and relatives have traveled a long ways to see your son, so the administrator has made a concession regarding the adult visitors. We will permit two visitors at a time but only for fifteen-minute alternating intervals during the four-hour visitation period. The first visitors may go up now and Mrs. Hastings will keep an eye on the clock and monitor how Leonard is taking to his company."

Betty, having stepped off to the side wishing to avoid being intrusive, observed the exchange between her friend and Mrs. Hart. When she did speak up, she directed her comments to Vinnie.

"You and Leo go first," she insisted.

Perhaps it was the momentary dip in her posture or the fleeting look of fatigue in her green eyes that attested to the strains of the hastily planned trip. Vinnie gave her neighbor and dear friend an empathetic look that said, "Yes, I know exactly how you feel." In response, Betty felt a faint blush warming her already subtly rouged cheeks.

"Well, truth be told," Betty admitted meekly, "I'm a tad tuckered out and would nearly kill for a cuppa."

"Oh, Betty, I'm sorry. How thoughtless of us," Vinnie commiserated with a pang of guilt. "By all means, you go ahead and get yourself that cup of tea. Would you like me to ask someone for directions to the cafeteria?" But the last question dangled in empty air. Betty had been on her mark, set, and ready to go taking off at a brisk pace in search of the restorative brew. She glanced fleetingly over her shoulder promising, "I shan't be long." But that was a promise she wouldn't be able to keep.

CHAPTER TWENTY

Vinnie and Leo were left standing open-mouthed in the lobby in the wake of Betty's departure, but it was time to see Leonard and their thoughts turned to him. They started toward the elevator then stopped. With all that had taken place, they had forgotten the other two bantering children in the lobby. It didn't take a rocket scientist to know hospital administration would not look kindly upon them leaving the children unattended.

Leo, always the gentleman, volunteered to stay behind and wait for Betty's return, but Vinnie could see the disappointment in his eyes. And Leo, knowing his wife so well, could almost smell the wood burning as she mentally weighed his offer. So before she could speak, he gallantly added, "Don't give it another thought, sweetheart." He patted her clenched hand, which eased under his reassuring touch. I'll be along as soon as I can."

A small smile creased her lips and extended outward. She looked appraisingly at her Leo's handsome face. After seven years of marriage, her husband was an open book. Today's chapter told her he was chomping at the bit. Her stallion was as anxious for the visit to Leonard as she was. She could not, with a clear conscience, leave him behind. She made up her mind. There would be no further discussion of the matter. She, too, would stay and await Betty's return.

Lenora and Bobby were busily chatting about the trip from Louisiana. Bobby boasted that the captain, the most important person on the whole plane, had let him sit in the cockpit before the flight and presented him with a set of wings.

"You've already told me that three times." Lenora responded with exasperation. She hadn't been asked to the cockpit and assumed it was because she was a girl. The truth was she really didn't care. However, when Bobby said something about the attentive stewardess in their cabin being only a waitress for the passengers and the pilots, she had felt compelled to come to the defense of the young woman who had been so nice to her. Lenora confidently announced, "I bet that pretty stewardess is also pretty smart and she could fly the plane all by herself, if she had to. But because she's a girl, they won't let her. Someday girls will be able to do whatever the boys do, and probably do it better!"

"This is worth the price of admission," Leo remarked as they eavesdropped on the youngsters' animated conversation. He and Vinnie were both enjoying the impromptu entertainment when an unfamiliar figure in white approached. Her demeanor, like a brand new Hoover, sucked any remaining particles of light-heartedness out of the air. A pall descended when she delivered her message: "Dr. Hart would like to see you both in his office as soon as possible."

Looking at the messenger, then looking back at the children, the split-second decision was made to leave the children unaccompanied in the lobby.

"We'll be right with you," Leo said to the attendant and directed his attention back to the children.

"Listen to me very, very carefully. I want the two of you to sit here and behave yourselves," he instructed in a firm tone that was barely above a whisper and left no room for argument. Bobby snapped to with a confirming "Yes, sir," but Lenora hesitated a fraction of a second too long. Frown lines creased Vinnie's forehead as she tried in vain to read her daughter's mind. She abandoned the task and relied on the standard, "That goes for you, too, young lady! We have to talk to Leonard's doctor and we don't want to have to worry about you."

Only those with extraordinary auditory prowess would have been able to hear the miniature wheels in Lenora's mind spinning faster than the speed of sound. When the rotations slowed to a semi normal rate, Lenora's changed facial expression resembled the fabled cat that swallowed the canary.

"I give you my very biggest promise that you won't have to worry...cross my sweet little heart," and she proceeded to do just that in demonstration of her earnestness.

Lenora watched her parents dutifully follow the somber lady until all were out of sight. She jumped up and counted to ten using the one-Mississippi, two-Mississippi method her Aunt Adele had taught her. Then she walked on her tippy toes to peek down the hallway. The breath she had been holding whooshed from her delicate lungs--the coast was clear. Having little time to waste, she did a quick about-face and headed toward Bobby.

He saw her coming and his body instinctively stiffened. He recognized the mischievous expression on that otherwise angelic face and knew trouble with a capital "T" was coming. She headed him off before he could voice his budding protest.

"I think we should go see Leonard." It was a statement, not a suggestion. If Bobby had been wiser, he would have observed Lenora's stance of hands on hips, and not opened his mouth.

"Are you completely off your rocker, Lenora? We're not goin' nowhere. We're gonna sit right here like we was told." He leaned back forcefully in his seat with his rigid spine butted against the chair. He resolutely crossed his long arms over his puffed-out chest and pouted with a frown of finality.

Lenora was not deterred in the slightest. She lavished Bobby with a smile befitting any aspiring ingénue, but he was too naïve to grasp the significance of the gesture. He could not fathom why she was standing there looking at him all girly-like when he had clearly laid down the law. He was venturing into unfamiliar territory here, so maybe he hadn't done it quite right. He could pretend to be a military officer and bark out orders like a general. Surely that way Lenora would have to listen.

An invisible light bulb suddenly flashed on above Bobby's pomade-slickened hair. He remembered exactly with whom he was dealing. He lightly smacked his right-hand palm against his forehead. "Ugh, Bobby Steele," he admonished himself, "you're a big dope." He had been stupid to think that as the man in this equation, his word was final. There would be no such luck when dealing with Lenora.

Admitting to himself he could not win the battle, let alone the war, he changed his strategy, but his words came out pleading. "But you promised your parents."

"Silly-nilly boy, I promised them they wouldn't have to worry… and they won't. I always keep my promises. God would be very upset with me if I didn't."

"Lenora," he said in frustration laced with an obvious tinge of admiration, "you're crazier than a bedbug."

CHAPTER TWENTY-ONE

As Betty wound her way through the maze of corridors, it was not long before miniature bells of discomfort began their warning chimes. "This is taking much too long," she reasoned under her breathe and slowed her pace to a crawl. She began to feel light-headed and her stomach growled ferociously. She chided herself for skipping breakfast earlier that morning, but her primary concern had been the children. Making sure Lenora and Bobby were fed, properly dressed, and ready for the flight had been her number one priority. She had very little time for herself and breakfast was a mere afterthought.

Now, as she continued, slowly putting one foot in front of the other, she noticed her surroundings were strangely void of normal hospital hustle and bustle. There were no voices to be heard, nor the beep or wheeze of loud medical machines providing their life-sustaining services. The fingers of anxiety reached out and tapped her on the shoulder. So forceful was the sensation that she feared looking back, but curiosity proved the more overpowering of the two emotions. Tentatively, she turned. Visibly relieved to find no one behind her, she inhaled deeply and found the hospital smells somewhat comforting. She took a step forward and everything went black.

When she awoke, Betty groaned and cautiously opened her eyes. She had no idea how much time had passed or where she was. She was in a prone position. Her hat and gloves had been removed and a damp cloth lay across her forehead. She tried to sit up.

"Take it easy, Mrs. Steele," a soft voice instructed.

"Goodness gracious. What in Heaven's name am I doin' here and exactly where is here?"

"You're in the nurses' lounge. One of the guards found you outside our door and asked if he could bring you in. While he checked your ID, we checked you over. Your pulse was racing a bit, but everything else seemed fine."

Betty noticed the table next to her. There was a large cup sitting there. She eyed it suspiciously. The other woman laughed. "You kept moaning the word "tea," so we wanted to make sure it was ready when you were."

CHAPTER TWENTY-TWO

Unbeknownst to Lenora and Bobby, they still had an audience of one in the lobby. A spectator witnessed the verbal sparring match between the miniature opponents from his vantage point across the room. He took pity on the young boy, easily recognizing he was no match for the half-pint dynamo in the pink crinoline dress. He tittered as he watched her standing erect with hands on hips, impatiently tapping the toe of her patent leather shoe.

"Robert William Steele, are you going to sit there like a bump on a log or are you coming with me?" The uniformed gentlemen decided it was time to make his presence known and throw the little guy a life preserver. Bobby was in way over his head.

"Good afternoon," he said approaching the pair. My name is Captain Gabe and right now I'm on duty here. Can I be of assistance?"

Lenora stared at the captain, her mouth slightly agape and her eyes filled with wondrous awe.

He addressed Lenora. "I know your brother quite well. I have been a frequent visitor at his bedside and he has asked for you many times. I can certainly understand how anxious you are to see him. And even though your immediate intentions are based on your genuine concern for your brother, I don't think it's a good idea for you to be traipsing around the building by yourself or with Bobby.

However, it would be my privilege if you would permit me to be your personal escort."

Lenora's feet felt cemented to the floor. "H-e-l-l-o, Gabriel," she stammered. "It's...it's an honor to meet you," she added sounding much older that her five years. Bobby shot her a questioning glare. She, in turn, only had eyes for the striking gentleman. She swallowed hard. "I...I love your wings. They're more beautiful than I ever imagined."

Bobby's ears perked up when he heard the word wings. Now here was a subject he could personally relate to. Being on safer ground, he jumped in with both feet not wanting to be left out of the conversation. "Yeah, nice wings, sir...My dad has them, too. He's a major in the Air Force, but he's back at the base in Louisiana training guys for the war."

Lenora executed an exaggerated roll of her hazel eyes in response to Bobby's unsolicited comments. She and the good captain exchanged conspiratorial smiles. After all, Bobby was a boy, and more often than not, boys didn't have a clue.

CHAPTER TWENTY-THREE

Vinnie and Leo's escort left them at the entrance to Dr. Hart's office. Leo turned the handle and pushed inward, letting Vinnie enter first.

"May I help you?" the secretary asked with an authoritative air.

"We were told Dr. Hart wanted to see us as soon as possible."

"I'm sorry, Mr. DiTrapani, but neither Dr. Hart nor I sent for you."

"I beg your pardon, madam," Leo countered with ice creeping into his voice. "One of your staff made a point of seeking us out and we want to know what's going on with our son."

"No one summoned you from this office, sir," she replied somewhat tersely.

Leo's eyes burned into hers. A pregnant pause hung in the air. She was the official gatekeeper and it was her responsibility to decide who passed through the invisible barrier and who did not. The power was hers and this time she chose to reconsider. Her voice lost some of its starch.

"Please be seated and I'll see if the doctor can see you for a moment." Leo and Vinnie chose to remain standing.

The secretary pushed a button on the small rectangular box on her desk. They could hear its resonating buzz sounding within the doctor's inner sanctum. In response, Dr. Hart pushed the lever on the box's twin which rested on his tidy desk. "I already know there's an emergency in surgery. They called on my private line," he announced. "I'm coming." A fraction of a second later, heavy footsteps were heard pounding the floor and the inside door flew open. Dr. Hart barreled toward the couple, who defensively parted like the Red Sea.

The doctor bellowed, "I don't know how long this is going to take." If the doctor was surprised to see the DiTrapanis standing in the office, it did not register in his preoccupied eyes, but he could recognize the panic in theirs.

"Everything is status quo with your son," he volunteered on the fly, lowering his voice with an unexpected degree of compassion. Then he was gone.

The doctor's hasty departure zapped the air out of the room. Vinnie unsteadily took a seat and the silence became deafening. When the phone rang suddenly, the three remaining occupants of the office were visibly startled.

"Yes," the secretary acknowledged into the black mouth piece, "I'll send them to collect Mrs. Steele." Vinnie and Leo's eyes met questioningly "Our Mrs. Steele?"

"It seems your friend," the secretary informed them, "was found by security in an unauthorized portion of the building and had succumbed to a minor episode of sorts."

Vinnie looked panic stricken, but the secretary added, "There's no need for worry. She's feeling much better and recuperating in the nurses' quarters. I'll have a security person bring you to her location and she can be released into your care."

Leo shook his head, thinking of poor Betty, desperate in her quest for a simple cup of tea. With tired eyes he looked upward. "I love you dearly, Lord, but on occasion you exhibit a very strange sense of humor."

CHAPTER TWENTY-FOUR

Bobby blanched when Lenora took the captain's hand. His instincts assured him Captain Gabe was one of the good guys, but he knew that leaving the lobby was against orders and a good soldier always obeyed commands. Bobby was not going to budge from his seat even if his full bladder continued to complain. He would just sit tight, cross his legs, and wait for Lenora's return. Maybe she'd be real quick and no one would be the wiser.

Lenora gazed into Gabriel's magnificent eyes when she took his offered hand. The tingling warmth traveled through her delicate fingers and coursed through her entire body. She sighed, deep lines furrowing her pale brow. "Are you here to take my brother to Heaven?"

"No, no I'm not. Under normal circumstances, escorting people to our Lord is not part of my job, but I'm here because He told me you asked Him to send an angel...one who could fly here on his own."

"Thank you for coming," she beamed.

"It's both a pleasure and an honor, Lenora," he said affectionately, the glow of his aura increasing with the radiance of his smile.

When they reached Leonard's room, the three-year-old could sense his sister's arrival. He started kicking his sock covered feet, and tried to sit up. Mrs. Hastings, ever watchful, left her chair to attend to her patient. If he became too active or agitated, it was her duty to sedate him.

When Captain Gabe stood in the doorway, Leonard quieted down. Mrs. Hastings, on the other hand, had a different reaction. Her body temperature rose markedly, and she used her right hand in a fanning motion to cool the sudden flash of heat. With his eyes intent, the captain greeted the boy's caregiver.

"Mrs. Hastings, good afternoon to you, madame. Could you possibly spare a moment of your valuable time to discuss something with me right outside?" The nurse's expression revealed her indecision, as she was obviously torn between her professional obligations and her overwhelming desire to comply with the captain's request.

The captain added, "I give you my personal assurance, it is perfectly alright. The little one is quiet now, and he won't be out of your sight for a moment."

The captain led Lenora into the room, releasing her hand and tweaking her button nose. He then reached toward Mrs. Hastings, lightly touching her elbow to usher her from the room. Lenora put her hand to her mouth to stifle the escaping giggles. This was the best trick ever. She must be invisible because the nurse neither saw nor heard her.

Lenora took off her shoes and climbed into the crib with her brother. He reached out his tiny arms and she pulled him close to her heart. When he was born, he had stolen a piece of that heart and was granted its ownership forever. She kissed his cheeks and the bandages on his wrapped head.

"Home, Lenora…take me home," he pleaded. She rocked him back and forth cooing, "Soon, Leonard, soon."

Captain Gabe allowed the children ten minutes together, then from the hallway, he nodded his raven head, signaling to Lenora that the visit was at an end. "Listen to me, Leonard," she said softly, but with conviction, as her hazel irises melded into his baby blues.

"I promise you," she said crossing her heart for the second time that day and truly meaning it, "there's no reason for you to be afraid. Mommy and Daddy are here for you and so is Gabriel."

Upon hearing his name, the captain winked a knowing eye in their direction. "Big...big wings," Leonard said, staring at Gabriel. The little boy raised his arms to illustrate the largest of sizes.

"Yes, Leonard, the biggest and bestest of wings."

When the visit with her brother was concluded, Lenora was returned to the lobby just in time to head off the posse of five frantic adults, which included her newly arrived grandparents. She had followed Gabriel's instructions and scooted ahead of him, but when she turned back hoping for his support, he was gone. Resigned, she stiffened her upper lip and prepared to face the music alone.

Vinnie and Leo rushed to meet Lenora. First came, "Are you okay, sweetheart?" That was immediately followed by, "You're in big trouble now, young lady. When you get home you won't be leaving your room for a month of Sundays. You scared us half to death. We've told you time and time again never to go off with a stranger."

Lenora raised her bowed head, an impish gleam in those curly-lashed eyes. "Mommy and Daddy," she said with an implied reprimand of her own, "You know I would never, ever go off with a stranger. I went with Gabriel and he's my friend. He's the angel God sent to watch over Leonard."

The adults did not have time to digest Lenora's statement because Mrs. Hart reappeared. "Is something else wrong? I see that Mrs. Steele has made a full recovery, but visiting hours have started and Mrs. Hastings said no one has been upstairs."

"No," Vinnie replied. "Everything is fine now." She looked at Leo and he nodded. "We're going to let Leonard's grandparents go up first."

CHAPTER TWENTY-FIVE

Over the weekend, the Giamontes and Betty visited Leonard as often as time and the hospital would allow. On Monday, August 13, the Giamontes, with Lenora in tow, and Betty with Bobby, would be going their separate ways. It was a bittersweet parting amid many tears.

With everyone's departure, Vinnie and Leo experienced feelings of abandonment and isolation. Leonard's accident had torn though their lives like a tornado. It was only the two of them and they wondered if they'd ever be able to pick up the pieces.

Days turned into weeks, and the weeks flowed into months. The theory that no news was good news did not apply to their son's situation. It only served to increase their emotion-laden speculation, which was running at an all-time high.

In September, they missed Lenora's first day of school in California. They wrote to tell her how proud they were of her. Mrs. Giamonte had sent a picture of Lenora going off to school in one of the many new outfits she had sewn for her granddaughter. Vinnie kept the picture in her pocket next to her rosary beads.

Their visits to Cafe Miguel decreased as their finances dwindled. Leo's pride had gotten in the way of his asking Vinnie's parents for money. They seriously discussed giving up the house in Louisiana, but Leo would have to leave Texas to close up the place and arrange the move to on-base housing. With nerves already frayed, leaving his wife wasn't an option.

Overhearing one of their conversations at Leonard's beside, Mrs. Hastings apologized for "butting in," and suggested the couple might ask the Red Cross for assistance. Leo dreaded asking for help of any kind. He had refused to ask his in-laws for money, but he couldn't allow himself to be prideful any longer. So with hat in hand, Leo and Vinnie had their first and last meeting with the charity they found not so charitable.

They were kept waiting an inordinate amount of time but took that in stride. Leo said partly joking, partly serious, "I guess beggars can't be choosers." He rubbed his rumbling stomach and asked his wife a silly question. "Bet you can't guess what I'm thinking about?"

"Leo DiTrapani, I know you all too well," his wife answered. "I can hear your stomach growling, so I don't have to be a mind reader to know, and just because you read stories in the newspaper about the Red Cross generously providing coffee and donuts to people during disasters doesn't mean we'll graciously be offered any."

The offer never came. Gracious or otherwise.

The director finally arrived with a preoccupied air. He took only a few seconds to look at the information on his desk pertaining to the couple. "There's nothing we can do for you," he said, looking sternly at Leo. "You're part of the military and you're entitled to food and housing at the base."

"Excuse me," Leo countered, attempting to control his rising anger. "The base is more than ten miles from the hospital and the only means of transportation we have are the feet we walked in on. Aside from the distance, the military would provide for me, not my family. What's my wife supposed to do?"

"I'm sorry, Mr. DiTrapani, but you're a member of the armed services and, as such, you and your family are their responsibility."

He rose from his chair and headed toward the door. "Now, if you'll excuse me, I have other business to attend to."

Leo jumped up to grab the retreating figure, but Vinnie forcibly held him back.

"Let him go, Leo. We don't have the money to bail you out of jail and you won't do Leonard much good in a stockade if the Air Force gets involved. We've been foolish, you and I. Foolish to place our faith in a bureaucratic system when we should only be placing our faith in God."

CHAPTER TWENTY-SIX

D r. Hart and a panel of three other doctors met every four days to discuss the hospital's youngest patient. They scrutinized x-ray after x-ray searching for anything remotely positive to indicate the puncture lifting. Optimism had faded as the end of September approached, but it was then that a change in the pictures was detected. The four doctors reached a consensus...there was more probability of the V-shaped indentation collapsing than lifting. That would mean Leonard's days as a normal functioning three-year-old were numbered if nothing was done soon. With the collapse, the child could end up mentally impaired or in a complete vegetative state.

The doctors made the last-resort decision to construct and insert a metal plate to provide what they hoped to be adequate protection for the child's brain; but they had never performed such a difficult operation on a cranium of diminutive size. Leonard's skull was measured and the plate expeditiously prepared. The operation was scheduled for Monday, October 8, to coincide with the arrival of Dr. Reese Warren, a senior neurosurgeon from Walter Reed Hospital in Washington, D.C. Dr. Warren regularly traveled to the country's military hospitals consulting on the more complex cases and performing the most intricate surgeries in his field.

Dr. Hart, who now often referred to Leonard as "the little tyke," and his entire staff had grown extremely fond of the child. He had no qualms about Dr. Warren doing the actual surgery. Even though he had an impressive résumé of successful operations himself, he confided only to his wife how relieved he felt, in this one case, to be handing the reins over to another doctor. With all in readiness, the operation would take place at 8:00 AM Monday morning.

At the O'Malley's, on the Sunday night before the surgery, no one had slept soundly. It was strange not to hear the landlord's sonorous snores reaching the upper level, but their absence only added to the tension of the endless night.

Having decided to attend six o'clock Mass on Monday morning, Vinnie and Leo got up in darkness and dressed in a strained silence. Not a word was spoken when they descended the stairs and exited the house. Hand clutching hand, they made their way through the streets to the church and up the cement steps. As the couple passed through the door, Leo took off his hat and transferred it to his left hand. He rested his other hand resting on the small of his wife's back, ushering her toward the altar, where he preferred to sit.

Vinnie's steps suddenly became lethargic. The full impact of the impending operation assailed her like a physical blow. Dr. Hart had done his best to go over the procedure with them step-by-step, but that didn't reassure them. Even as laymen, Vinnie and her husband understood the most infinitesimal slip of a finger during surgery could prove catastrophic to their son.

Her body began to tremble and Leo gripped her arm in support. Rivulets running over the rims of her eyes impaired Vinnie's vision, but on the periphery she saw a man she recognized. He was standing in an alcove in front of a magnificent painting of the Blessed Virgin Mother. She stopped in her tracks.

The young man in uniform was reverently lighting a candle. Reluctant to move, Vinnie reached into her purse for the handkerchief always neatly folded at the bottom. Extracting it, she dabbed her sodden eyes and returned her focus to the young man.

To her profound dismay, the area in front of the beautiful canvas was now empty, but the newly lit candle blazed invitingly. Vinnie moved toward the side altar. Leo opened his mouth to question their change in course, but when his eyes beheld the painting of Our Lady of Perpetual Help holding the infant Christ Child, no explanation was required.

Jointly, they put a flame to a long, thin taper. Each took a turn lighting the wicks on its left and right, completing the trinity. The Mass had started, but it was here they knelt with heads bowed. Their tears surged like storm waters, but Leo was not ashamed. He cried openly as his lips moved in silent prayer.

Vinnie's eyes were shut tightly, but her sobs were audible. She started to tremble again, but was instantly warmed by an intense radiance coming from above. Her spirit felt as if it were bathed in a golden ray of the sun. She was compelled to raise her head and look up. When she did, she was drawn to the compassionate eyes of the Madonna. There was a flicker of golden light in the beautifully painted orbs that now bored into hers. The hypnotic golden irises on the canvas intensified their penetrating gaze and Vinnie's heart was filled with their words.

"We, as women, are not immune to the pain and sorrow that can accompany the gift of motherhood, but know that we are blessed and our precious gift is worth whatever price our bodies and hearts will be asked to pay. You have a remarkable life ahead of you. You will be given much, and in return much will be asked. For today, the Lord seeks nothing more from you than your faith. Go in peace. Your life and son await you."

Chapter Twenty-seven

At the hospital, Leonard had been sedated and prepped for surgery ahead of schedule. It was already agreed that his parents wouldn't see him prior to the operation. The only visitor allowed would be a priest.

It was not uncommon for the attending hospital priest to administer the "Last Rites" to Catholic soldiers who would never be leaving the hospital. In most cases, his would be the last face these men saw before entering the kingdom of Heaven. There was an ache in the priest's heart when he entered Leonard's room. God hadn't shared His intentions with the clergyman so he didn't know if this sleeping child would be among those called home today.

"In name of the Father, Son, and Holy Ghost, I bless you, Leonard." The priest anointed the child's head with oils and holy water and continued to pray. To the Lord, he said, "Thy will be done on earth as it is in Heaven."

Gabriel hovered over the clergyman's shoulder. Next it was his turn to go to work.

CHAPTER TWENTY-EIGHT

Later in the operating suite, Dr. Warren and his team were suited up and scrubbed, but Dr. Hart could see something was bothering the visiting surgeon and questioned him.

"Reese, there seems to be something on your mind. Are you having second thoughts about proceeding?"

Dr. Warren spoke candidly to his colleague.

"As a matter of fact, Charles, I am. Something has been gnawing at my gut since we scrubbed, and I've been in this business too long to ignore it. The patient may be on the table, but I would prefer one more x-ray before we go in. Make it two. Have it done STAT."

His request was promptly completed. Dr. Warren put the two new x-rays on the board and carefully examined the interior view of his patient's cranial lobe. He continued to stare and muttered to himself. Dr. Hart, unnerved by his fellow surgeon's reaction, cautiously approached.

"What's wrong, Reese? From the look on your face, it can't be good. Don't tell me we're already too late to save the child!"

"Look carefully, my good friend," Dr. Warren replied. "As a learned physician, tell me exactly what you see."

Dr. Hart looked at the first x-ray, did a double-take, and then immediately studied the second. His mouth dropped open. He moved back to the first film, not being able to comprehend the images before him. Then he became agitated.

"What's going on here, Reese? These pictures are of a perfectly healthy child's brain."

"Yes, they are, and they're Leonard DiTrapani's. I don't know for sure what happened here this morning, but my best guess tells me you and I witnessed an honest to God, blessed miracle. And I, for one, have never been happier."

Dr. Warren slapped his open-mouthed associate heartily on the back. "Well, Charles, since it's obvious my professional services here are no longer needed, I'll be on my way to some other patient who really does need me. And if you or anyone else has any further questions, I suggest you take them up with the Almighty. He's the one who is clearly in charge here."

He headed out of the room with a jaunty step and tossed his unsullied scrubs in the appropriate receptacle. When he left the premises, he was grinning ear to ear. This was a story he couldn't wait to tell his children and grandchildren...over and over again.

CHAPTER TWENTY-NINE

When Vinnie and Leo came through the hospital entrance, they found Mrs. Hart waiting at the door. She could see their anxiety ignite.

"Please don't be alarmed, Mr. and Mrs. DiTrapani, but my husband would like to see you." Before they could take another step, they saw Dr. Hart rushing toward them.

This was the clichéd straw that broke the camel's back, or in this case, Leo's. His face turned a deep shade of red and a single vein popped on his forehead. "What's happened to our son?" he roared as he reached forward to grasp the lapels of the doctor's lab coat.

Dr. Hart, having played football, instinctively took an evasive step sideways. Seizing the opportunity, the doctor's wife swiftly inserted herself between the two men.

"No, no, Mr. DiTrapani. Please calm down. We have wonderful news to relay," she said, trying to gain Leo's full attention.

Before Vinnie or Leo could say another word, Dr. Hart shouted, "There will be no operation. Your son is fine, absolutely, unequivocally one hundred percent fine."

Vinnie and Leo looked at one another. Their faces had gone white and neither seemed capable of remaining on their feet.

"Please have a seat," Dr. and Mrs. Hart said at the same time and guided them to nearby chairs.

"Apparently I'm not handling this as well as I'd like," Dr. Hart said in apology, "so let me start at the very beginning.

"The team was ready to go and your son prepped, but Dr. Warren insisted on taking a last x-ray before the procedure. Between the time the first pictures were taken earlier this morning and the last ones taken pre-op, a mir… a phenomenal thing occurred. The indentation that was so dangerously close to your son's brain lifted of its own accord. The fragile bones surrounding the area have knitted themselves into the pre-trauma position.

"There's no plausible medical explanation for what happened here today, so I'm not even going to attempt it. We'll check Leonard again tomorrow and if nothing has changed, I see no reason why we can't start preparing him for discharge."

Leo folded Vinnie into his arms and they held each other, weeping unrestrained tears of relief and joy. The couple never heard the doctor and his wife excuse themselves nor the approach of the gentleman in uniform.

"Please forgive me for intruding yet again," Captain Gabe said. "The hospital is abuzz with the news of Leonard's recovery. The jubilation of the staff is contagious. They want to plan a little party for him; but I'm sorry to say, I won't be here for the celebration. My new orders have come through and I've been instructed to return to home base. I didn't want to leave without saying good-bye."

Vinnie reached out for the captain's arm. Her tear-filled eyes searched his.

"You were there this morning, weren't you? And none of it was my imagination."

The captain's broad smile melted away as his intense eyes melded into hers.

"Mrs. DiTrapani, some questions are better left unanswered. Remember that God doesn't fail to hear our prayers, but he doesn't always answer them in the way we hoped. Miracles and adversity take many shapes and forms. God has purpose in all that He does or seemingly doesn't do. We must trust in Him."

The captain's smile reignited. "Now, on a lighter note, I can wholeheartedly say that it has been an honor to have met you and your wonderful family, but I must be on my way."

After an emotion-filled hug from Vinnie and a grateful handshake from Leo, the captain headed for the door with a bounce in his step. He turned back once, proudly saluted the DiTrapanis and walked outside into a brilliant rainbow of light that engulfed him. A second later, he was gone.

Two days later, Vinnie and Leo, along with their perfectly healthy and happy son, left Brooke. Vinnie, holding Leonard's hand, glanced up. She was drawn to a particularly brilliant sunbeam. Following its path through the clouds to the bountiful sky, she felt renewed in her faith. She made the Sign of the Cross. Leonard waved and threw a kiss skyward, aiming at the wings only he could see.

BOOK III

CHAPTER ONE

October 1951 to May 1954

With Leonard's accident and its aftermath, it wasn't until the last week in October 1951 that the four DiTrapanis were once again under the same roof back in Louisiana. They took renewed pleasure in what Leo referred to as "simple, everyday life," but rarely was life simple.

For Leo, an important decision loomed on the horizon. In February his commitment to the military would formally end. His superiors hounded him to reenlist in the Reserves, but when Leo didn't respond in a timely manner, a man of higher authority called Leo into the office for a little heart-to-heart.

"Have a seat," the captain urged Leo, motioning to the single chair facing his desk. The officer made a pretense of scanning the papers in front of him before he looked up at Leo.

"Leo, my boy," he said in the supportive tone of an uncle rather than a man of senior rank. "Although I haven't been able to say anything before now, I have it on good authority that upping your enlistment will mean a promotion for you and, of course, a pay increase to help with that growing family of yours. All you have to do is put your John Hancock right here on the dotted line and it will be a done deal." While flashing an unnatural grin, the captain slid the papers and a pen toward Leo.

Leo took the papers in hand. "No disrespect to you, sir," he said while perusing the sheets of very fine print, "but I was taught never to sign anything without reading it first."

A scowl arose on the officer's face, but was promptly replaced by a look of comradery. "Of course, my boy, go ahead and read every word. After all, if you can't trust Uncle Sam, who can you trust?"

Leo understood the question was rhetorical and did not reply. Instead he continued to read. When he finished, he looked up and said, "Something is missing."

The captain harrumphed. "The form is standard, Leo. The only thing missing is your signature."

"Well, that's the problem, sir. It's standard. There's no mention of a promotion."

"Your promotion is something that will be taken care of down the line at the appropriate time."

"Once again, with no disrespect meant to you or the Air Force, I think now is the appropriate time. I sincerely appreciate all the Air Force did for me when my son was injured, but this Korean situation isn't showing any signs of being resolved. I've been extremely fortunate during my service time and I'm not sure if I'm willing to tempt fate. If I don't see something in writing, you won't be seeing my signature on this paper."

"Young man," the captain addressed Leo sternly, "that's not how things work around here. I give the orders, you carry them out."

"Not anymore," Leo answered as he rose from his chair. He picked up the papers and tore them into pieces. With a well-aimed flick of his hand, the remnants cascaded onto the desk.

"Captain, this pigeon," he said pointing to himself, "is flying the coop when my time is up. I'm sorry we couldn't come to an understanding, but I think, in view of all the circumstances, my only commitment should be to my family and God." He saluted and turned on his heels.

With Leo returning to civilian life, the family had to decide where their next move would take them, literally. Vinnie didn't see any point in returning to the apartment in Queens. Without her parents there, nothing would be the same. In her heart of hearts, she had known that once they left New York, coming back would not be an option.

Since Lenora had loved being in California with her grandparents, she and her grandmother teamed up to persuade the family to move there. The outcome was highly predictable.

In March, 1952, the DiTrapanis once again packed up their possessions and prepared them for shipment. They were heading west, to the wide-open spaces of California. The family said tearful good-byes to all those in Louisiana who had become their extended family in the tight-knit military community. Leaving the Steeles was the hardest of all, but they too were entertaining thoughts of moving to the West Coast when Major Steele retired.

Their larger items would have to be shipped through a moving company, but Leo loaded their newly purchased 1948 Nash 600 (which he bought from a little old lady who only used the car to drive to and from church for Sunday Mass and Wednesday night bingo) to the rafters with items they wanted to keep with them.

While the right passenger door was still open, Bobby awkwardly leaned in. He surprised both himself and Lenora by quickly kissing her on the cheek. Only Leonard had time to witness the encounter and he scrunched up his face. He thought Bobby must be crazy to kiss any girl, even if that girl was his own sister.

Mrs. Goldberg and the Steeles tearfully waved their good-byes until the brown car became a speck on the horizon. "Go with God's blessing," Mrs. Goldberg said, softly wiping her eyes.

For many miles Lenora sat in the backseat, a grin glued to her face. She thought about her departure and Bobby's unexpected kiss. Several times she put her hand to the exact spot his warm lips had touched. Perhaps, just maybe, boys weren't such silly creatures after all.

It was a long and stimulating road trip for the family. Leo and Vinnie made it as entertaining and educational as possible for the children by stopping at points of interest along the way. The last day of their travels, however, was a little daunting. Every few miles, to the dismay of the other three passengers, Leonard would ask, "Are we there yet?" Lenora finally gave her brother the sternest look she could conjure. "Sorry," he whispered and covered his mouth with both hands.

Upon reaching the San Fernando Valley in California, they drove directly to Pacoima, a neighborhood of the City of Los Angeles, where the Giamontes had purchased a single-story house. The temperature of the Valley was welcoming; but not as welcoming as the Giamontes, who met them with exuberant hugs and kisses. Vinnie didn't remember the last time she saw her parents so relaxed. Their aura was positively glowing.

As agreed before the move, the DiTrapanis would reside with Vinnie's parents while looking for a home, but the Giamontes weren't the only newly established residents of the area. Cousin Carmine "the carpenter" had sold his business in Queens the year before and moved his family lock, stock and barrel out West. Construction was on the rise in the Los Angeles area, and the consistently pleasant temperatures made it an ideal place to set up residence and reestablish his business. His new company, Cione & Sons, was already doing better than Carmine anticipated and he continued the tradition of family discounts. As a result, after several months of unsuccessful house hunting, the DiTrapanis decided to avail themselves of Carmine's services and build a new structure.

The family chose a quarter-acre tract of land two blocks east of the Giamontes. The plot was covered with lemon and orange trees bearing the fullest of luscious fruit. Upon surveying the property with Cousin Carmine, Lenora's hazel eyes welled with tears when she understood that the land would have to be cleared for construction.

"But Cousin Carmine," she croaked, the sadness traveling to her voice, "God placed those trees here and maybe He won't be happy with us if we take them down."

Carmine's mouth curved into a smile as he explained. "Ah, *piccola mia* (my little one). God created people, knowing that we all need places to live. He understands that we all can't possibly live together, and the more people there are, the more houses will have to be built." And the larger your old cousin's bank account, he thought to himself.

"With this particular piece of land," he continued, his eyes taking in the lush parcel, "I don't think we have to worry. Since it's for you, I'm sure God wouldn't be upset in the slightest. As a matter of fact, He may even be happy if we leave some of the best trees standing in His honor."

Carmine took Lenora's hand and showed her exactly where the new house would be and asked if she wanted to choose the perimeter trees that would remain. There was a pause while Lenora weighed his words.

"I don't think God would want me to do that, Cousin Carmine. I'm only a little girl and it's up to Him to decide what lives and what dies."

Carmine, who was customarily known to have an answer or two for everything, found his tongue tied. Mentally shaking away the unfamiliar sensation, with regained composure came a broadening smile and response.

"Okay then, I tell you what, *bambina*. I'll ask God which trees he wants me to save and if the Big Guy has the time to answer me, I'll do whatever He says. Is it a deal or what?" Carmine asked, extending his calloused hand for a confirming shake.

"Deal," she agreed with a satisfied giggle, putting her petite hand into his and sealing their agreement.

On the work front, Leo was fortunate to secure employment with a printing company in Burbank. He worked the required forty hours a week, but always volunteered to come in early or stay late.

It took six months for the house to be completed and Vinnie's full-time occupation returned to that of mother, wife, and homemaker.

Their first fifteen months in California flew by, bringing them into 1953. As a five- year-old, Leonard would be attending school in the fall. Lenora had been enrolled in the public school system at Beachy Elementary and remained there throughout the second grade. Having watched, with heightening degrees of excitement, the construction and completion of the nearby St. Genevieve's Catholic School, she asked her parents if she could "please, pretty please" transfer to the new school.

"Beachy is a good school, Mommy, and it's more than okay if Leonard goes there. Most of the teachers are very nice, but I'd like to go to school where the nuns are the teachers. I'm sure the nuns are a lot closer to God than the regular teachers, and that's where I need to be."

Her inquisitiveness about and love of God had not diminished but had grown and deepened. The parochial school heartily welcomed the exceptionally devout child, and Lenora flourished in her element.

In celebration of her devotion to God, a year later, on May 9, 1954, two months shy of her eighth birthday, Lenora experienced one of the most auspicious and eagerly awaited days of her young life. It was the day she made her First Holy Communion, the day she received another of the Church's sacraments, strengthening the ties that had always bound her to God.

In preparation for the event, the children studied their catechism, learned the Act of Contrition (a prayer of repentance), and informally practiced their first confessions with the nuns substituting for the ordained priests of Mary Immaculate Parish. Learning their lessons well, the students knew sins came in all shapes and sizes. Mortal sins were the worst and covered a broad spectrum from the hateful act of willfully taking a life to purposely, with forethought, eating meat on Fridays. Venial sins were the less severe and included lies, disobedience, answering back, and stubbornness.

Lenora knew of many adults who thought children "should be seen and not heard," but buttoning her lips was often a difficult task. On occasion she skirted the truth because she did not wish to displease God by telling a fib and she weighed situations carefully in order not to be deliberately disobedient. She chose to honor her parents as well as her Heavenly Father.

She was cognizant of her own strong will. That term sounded so much better to her than "stubbornness," which fit into the little sin category. During her practice confession with Sister Bernadette, she was her usual candid self.

"Forgive me, Father, for I have sinned. This is my first confession. Grandma always tells me I'm a girl with strong will, but sometimes Mommy says I'm just plain stubborn. Since that's part of the veal sins, I guess that means I'm a little sinner. But I promise I'll never ever be a big sinner.

"Oh, there's one more thing. It wasn't on the list, but I probably should tell anyway. Some nights I forget to brush my teeth. Usually that's only because I'm in a hurry to say my payers. Amen."

The nun had to suppress a laugh. She was certain the child kneeling on the other side of the darkened screen had to be the one and only Lenora DiTrapani.

"What some perceive as stubbornness in you, my dear child, is not a sin," the Sister assured her. "You have great faith and determination. They are both gifts from God and will serve you well. Now as for your evening rituals, I'm certain God doesn't mind waiting for you a little longer while you brush your teeth."

On the ninth of May, outfitted in an original Giamonte dress of white dotted swiss, accented with short puffed sleeves and belted with a satin sash, Lenora knelt before the altar. She understood the Latin words as Father Joseph Bellman, their favorite parish priest, dipped the sacramental host in the wine within a special golden chalice.

The texture of the wafer she found odd at first; it felt like a circular piece of cardboard resting on her tongue. Then she remembered that this small host symbolized the body of Christ, who died on the cross for her. A deep feeling of happiness flowed from her heart as the wafer dissolved in her mouth. She made the Sign of the Cross. "I love you all," she said contentedly, "the Father, Son, and even the Holy Ghost."

CHAPTER TWO

Summer 1954

School let out for summer break the third week in June. Lenora was excited yet wistful. There were lots of activities to occupy the summer months. There was no homework to do before or after dinner and the stimulating sunlight lasted well into the evening hours, so there were no hard-and-fast restrictions on playtime.

Television viewing time also increased as the children's bedtime was extended beyond the 8:00 PM curfew. Lenora would also have plenty of time to spend with her classmate and "bestest friend," Mary Margaret Newman. Just the same, the excitement of summer's awaiting adventures were tempered by Lenora's sad thoughts of not having classes with Sister Bernadette or the unique serenity she felt within St. Genevieve's walls.

Most summer Sundays after ten o'clock Mass at Mary Immaculate, the DiTrapanis, accompanied by numerous family members, including three generations of Ciones, traveled to Pop's Willow Lake Resort, where they would picnic, swim in the crystal blue waters, or frolic on the warm, sandy beach. Both Lenora and her brother swam like fishes, having been taught early on by their parents.

Carmine commented that eight-year-old Lenora resembled a mermaid and that pleased her no end. After all, mermaids were always beautiful and could gracefully outswim the other inhabitants of the sea. Often she and Leonard were seen swimming side-by-side, looking like a mother dolphin and its offspring. Carmine would teasingly yell across the beach to Vinnie, "Hey, Vincenza, I swear those kids of yours have gills instead of lungs."

During the weekdays the children were invited to refresh themselves in the cool water of Mary Margaret's pool. Her given name was Mary Margherita, but sometime during her early years in school it was mispronounced as Mary Margaret and she preferred the more Americanized version. Lenora found Mary Margaret and her family most interesting. Her father ran a successful real estate business, making them more affluent than other families living on Sandusky, hence their larger house, built-in pool, and Mexican housekeeper. Nonetheless, the Newmans were down-to-earth people, attending Mass, church functions, and often hosting neighborhood gatherings.

Lenora knew her own mother was pretty, but Mary Margaret's mom was a different kind of pretty, with the darkest long hair framing a perpetually tan face and immense dark eyes. Connie Newman had not been born in America, but instead of coming from Europe, as Lenora's own relatives had, the exotic-looking woman came from a small island off the southeast coast of Florida called Cuba. She had proudly become a naturalized citizen of the United States and insisted that "only English" be spoken in their household.

She reprimanded the housekeeper whenever the woman lapsed into Spanish. "Maria, you are fortunate to now be living in the U. S. of A. and must show your respect to your new home by speaking its language." In spite of her honorable intentions, whenever Mrs. Newman got excessively excited or upset, she too reverted to her native Spanish, speaking rapidly and gesticulating with her prettily manicured hands.

A large room in the back of the Newman's house had been converted to a professional studio, where Mrs. Newman gave dance lessons. As the often-told story went, eighteen year old Connie, whose given name was Consuelo Rosita Fuentes Vega, immigrated to the U.S. accompanied by a chaperone, a superb singing voice, a gift for music and dance, plus a few well-placed connections. Through a friend of her father's, in New York she auditioned for a gentlemen who was becoming well known as a connoisseur of pretty young talent. This gentleman, whose name was Xavier Cugat, a Catalan-Cuban maestro, was credited with bringing Latin American music and its rising popularity to the States.

Consuelo nervously auditioned for Mr. Cugat and he was impressed by her performance. He saw a moldable raw talent, and he was the accomplished artiste who could develop that talent. With an imperceptible nod of his head, she was hired. Taking her under his professional wing, Tio (Uncle) Cugie, as she later came to refer to him, treated Consuelo with the respect due the Fuentes family.

In the early days of her career, Consuelo, whose off-stage name became Connie, immersed herself in show business on the stage and off. Rather than getting her own apartment, with the attentive chaperone as her only companion, she elected to room with a group of young ladies all enthusiastically starting out in show business. She and her chaperon shared a bedroom with a southern gal named Luanne (Lu for short) who was extraordinarily beautiful on both the inside and out. Lu was also the fiancée of Cugat's primo pianist, Victor Giamonte.

During her career, Connie shuttled between New York and Los Angeles with the flamboyantly gifted showman, his talented musicians, crew, and second wife, Carmen. In early 1946 following a performance in California, Connie was introduced to a handsome

young man by the name of Roger Newman. Three months later, the
strikingly good-looking couple were married in a civil ceremony, and
as requested by her husband, she bid a fond but tearful farewell to
Tio Cugie and her life as an entertainer. Mary Margherita was born
on their ninth-month wedding anniversary.

On summer afternoons in 1954 at the Newman's, the children's
activities in the pool were monitored by the housekeeper, Maria. She
was there in the capacity of would-be life guard and assigned "to keep
an eye on the children." Instead, she reclined in a chaise lounge a safe
distance from the pool with her dark eyes glued to a Spanish magazine.

Six-year-old Leonard wasn't very fond of Maria. She had a habit
of yelling at the children whenever Mrs. Newman wasn't in earshot.
He didn't understand what she was saying but her tone didn't require
translation. In reprisal, he would frequently cannonball into the
water, hoping to douse her with the residual spray. He was tempted
to flounder in the deep end of the pool pretending he had a leg
cramp, or worse, to see exactly what action the housekeeper would
take. Would she simply scream for help or heroically dive in, clothes
and all? He wondered if she would take the time to remove those
ugly black shoes she wore every day. Maybe the shoes would prove
useful after all, and help her sink to the bottom.

"Don't you dare!" Lenora admonished her brother whenever she
saw that mischievous look appear on his sun-flecked face. "I've told
you the story about the naughty boy who cried wolf and you surely
don't want to end up like him. Besides, it would make me feel bad
if I really had to tell Mommy on you!"

Leonard usually abandoned his not-so-good ideas, but not
without complaint. "C'mon Lenora, give a sweet little kid like me
a break!" Instead, she would dunk his blonde head under the water
and count a quick one, two, three.

Lenora, on the other hand, did not have to pretend when it came
to her own leg cramping. Her brother teased her whenever she ran

out of steam before him. Other times he became concerned when a Charley horse or "Charlene" horse (as Mary Margaret preferred, stressing gender correctness) caused a cramp in her leg. Being a strong swimmer, she was never physically in danger. She would use her arms and left leg to propel her to the ladder and would sit on the edge of the pool and massage the affected limb. As soon as the cramp passed, she somersaulted back into the pool, pretending she was a hungry shark heading straight for her bite-size brother.

In the fall, when school was back in session, there was less time to swim. Mrs. Newman's dance classes coincided with the school term so she was busy with her novice and continuing students. Mary Margaret did not share her mother's enthusiasm or talent for the disciplined art. She preferred playing house, but not in traditional way. In her version of the game, Mary Margaret was the neighborhood realtor and she pretended to sell houses to her playmates. She confided to Lenora that she always saved the nicest houses for herself.

Mrs. Newman, noticing that Lenora took particular interest while watching the lessons, thought her curiosity should be nurtured and offered the child free dance lessons.

"That's very nice of you Mrs. Newman," Lenora responded to the generous offer. "I think I would like that very much, but I couldn't take lessons without paying you something. I don't have much money of my own, but I could come over on Saturday mornings and help Maria around the house."

Mrs. Newman was tempted to laugh, but suppressed the urge when she saw the serious expression on Lenora's face. "I think that would work out fine," she managed to say, but a rogue chuckle escaped her lips. She feigned a cough and graciously said, "Excuse me, Lenora. I'm sure Maria would simply love having a little helper." Lenora was too excited to catch the humorous irony in Mrs. Newman's voice.

CHAPTER THREE

Fall to December 1954

The summer ended too soon as far as Mary Margaret and Leonard were concerned, but Lenora was glad to return to school in September. Once the school year started, time seemed to pass too quickly. Halloween had been fun with costumes and lots of candy. Thanksgiving was as festive as always with family and all the delicious food. Now, in a blink of an eye, the calendar read December. St. Genevieve's and Mary Immaculate joyously started preparing for Christmas.

Lenora continued to spend much of her free time at the Newmans, but had curtailed her dance lessons. She had loved the classes and, although not the most gifted of Mrs. Newman's students, she was definitely the most enthusiastic. But truth be told, the dancing brought a growing fatigue to her legs, a fact she did not share with even her best friend, Mary Margaret. So at the tender age of eight, she made the decision to hang up her dancing shoes until her body grew stronger.

Finally, the long-awaited eve of Christmas arrived bringing with it the greatest of gifts for the DiTrapani children, in the form of a five-year-old Rough Collie named Duchess, who looked exactly like the popular canine star Lassie. Since Lassie's television debut in the fall of that year, every Sunday evening at 7:30, Lenora and Leonard sat mesmerized, along with hundreds of other children, their tow heads positioned two feet in front of their fifteen-inch Zenith console, enthralled in the collie's adventures. As was the case with most youngsters who viewed the show, they too wished they had a "Lassie" of their very own.

The DiTrapani's adoption of Duchess was a story worthy of the original televised series. The dog's owner, Duncan (no one was exactly sure if it was his first name or his last because he was simply known as Duncan), was an elderly gentleman whose failing health was forcing him to move north to San Jose to reside with his only grandchild and her three energetic children. His granddaughter stipulated that although he was welcome to come live with them, because of her husband's severe allergy to animals, Duchess was not.

However, being of sound mind and kind heart, Duncan knew this was for the best. He could not, in good conscience, subject his faithful companion to the consequences of a life with his overly exuberant great grandchildren. He would have to find his beloved Duchess a new home and would be obsessively selective in doing so.

A parishioner of Mary Immaculate, sympathetic to Duncan's plight, had suggested the DiTrapanis as candidates. During a telephone conversation, the family was invited to Duncan's small one-story bungalow on Christmas Eve. Duncan instantly liked what he saw.

The children had been warned to be on their best behavior, so they sat quietly on the faded chintz couch, with hands in their laps and feet on the floor. Duchess wasted no time in approaching the little boy, who looked entirely uncomfortable in his dress clothes. She sat down in front of him, offering her right paw in a welcoming fashion. The boy's surprised blue eyes and accompanying smile grew wide with glee.

Duchess then moved on to the pretty little girl, who Duncan easily surmised was the elder of the pair. As Lenora raised her hands to pet the Collie, the dog laid her head in Lenora's lap. Duchess's bright canine eyes looked adoringly into the girl's. The adoration was reciprocated.

The old man pushed himself up from his well-worn chair and ambled down the hall into a small bedroom. He came back with Duchess's lease and a big red bow. Duncan handed them to Lenora.

"Now you take care of my best girl, lass, and she'll take care of you. In the spirit of love that is Christmas, I'm giving you the bow because Duchess is my most cherished possession and she's my gift to you and your family."

Lenora and Leonard jumped off the couch, their arms encircling Duncan's arthritic legs. "Thank you, thank you," they caroled.

"You're quite welcome," Duncan replied, enjoying the tenderness of the moment. "Now, off with you… shoo," he said with a flick of his hand. "It's time for this old man to take his daily nap."

Duncan walked them to the door and watched as the children slid into the backseat of the car and tried coaxing the dog into joining them. Duchess refused, firmly planting her hind quarters on the curb. She turned and looked questioningly at Duncan.

"It's okay, girl," Duncan told her, while stoically holding back the emotion threatening to clog his throat. "You go with the children and watch over them."

Duchess woofed softly in reply, turned, and leaped into the car, positioning herself between Lenora and Leonard.

Duncan moseyed to his bed and laid atop its spread. He looked at the picture of his wife, in its place of prominence on the nightstand. He spoke to her as he did every day.

"This was the second hardest thing I ever had to do in my life. The first, my dearest, was saying good-bye to you when God decided it was time to take you home, but I think our Heavenly Father has a plan for my other girl and being with the DiTrapanis is part of that plan.

"Now, I'm going to close my eyes and rest. Hopefully, when sleep comes, you'll be with me in my dreams."

In the DiTrapanis' car, Duchess hadn't looked back again. As her master Duncan had instructed, she would take care of the new people in her life. She nuzzled Lenora and Leonard as they drove the short distance to their house. It only took a couple of hours for the DiTrapanis to fall head over heels in love with the canine and she with them. Within days, Duchess had them trained.

She would rough and tumble outside with Leonard, obediently fetch the ball, but often refused to relinquish it to the waiting six-year-old. When she sensed Leonard losing interest, she would drop the ball at his feet and bounce on her front paws, barking as if to say, "What are you waiting for?"

Duchess made a night-time practice of remaining in Leonard's bed until he fell asleep…a task that was usually accomplished within ten minutes. As soon as the dog heard his breathing slow into the rhythm of peaceful slumber, she would silently leave and go to Lenora's room.

Every night Lenora took her time brushing her teeth and waited for Duchess's arrival so they could say their prayers together. As soon as she made the Sign of the Cross, Duchess would bow her furry head and cross her right paw over her left. The Collie would not raise her head again until Lenora said "Amen."

With prayers concluded, Duchess would inch as close as possible to Lenora. Cuddled together, two girls would drift off to sleep.

CHAPTER FOUR

The New Year 1955

Christmas joy evolved into New Year's cheer and on Friday, the eve of 1955, the children would be allowed to stay up to welcome in the incoming year with family and friends gathering for the annual celebration at the Giamontes. As forecasted, there was an unseasonable drop in temperature, with sporadic rain and the rare possibility of that rain turning to snow. The DiTrapanis arrived early to help with the preparations. They were there for perhaps ten minutes when a rap, tap, tap sounded on the door. Lenora eagerly ran to answer it. Her eyes widened when she saw her Uncle Victor and Aunt Lu on the step. Victor, Vinnie's eldest brother, was decked out in a light charcoal topcoat and matching Homburg and his attractive wife, Lu, was caressed by a new sable stole Victor had given her for Christmas. As Lenora's aunt bent down to hug her, the little girl encircled her in her tiny arms, resting her face against the silky, dark fur.

Victor and Lu still resided in New York but he was in town recording an album with songstress Eartha Kitt. Victor was an accomplished pianist in his own right and his name appeared on numerous album credits.

Lu, having given up her career as a showgirl when they married, was perfectly content to accompany her talented husband whenever the opportunity arose. Lu put their coats on the bed in the master bedroom and, donning an apron, joined her mother-in-law and Vinnie in the kitchen.

Lenora was delighted when her Uncle Victor volunteered to take on the duties of doorman and proclaimed her his official assistant. She would help with the coats as other guests, including Cousin Carmine and his expanding brood, arrived in shifts. Since the rain had held off, Lenora's brother and cousins were remanded to the front yard to await new arrivals. Soon they found that boring and decided a game of tag would be more to their liking.

As part of the extended Giamonte family, the Newmans had been invited to partake in the holiday gathering. Traditionally they spent the holidays in Cuba, but the government there had become unstable, with political gangsters dangerously vying for power. Despite Connie's insistent and frequent requests that her parents relocate to the United States, they refused to leave their homeland estate. The Newmans' trips to Cuba had become few and far between, but ties of the heart kept them close.

The Newmans arrived bearing dishes of both ethnic staples macaroni and cheese and black beans and rice. It was Mary Margaret's job to knock on the door as her parents balanced the oven-hot trays. In response to her energetic rap, a distinguished-looking gentlemen opened the door. When Mrs. Newman looked up, her large dark eyes grew noticeably larger, and her slender jaw dropped as she recognized the handsome man who had been Tio Cugie's pianist. The casserole she was carefully holding almost dropped as well. It had been almost ten years since they had seen one another.

"Ay! Victor, is it really you?" she sputtered, her accent noticeable in her excitement. His smile was filled with charm rather than surprise. Having heard about his sister's neighbors through the family grapevine, he had suspected that Connie Newman might well be the former Conseulo Fuentes.

"Si, Senora Consuelo," he said executing the perfect bow he normally reserved for royalty.

Vinnie and her sister-in-law, Lu, simultaneously wiping their hands on their aprons, rushed from the kitchen. Lu, hearing a familiar voice from her past, pushed passed her husband like a football running back. Grabbing the baking dish from Connie's unsteady hands, Lu pushed it into Victor's. Forgetting everyone else, she wrapped her arms around her long-lost friend from her early days in show business. The women hugged, separated for a second to look at one another at arm's length, and then hugged once again.

The evening continued on a celebratory note of gaiety. The dining room table, serving as the center of the delightful buffet, was heavily laden with varieties of aromatic foods, and the poignant scent of garlic permeated the air. Cousin Carmine manned the makeshift bar in a corner of the room and beverages flowed, as did the vintage homemade DiTrapani red wine. Every Christmas the relatives back East, who were still practicing the art of winemaking that had been passed on for generations, would distribute the finished product both near and far for the holidays.

When everyone had eaten their fill, Mrs. Giamonte drafted family members into clearing the dining room table and resetting it for the desserts. At her suggestion, Victor took his seat at the piano. He patted the space besides him on the bench, motioning for Lu to join him. Lu scooted close to her husband, leaving enough space on the end of the seat for Lenora. Victor's long, slender fingers glided lovingly over the piano keys and the threesome on the bench were soon surrounded by appreciative listeners. Connie stood behind Lu, her hands affectionately on her friend's shoulders. It was reminiscent of the good old days, as Connie's trained soprano accompanied Victor's skillful playing. Victor contemplatively glanced to his side and then to the enthusiastic group cozily gathered around him. He considered himself a very lucky man. He was fortunate in his professional pursuits but far luckier in love, the unconditional love of a large family and an adoring wife.

Connie, too, became lost in thought. It was such a really small world. It was utterly amazing that Victor Giamonte, a virtuoso pianist in the world of music, was the elder brother of her good friend and neighbor, Vinnie. When she had first met Vinnie's parents, the name Giamonte rang a distant bell, but she never put two and two together. Now on this last day of December 1954, the three companeros were reunited and embraced by the warmth of a rekindled friendship and a family's love.

Little Leonard, wanting to be like the adults, but tired from the day's activities with the younger family members, struggled to stay awake. Long before the clock reached twelve, his red-rimmed eyes grew heavy and he drifted off to sleep. After the stroke of midnight wishing everyone health and happiness for the coming year and bestowing hugs and kisses all around, Vinnie and Leo gathered their children in preparation for the two-block drive.

Leonard, still small enough to be carried in his father's arms, nuzzled into Leo's chest and was fast asleep as they walked down the front porch steps. The rain had come and gone and now a cold wind blew against their faces, but the family was adequately bundled against the unusual frosty temperature.

Vinnie held Lenora's hand protectively but did not see the patch of ice waiting ominously in their path. Both the ladies began to slide, but Leo, with his lightning fast reflexes, maintained his hold on his son while grabbing his wife with his right hand. Vinnie regained her balance and remained upright, instinctively tightening her grip on Lenora's hand. Despite her best effort, the little girl's right leg slipped out from under her, bringing her knee in contact with the cement walk. Easing herself from her mother's grasp, Lenora got to her feet.

The little girl was more startled than hurt as she leaned down to brush the dampness and sidewalk grit from her leg. In response to her parent's swift questions about her well-being, she hastily assured them that she was "perfectly fine."

The remainder of their trip home was uneventful. Duchess, having heard the familiar sound of the car motor from a block away, automatically started wiggling her hindquarters like an exotic hula dancer. Normally she would have rushed up to greet her family as they entered the door, but tonight her senses were on alert and she deliberately stayed in the background.

Leo headed to Leonard's room to deposit his sleeping bundle while Vinnie led her daughter to the kitchen. There she helped Lenora out of her coat and had her sit on the white wooden chair. She kneeled down to get a better look at the little girl's knee but Duchess, who had stealthy crawled into the room, took that moment to insinuate herself between the ladies. The dog carefully nudged Vinnie aside with her head and planted herself directly in front of Lenora, oblivious to anything else in the room. Very gently she began licking the little girl's right knee.

Perhaps it was the latest of the hour, but Vinnie was not amused by Duchess's intrusion.

"Out," she ordered the dog more sternly than intended and pointed in the direction of the hallway. Duchess turned and stared at Vinnie. Their eyes held.

"Please, girl," Vinnie added with a softened plea. "I need to tend to Lenora." The canine returned her watchful eyes to Lenora.

"It's okay, girl," Lenora said, caressing the satiny blonde fur. "Listen to Mommy. She knows what's best for us and I'll see you later." Duchess dutifully stood on all fours and exited the room.

Once again kneeling before her daughter, Vinnie took a studied look at the girl's leg. She found no visible abrasions requiring the application of iodine, but thought a thorough cleaning of the area was in order. She lightly lathered a soft dampened washcloth with Ivory soap and tenderly cleansed the knee. She rinsed the cloth in warm water and wiped again to remove any soapy residue. With a clean fluffy towel, she patted the area dry.

Lenora had remained quiet during her mother's administrations, but started yawning.

"Mommy, I hope you're feeling better now that you can see for yourself that there's nothing wrong with my leg, but I'm very sleepy and would like to go to bed." Vinnie walked Lenora to her bedroom and helped her into her pajamas. Leo joined them. They listened to her prayers, in which she wished God a happy new year, and each kissed her cheek goodnight. She was in the land of dreams before her parents reached the bedroom door.

Duchess, meanwhile, was unobtrusively sitting a distance down the hallway awaiting her turn. When all was quiet, she entered Lenora's room. Rather than jumping on the bed, as was her custom, she sat along its side, inching her front paws and head as close to Lenora as possible. The dog's attentive eyes were filled with sadness as they watched Leonora sleep. Duchess bent her head forward as she did on the evenings when the pair said their prayers together. Soft, long whines resonated from deep within the dog's throat. It looked and sounded like she was praying.

The next morning, the languid sun rose at 6:58 AM over many a sleeping household in California, including three exhausted members of the DiTrapani family. Leonard, having fallen asleep at his grandparents, was well rested and up at the crack of dawn. On rare mornings like this, when he was the only one up, he would find a way to entertain himself and pretend he was actually old enough to be alone and unattended.

However, this first day of the New Year was markedly different. He awoke with something uncomfortably pressing on his mind and bolted from his comfy bed. He was a young man on a mission, and headed to Lenora's room, where his sister and Duchess slept snuggled together. The Collie's ears, perpetually alert, stood up straight as she heard the patter of bare feet racing down the hall.

Despite the heaviness in Leonard's stomach, his heart smiled as he came through the doorway and saw Duchess's golden-tipped tail wagging energetically back and forth in greeting. He soundlessly approached the pair, and for a few seconds he stood next to the bed watching his sister sleeping peacefully. To him, her hair looked like a golden halo on the plumped pillow. Even in sleep, she was the prettiest girl he had ever seen.

Duchess nudged Leonard's elbow and he speedily corralled his wandering thoughts. His mind returned to his original purpose and he extended his hand and softly but persistently tugged on the long sleeve of his sister's red pajamas.

"Lenora, wake up, would ya please? Are you okay? I had a bad dream last night that you fell and hurt your leg. Please wake up, Lenora. I got a really bad feeling in the bottom of my tummy."

Lenora leisurely stretched her arms above her head then wiped the sleep from her eyes.

"I'm fine and dandy, little brother," she managed to say before a wide yawn escaped her lips. "You fell asleep at Grandma and Grandpa's last night and Daddy carried you to and from the car. I slipped on some ice when we left their house, so that's probably what you dreamed about."

She tossed off her covers and pulled up the leg of her pajama bottoms and the two flaxen heads leaned forward, simultaneously inspecting Lenora's knee.

"See, not even a scratch." She leapt out of bed and reached for the pink bathrobe hanging on a child's-height hook near the door. Her brother did not see her wince as the pain in her right knee traveled up her leg to her teeth.

Breakfast was scrambled eggs extra dry, fried potatoes seasoned with diced green peppers and chopped scallions, and a large plate of buttery rye toast. Duchess lay patiently under the table inches from Leonard's chair, knowing full well crumbs of food would be coming her way. Conversation at the table centered on their New Year's Eve gathering.

The best holidays were those shared with family and close friends. For Lenora, it was the most wonderful of surprises to find out that Mrs. Newman, who rated highly on her favorite people list, and Aunt Lu and Uncle Victor, who she ardently adored, had been good friends and worked together in show business long before she was ever born.

Midway through the meal, both parents inquired about Lenora's leg, but she evaded the question. She deftly brought the subject back to Mrs. Newman, her uncle and aunt, rambling on about small worlds.

"Did you know that Uncle Victor only works with people who have really funny names?" she asked, looking at her parents. As was her habit, she didn't wait for an answer. "Mrs. Newman asked about the people he'd been working with. He told her there was Tennis Ernie Ford, Ethel Mermaid, Ski Nose Hope, and someone called Jimmy. They laughed about his schnoz (whatever that is), and said Jimmy's best friend was a Mrs. Colliebash who he always said good-night to. Then they talked about the time they worked together for a man named Cougar. Uncle Victor said how much he liked all these people so I know I'd like them, too. Maybe one day I'll get to meet them."

"That would be wonderful, sweetheart," Vinnie said. Your uncle is definitely a talented man and is famous in his own right."

"Mommy, do you think someday I'll be famous?"

"You never know, honey," Vinnie answered.

"It wouldn't surprise me one bit," Leo chimed in. "After all, you come from a very talented family."

. When breakfast was finished, Vinnie topped off Leo's coffee while he perused the morning paper. When Lenora got up to help clear the table, she avoided putting her full weight on her right leg. Vinnie's maternal radar went on alert.

"Lenora, is your leg okay?" Not receiving an immediate reply, she looked into her daughter's shadowed eyes. Leo, having heard his wife's query and not hearing a response from his daughter, put his newspaper aside and studied his little girl.

"We need you to be totally, one hundred percent honest with us, sweetheart," he said to her with a semi-stern look tempered with compassion. "If something is wrong, we have to know about it."

Leonora released the breath she was holding. With a sigh of surrender, she answered.

"I'm really sorry," she said, apologizing as though it might somehow be her fault. "I wanted it to be okay and I didn't want you to worry, but my leg does sorta hurt when I stand on it." Vinnie and Leo glanced at each other, wondering why their daughter would choose to carry this weight upon her small shoulders.

"There's no need to be sorry," they earnestly said in tandem. "It's a parent's job to worry about their children," Vinnie reassured her, easing Lenora into the same chair as the previous evening.

"You never have to be afraid to tell us anything ever," Leo promptly added. "Do you understand what we're trying to say?"

"Yes," she replied, barely above a whisper.

Both parents examined her right leg. "Where does it hurt, honey?"

"Mostly my knee, but when I stand up, my whole leg feels kinda funny." Lenora's leg was sensitive to her mother's touch, but there were no bruises or swelling visible to the naked eye.

"I think maybe you should take it easy today and give your leg a chance to rest. Even though there are no cuts or bruises on the outside, you could have hurt it on the inside and maybe that's why it's bothering you."

"Thank you, Mommy. I'm sure that's all it is. I'll be especially quiet and rest up so I'll be as good as new in time for school on Monday."

While Lenora was in her room dressing for the day, Vinnie conferred with Leo. To be on the safe side, they called the doctor, but it was a holiday weekend and his long-time housekeeper, Miss Alice, answered the phone. Dr. Stevens was up in San Francisco visiting his wife's family, but would be back in his office first thing Monday morning. Having worked for the good doctor for many years and knowing the DiTrapanis personally, Alice felt confident in advising them to just drop by the office on Monday afternoon. She would leave the doctor a note to that effect and wished Vinnie and her family a happy new year.

Sunday the family went to ten o'clock Mass and Lenora made a concentrated effort to walk as normally as possible. She knelt in the thinly padded pew, shifting her weight to her left leg. When she prayed, she did not ask God to make her leg stop hurting. She would never ask God for anything for herself, but decided perhaps asking something for her parents might be okay in God's eyes.

"Please help Mommy and Daddy not to worry about me. Father Bellman says we should 'cast our cares' onto you, God. That means for us to stop worrying about things and let you take care of them. I know my parents and other adults don't always do that. I guess you have to consider that adults are really just your grown-up children. They sometimes have a problem doing what they're supposed to do...the same as us little kids."

CHAPTER FIVE

Monday, January 3, 1955

Before going to bed that night, Lenora begged her mother to let her go to classes the next day. She had so been looking forward to seeing her third-grade teacher, Sister Francis as well as her last year's teacher and good friend Sister Bernadette. She was eager to tell them all about the holidays and in particular about the canine addition to the family. Looking into those big pleading eyes, Vinnie relented.

Their normal schedule resumed Monday with Vinnie preparing breakfast and getting the children properly readied for school. Leo had gone into work earlier than usual so he would be able to go with the family to see Dr. Stevens.

At three o'clock, Vinnie and Leonard met Leonora outside the oak doors of St. Genevieve's. Moments later, Leo slid his Nash up to the curb. The children chatted animatedly in the backseat of the car as they traveled the few blocks to the sprawling, honey-colored ranch where Dr. Stevens combined his residence and office.

"Leonard," Lenora said, lowering the volume of her voice, "you're not going to believe what Mary Margaret told me. She said Chester Garrity and some of the older altar boys got caught drinking the sacramental wine after yesterday's last service. All of them had to go to the monsignor's office this morning with their parents. I didn't see any of them at school today."

"Boy, are they in big trouble," Leonard acknowledged. "You know how the monsignor is. I bet the old man padded their behinds real good and they probably peed in their pants. Maybe they didn't come to school today because they can't sit down."

"I bet you're right," his sister agreed. "But if the monsignor hears you calling him 'the old man,' you'll be the next one peeing in your pants."

At Dr. Stevens's, Leo followed the circular driveway to the office entrance. He rang the bell and the family entered the side door into a small but cozy waiting area. They were seated only a few minutes before Mrs. Stevens poked her head in, letting the DiTrapanis know the doctor was finishing up with a patient. The ladies exchanged pleasantries and Mrs. Stevens excused herself when a ringing phone summoned her away.

Dr. Stevens opened the inner office door and escorted out a young, gangly male with a prominent case of acne. The doctor's navy suit jacket hung on the coat rack behind his desk but he looked every inch the professional in his vest, tailored pin-striped pants, and conservative navy tie. Women of all ages found the sexagenarian particularly dashing with his perfectly groomed head of white hair accented by a snowy, manicured mustache with its waxed ends pointing upward. Lenora wondered if the hair on his lip tickled the doctor's pleasantly large nose, but figured it would be impolite to ask.

"Just swab that sore throat with some tincture of Argyrol in the evening and gargle with warm salt water three to four times a day," the doctor instructed his departing patient. "If that doesn't do the job, young man, despite your advanced years of eighteen and some odd months and your vigorous arguments to the contrary, those tonsils may have to come out, and remember to use plenty of soap and water on that face of yours. Give me a call in a couple of days and let me know how your throat is doing. My regards to your parents." He then gave his full attention to the DiTrapanis.

"I understand the little lady here celebrated a bit too much on New Year's Eve and took a spill on the ice."

"Dr. Stevens," Lenora questioned, "how can you celebrate too much and what does it have to do with me slipping on some ice?"

"Don't mind me, Lenora, it was simply an old man's attempt at humor. Now, Mrs. DiTrapani, if you'd accompany this young lady into the examination room, we'll take a look-see at her leg."

Vinnie did as the doctor asked. When Lenora was seated on the examination table, Dr. Stevens lifted the stethoscope dangling around his age-creased neck and, as was his practice, warmed it in the palm of his hand before listening to Lenora's heart and breathing. He instructed her to take a few deep breathes and let them out slowly. Next came her temperature and pulse.

"Everything sounds tip-top," he assured his young patient with a grandfatherly grin before turning his attention to the leg. The right knee had remained tender and Lenora flinched when the doctor applied pressure to the area.

"I think it best if we x-ray the knee," he said to Vinnie.

"What's an x-ray?" Lenora questioned the man who had been her physician since their move to California.

"Well, it's actually just a camera, bigger than the Brownie you probably have at home, but it can see inside your leg and it will give us a picture of what's going on under the skin. But I give you my word that my picture taking won't hurt in the slightest and we'll be done in a jiffy." Dr. Stevens was a man of his word.

The family sat in the waiting room while the doctor developed the film. He had taken shots from different angles, but didn't like the images staring back at him. Perspiration glistened on his lined forehead. He considered himself a reasonably good doctor. He had learned a lot during his career, but this was something far beyond his general practice.

Dr. Stevens sighed deeply as he put the x-rays down. He then went to his office to make a crucial phone call.

CHAPTER SIX

With the call concluded, Dr. Stevens walked to the door adjoining the waiting room. As he did so, he caught his image in the wall mirror. "You're getting too old for this, Aloysius Stevens," he said to his reflection. "I may be taking the cowardly way out, but I'd rather leave this in the hands of the experts, God in particular."

His feet felt like lead, making the last of his steps laborious. He opened the door and asked Vinnie and Leo to come into his office and then his weary eyes went to Lenora.

"My dear, would you be kind enough to keep an attentive eye on your brother while I converse briefly with your parents?"

"You go ahead and do whatever you have to, Dr. Stevens," she said as if giving him her permission. And I promise I'll keep both my eyes on my little brother, not just one."

Dr. Stevens ushered the couple into his office. Its interior was neatly compact, with a place for everything and everything in its place. Dr. Stevens gestured for them to be seated in the subtly printed beige chairs angled in front of his desk. He then settled uneasily into his toffy-colored chair, sitting on the edge of the leather seat with his arms leaning on the desk. He tented his brown-speckled hands in front of him.

"Well, it certainly doesn't take a Rhodes Scholar or even a medical degree to read the questions clearly displayed on your faces so I won't waste time beating around the bush. There appears to be more to Lenora's injury than meets the eye. I simply don't have the expertise to do a proper evaluation."

Questions swam in the parents' worried eyes, but Dr. Steven's held up his own hand before the questions were spoken aloud.

"Mr. and Mrs. DiTrapani, I don't have the answers to your questions, but I do know a specialist who would. I am recommending that you take Lenora to see Dr. James Segal at Children's Hospital in Los Angeles. As your long-time family physician and friend, I've taken the liberty of making an appointment for nine AM tomorrow morning with Dr. Segal. We'll talk again after you meet with him."

After walking with the DiTrapani family to the outside door, the doctor returned to his chair. He was glad they were no other patients waiting for his undivided attention, because his thoughts were on the darling little girl who had moments ago left his office. His wizened eyes misted and his knowing heart began to ache.

CHAPTER SEVEN

Tuesday, January 4, 1955

For the rest of Monday and the next morning, Vinnie and Leo made a Herculean effort to act as normal as possible. Despite their best attempts, apprehension filled their every thought, but neither gave voice to those inner ruminations.

Their tentative plan Tuesday morning involved Leonard being dropped off at his grandparents and taken to school by the Giamontes, while the other three members of his immediate family made the fifteen-mile trip to Los Angeles. Leonard, however, had other ideas and disagreed with the proposed agenda. After breakfast, he pulled his sister into the hallway out of earshot of his parents.

"Lenora, I need to go to the hospital with you." His pale blue eyes, brimming with worry, pleaded with her. "I have that awful feeling in my tummy again, and I'm scared that if you go without me, you won't come home."

Her hand reached out for her brother and she lightly ruffled his hair. "Leonard, I promise you I will be back. Have I ever lied to you?"

"Well, no." His eyes gleamed as he remembered the times his sister had masterfully skirted the truth. Easily reading his thoughts, her eyes and heart united in laughter but her voice remained calm and soothing. "I may not be back right away, little brother, but I'll be coming home to you...saint's honor." Lenora sealed her pledge by crossing her right hand over her heart.

There was relatively little conversation in the car during the trip to the hospital. Lenora was uncharacteristically quiet. Sitting with her legs crossed at the ankles in ladylike fashion, she did not move or fidget. She was thinking about her prayers last evening. She and Duchess prayed as was their routine at bedtime, but last night she had a few direct questions for the Almighty. She stayed awake as long as she could waiting for a reply, but none was forthcoming. Now she was hoping God was not mad at her for asking Him so many questions. When she had the opportunity, she would ask Father Bellman what he thought.

When Vinnie turned to check on her daughter in the backseat, Lenora had a faraway look in her eyes.

"Are you okay, honey? You're not usually this quiet."

"I'm okay, mommy. I don't really feel like talking. Sometimes it's better to sit back and listen. That way if God is trying to tell you something, your ears and your heart are both open at the same time."

The DiTrapanis arrived at the hospital at 8:45 AM. Being early, they were prepared to wait. Instead, to their surprise, they were taken straight to Dr. Segal's office, where a young-looking physician sat behind a scarred desk engrossed in a mountainous stack of research papers.

When they entered, he shot to his feet and his six-foot frame agilely rounded the desk. He greeted them and proceeded as any congenial host would.

"Please be seated. Make yourselves comfortable." Lenora sat on her father's lap with his protective arm encircling her tiny waist.

The doctor's topaz-brown eyes sparkled as he spoke to the girl's parents. She thought him handsome, with his curly brown hair and dimpled chin. She took particular interest in the stray lock of hair that repeatedly fell above the doctor's left eye and counted the number of times his fingers absently brushed it back into place. But most of all, she liked his eyes. They were the same color as Duchess's and filled with compassion. Her grandmother Giamonte had once told her a person's eyes were the windows to their soul. Lenora now understood exactly what her grandmother meant. She had caught a fleeting glimpse of the doctor's soul and it was very pretty.

"And a special good morning to you, Miss Lenora," the doctor said, interrupting her musings. He directed his undivided attention to the little girl. "I'm very pleased to make your acquaintance." He noticed a faint blush blooming on her delicate cheeks. "I understand from my good friend Dr. Stevens you had some pictures of your leg taken yesterday; but he has asked that we take several more of those during your visit today. I hope that's okay with you." Lenora quietly nodded her assent.

Dr. Segal buzzed for the nurse, waiting as prearranged outside his door. He introduced the DiTrapanis to the short brunette with soft almond eyes perfectly set inside an attractive face.

"Ladies and gentleman, this is Nurse Catherine, one of our favorite staff members at Children's, and she'll be assisting our little lady today." He sent a reassuring wink in the child's direction.

"Nurse Catherine, would you please take Miss DiTrapani for her photo session." Lenora scooted from her father's lap and took the nurse's hand. She looked back over her shoulder at her parents nervously. She hoped they would be all right without her.

The two ladies walked down the hall side by side without Lenora uttering a single word. Nurse Catherine knew it was her responsibility to make her patient feel at ease. For five years she had been a pediatric fixture committed to the children in her care...all of whom were special.

In the early days of her career, she had worn her heart on her sleeve and was admonished by her superiors. One of her instructors sternly told her, "Catherine, you have the makings of a fine nurse, but if you can't control your emotions, you don't belong in this field." Rather than feeling discouraged, Catherine was determined to prove them wrong. With maturity and experience, she was able to form a thin shield of professional detachment that protected her heart...to a degree. She already knew things would be different with this child. She patted the child's hand twice. "My, my, you're a very quiet little girl," the nurse said breaking the silence.

"Not usually," Lenora piped up, looking quite serious. "My Mom says I'm a regular little chatterbox and that's one of the many things she loves about me."

"Then we have something in common," Catherine confessed. "My Mom used to call me Chatty Cathy because I always had a problem keeping my lips zipped. Even as an adult, it's a problem I've yet to overcome. I guess you and I are like two peas in a pod.

"Lenora," Nurse Catherine continued softly, with understanding wrinkling her normally unlined brow, "I'm sorry if you don't feel comfortable enough to be yourself today, but being in a hospital environment can make anyone, even grownups, uneasy." Lenora looked contemplatively at her new friend.

"Nurse Catherine, I'm fine. Really I am. I was at a very big hospital before when my little brother, Leonard, was in San Antonio. That's in Texas, by the way. So I sorta know how things work, but right now, I have an important reason to be quiet." Her brightening eyes looked up with her head tilted a fraction of an inch to the side. As if sharing a secret, she lowered her voice.

"I have to keep my mouth closed and my ears open. I'm waiting to hear from God."

CHAPTER EIGHT

After Lenora's departure, Vinnie and Leo had been accompanied to the cafeteria, where they sat on pins and needles waiting for the initial medical tasks to be completed. In the interim, Dr. Segal walked into the examination where his newest patient waited with Nurse Catherine.

Lenora had been quietly studying her ten bare toes. The expression in her eyes changed dramatically when her eyes focused on a pair of feet. The rest of Dr. Segal's appearance looked very professional, with his white coat and clipboard, but his red clown shoes were two of the funniest things Lenora had ever seen. Nurse Catherine, although quite familiar with the doctor's modus operandi, found Lenora's laughter contagious and joined her patient in a bout of girlish giggles.

Dr. Segal followed Lenora's stare to his colorful appendages. "Oh, my goodness, where did these come from?" the doctor exclaimed, feigning surprise.

Without missing a beat, Lenora commented, "My, Dr. Segal, what big feet you have!"

"Ah, yes, my little patient," he answered with a sly gleam of satisfaction. "All the better to make beautiful young ladies like you smile." The shoes had worked their magic once again. Like an old friend, they seldom let him down. "Are we ready to begin?" he asked, his lips still extended upward in a grin.

"We're ready," Lenora responded, her expression matching his.

As was his practice during the formal physical exam, Dr. Segal regaled his patient with funny stories from his childhood. One particular story would lead to the tale of the red shoes.

"My brother, Joe, and I are identical twins, which means we were born at almost the same time and we look exactly alike," the doctor said, beginning his trip down memory lane.

"If you looked just like each other, how could people tell you apart?" Lenora interjected.

"The only person who could always tell us apart was our mom. No matter how hard we tried to fool her.

"Moms are smart like that," she said in confirmation.

"Well, Joe and I really loved the circus," the doctor continued. "One summer when we were still quite young, the Ringling Brothers Circus came to our town, and the two of us snuck off to the fairgrounds where they were setting up."

"How old were you and Joe?" Dr. Segal.

"I guess we were about ten; but whenever we could, we'd hang around the encampment. We were good at making total pests out of ourselves. It didn't take long until the circus people would see us coming and say, 'Here comes trouble...double trouble.'

"I must admit, we were cute little rascals, and we were also persistent and probably pathetic enough that they finally gave in and gave us some jobs to do." He paused. There was an interesting look on his face as he recalled some of the oddest jobs he had back then.

"Go ahead, Dr. Segal," Lenora instructed, waiting to hear more. "I think I'm going to like this story.

"I hope you will," he said, returning to his tale. "Joe and I were always quick learners, and what we may have lacked in size, we made up for in enthusiasm. After a while, it was like we had always been a part of the team. Whenever the circus returned, so did Joe and I.

We learned to juggle, and do a multitude of tricks like this one," he said taking a shiny new quarter out of her ear.

"Wow!" Lenora exclaimed with her eyes all aglow. "Can you teach me how to do that for my little brother?"

"Let me give it some thought," he said stroking his chin. "It's a secret and you'd have to promise never to tell anyone."

"You can trust me, Dr. Segal. Really you can," she said with the utmost sincerity. The adults' eyes met over their patient's head. Each suppressed their inclination to laugh out loud.

"Now, if I may continue, young lady, here comes the part of the story that has to do with my special red shoes. Shall I go on?" Lenora's head bobbed a "yes."

"My most favorite clown in the world was one Mr. Emmett Kelly. He wore a perpetually sad-painted face, but he had an endearing charm and natural talent to make people laugh. Audiences of all ages loved his performances and I wanted to be just like him when I grew up. But the years passed by and Joe and I developed other interests and somewhere along the line, to my mother's relief, we abandoned our dream of running off to join the circus.

"Then when we were sixteen, our little cousin, James (who's named after me), got really sick. Joe made two trips to the hospital with me to visit James, but each time we got to my cousin's room, Joe's face turned an awful shade of green. He barely made it to the restroom before his lunch came up. Because of that, Joe refused to step foot in that hospital ever again, but I continued to go day after day, making a pest of myself. I must have asked the doctors and staff a million and one questions."

"Did your cousin get better, Dr. Segal?" Lenora asked with genuine concern.

"Yes, he most certainly did, and by the time James was well enough to leave the hospital, I knew that I wanted to be a doctor who specialized in children's medicine.

"Then during my first year here at Children's, I was running around like a chicken without its head, as I did more frequently than not. And who do you think I had the pleasure of accidentally almost running in to?"

"Who?" Lenora questioned, her eyes bright with expectation.

"None other than Mr. Emmett Kelly. Unbeknownst to me, he made it a practice to stop by the hospital when his busy schedule permitted so he could visit with the kids. I was so excited, I could hardly speak. When I was able to form a coherent word, I asked if he'd honor me by accompanying me on my rounds. His usual somber face broke into a smile that stretched all the way from his right ear to his left."

"That must have been a giant smile," Lenora ascertained.

"Yes, it was indeed," the doctor agreed.

"So when I saw Mr. Kelly, all my happy childhood memories of the circus came flooding back, along with my overwhelming desire to perform. Without having to say a word, Mr. Kelly and I fell into a companionable rhythm, working as a team before our captive audience of children. As we went from room to room, the atmosphere became charged with excitement and laughter filled the air. From the looks on the children's faces, I knew for a fact that laughter was its own kind of medicine. Being a good doctor didn't mean I had to forget all about being a clown. If I could combine my medical skills with the ability to make children laugh, I was certain it would make me an even better doctor."

"Of course, it would, Dr. Segal," Lenora admonished him. "I'm a kid and even I know that.

"I stand corrected, Miss DiTrapani," the doctor chuckled.

"Now, getting back to Mr. Kelly, when rounds were completed and it was time for him to leave, he swept off his hat, held it at his waist and bowed to me. Then ceremoniously he bent down and removed his red clown shoes. Holding the shoes out to me with his left hand, he touched his right hand to his heart then extended it to touch mine. No words were exchanged but none were needed. The shoes were a gift from the heart of one clown to another. It was one of the best days of my life and since that day, the red shoes are one of my most cherished possessions.

"And that's the end of my story, Lenora, and I thank you for being such a good audience. Now I'll let Nurse Catherine help you off the table."

Lenora viewed the good doctor with a look of confusion then amazement. "Dr. Segal, you told me that story so I didn't pay attention to what you were doing."

"That may be partially correct," the doctor admitted. "But I told you that story because it's true and I felt an overwhelming need to share it with you."

Lenora was contemplative for a brief moment then said, "Dr. Segal, do you know what?" "No, Lenora, I don't know what, but I'm sure you're going to tell me."

"Yes, I am," she said with a serious expression. "I'll bet God is very happy with you and He has a very special place waiting for you in Heaven."

The good doctor was taken aback by the words emanating from this pint-sized person. It was one of the few occasions he found himself at a loss for words. His face, however, did turn the same color as his distinctive shoes.

CHAPTER NINE

With the examination completed, Dr. Segal shepherded Lenora to the cafeteria to be reunited with her parents. His observant eyes registered the way in which the DiTrapanis' hands were protectively interlocked as he approached. It was a practice he would see repeated numerous times in the days ahead. Now as he drew nearer, the strained expressions on their faces became evident. He experienced a pang of guilt because he knew it would be necessary to extend their anxiety further. He empathetically addressed the couple.

"I'm returning our little lady to you for the time being, but I've scheduled a meeting in half an hour to go over Lenora's test results with my associates. Perhaps you'd like to grab an early lunch and meet me back in my office at 12:30 PM."

What Vinnie and Leo wanted were answers and their frustration showed.

"I'm sorry," Dr. Segal said earnestly, "but I make a practice of conferring with my colleagues before discussing any results with parents. If I may leave now, I'll be prepared for you at 12:30."

Vinnie and Leo sat numbly staring at the physician. Their daughter was the one to speak up. "It's okay for you to go, Dr. Segal. I'll make sure my parents are there on time."

When the meeting with his principal staff was completed, Dr. Segal sat at his desk reexamining his patient's test results. His forehead was furrowed in concentration and he had an all-too-familiar knot in the pit of his stomach. He reached for the telephone to dial Dr. Stevens, mindful that his elder colleague was anxiously awaiting the call. He dispensed with the social amenities when Dr. Stevens came on the line.

"Well, Aloysius, it seems our Lenora is in for one tough battle." The two doctors discussed their patient until Dr. Segal heard the intercom buzz on his desk. He knew the time was 12:30, even before his weary eyes sought the hands of the wall clock for confirmation. He met the DiTrapanis at the door and spoke to his secretary.

"Elizabeth, would be kind enough to take Lenora to the play area while I spend some time with her parents?"

"Of course, Dr. Segal. It will be my pleasure." The doctor escorted the couple into his office and asked them to be seated.

Dr. Segal was first and foremost a professional. He strode directly to his desk where he retrieved a long thin object. With the pointer firmly in hand, he approached the screen on the wall. With a flick of a switch, the x-rays of his young patient were illuminated. Only the minute pulsing in the doctor's right cheek belied his outward calm as he began his explanation of their medical findings.

"This is a picture of the interior of Lenora's right leg," he expounded, tapping the area with the pointer.

Vinnie and Leo's faces were matching portraits of confusion, their bewildered eyes intently viewing the contrasting print. They saw what resembled a giant octopus feasting on the knee, its greedy tentacles reaching out in every direction. Vinnie stiffened in her chair responding to the heightened state of alert her senses were now experiencing. She unconsciously bit her lower lip, her hand automatically increasing its grip on Leo's.

"The highlighted area represents a mass," Dr. Segal continued, "a diseased mass that has spread through most of the leg." Both parents sat in a stupor, their brains defensively refusing to interpret the doctor's words. Leo, laboring to form coherent syllables bellowed, "Mass... diseased mass...what on Earth does that mean?"

The prominent movement of the doctor's Adam's apple attested to the intensity of his swallow before he continued. He was a committed physician and felt a joyous satisfaction when his abilities enabled him to heal the children in his care. When the fates were unkind, in cases such as Lenora's, it never got any easier to be the bearer of catastrophic news. He knew there was no time left for treading water on this emotional sea. He took a deep breath and jumped in with both feet.

"This area," he pointed to the x-ray of the leg, "or mass as we call it, represents the perimeter of the area to which the diseased tissue has spread. There is no rhyme or reason to this affliction. We currently believe that an internal maturing cell or two within the knee went haywire at some unknown time causing an abnormal growth that multiplied itself repeatedly resulting in the extensive area we see on the screen. The name given this disease is osteogenic sarcoma and it primarily affects children and adolescents. I'm sorry, so extremely sorry to tell you Lenora has bone cancer."

Leo, nearly falling off his seat, felt like he had been sucker punched in the stomach. His faced turned crimson despite the fact the blow to his body had not been physical. Across from him, his wife eyes were possessed by fear. His face still vividly colored, Leo stammered, "I may not have a medical degree, Dr. Segal, but I do know that any diagnosis of cancer is the equivalent of a death sentence.

Dr. Segal, with his usually erect posture slumping several degrees forward, returned to his chair. He looked intently into Leo's eyes, then Vinnie's. "Right now, there is no known cure for the type of cancer your daughter has," he candidly answered.

A torrent of scalding waterworks streamed from Vinnie's eyes. It was becoming difficult for her to take a breath and an excruciating pain seized her chest. At first she thought it was a heart attack. That pain she would have found tolerable in comparison to having a child with an incurable disease. Only later would she realize what she had felt was the shattering of her heart.

Leo was oblivious to the tears coursing from his own stricken eyes. His stomach wanted to heave but he fought for control.

"Life is a precious commodity, Mr. and Mrs. DiTrapani," the doctor solemnly added, "and the life of a child the most precious of all. That's why I'm here, but I'm not going to lie to you and give you false hope. We've devised the only treatment plan plausible under these circumstances and that necessitates the immediate amputation of Lenora's right leg. In view of the extensive amount of diseased tissue, the incision will best be made directly below the hip. I'd like to schedule surgery for tomorrow morning. I think it's a good idea for her to remain at the hospital, starting this afternoon so I've arranged a room for her. Elizabeth will take her right from the play area.

Of course, you'll be allowed to visit her. She'll be here for a few weeks, but when she regains some of her strength, we'll follow up with a regiment of concentrated radium treatments in the hope of slowing down the cancer's progression. This disease is aggressive and will spread to other parts of her body."

Dr. Segal's voice faltered. "If there's a miracle in the offing, Lenora's life may be extended by another year. Perhaps two. Whatever the fates may have in store for your daughter, I give you my personal promise that we'll do everything medically and humanly possible to increase the length and quality of her life. The rest," he again paused, "is in God's hands."

Vinnie made a sound like a wounded animal. In response to his wife's guttural outcry, Leo was determined to ignore his own pain although his heart felt like it was being jabbed by a million tiny knives. He knelt protectively on the floor in front of Vinnie's chair.

At first she fought his attempts to hold her, beating her fists against his unprotected chest.

"No, Leo, no," she screamed. "This can't be happening. Why would God do this to us? Why would he do this to Lenora?"

Vinnie cries evolved into hysteria, the shaking of her body violent in its intensity. Dr. Segal swiftly summoned a nurse, requested a tranquilizer, and returned to Vinnie. His efforts to soothe the grieving mother were to no avail. When the nurse arrived, Vinnie forcefully pushed her away when she tried to swab Vinnie's arm with alcohol. The nurse and Leo were instructed by the doctor to "hold both of Mrs. DiTrapani's arms securely" while he administered the injection. He counted to ten, waiting for medication to take effect. He extended his hand to Leo and put several pills in his palm.

When the sedative took hold, Leo was able to take his wife into his arms. He methodically rocked her back and forth while their commingled sobs sliced through the inert air. Feeling like an intruder in their personal grief, Dr. Segal excused himself and he and the nurse left the room. Their departure went unnoticed.

CHAPTER TEN

Leo considered his options. He didn't have any. The next best course of action would be to take his wife back to the house. He requested a wheelchair to speed their exit, and another nurse helped him settle Vinnie into the padded seat.

"I'll help you take her out to the car," the concerned staff member volunteered.

Leo declined the offer and lowered his voice. "Please just tell Dr. Segal I'm taking my wife home and I'll return to the hospital as soon as possible. He'll understand."

The DiTrapanis were eerily silent during the ride. A pall had descended on them, sucking the oxygen out of the car. Leo concentrated only on the road before him. He was terrified of what would happen if his emotions were put into words. Vinnie, stared straight ahead, looking like a cement statue. When they arrived home, Leo assisted his wife inside the house with the sole intention of putting her directly to bed, but she vehemently refused.

"Do you really think I'm simply going to go to bed and forget the last few hours ever took place? It's not going happen, Leo, not in this lifetime."

"Then please at least sit on the couch for one second," he pleaded. He went into the kitchen for a glass of water and tried to coax her to take one of the pills Dr. Segal had given to him. Vinnie shook her head with childlike petulance and motioned for him to put the items in his hands on the coffee table.

"Honey, I'm going to call your mother to come stay with you while I go back to the hospital," he said not knowing what else to do.

"No, Leo. You'll do nothing of the kind. Let me be," she demanded. Her eyes met Leo's and her voice broke. The bravado was gone. "I can't face anyone right now....not even my mother."

"Are you sure you'll be okay?" he questioned with increasing worry.

"The only thing I know at this moment is that I'll never be okay again. Not for as long as I live."

Bereft of speech, Leo brushed away the droplets of tears trickling down his own cheeks. As he did so, he glimpsed his reflection in the mirror above the couch. The man he saw staring back at him was impotent, a man who could do nothing to help his wife and even less to help his daughter. Suddenly overcome with the desire to flee, he dropped a kiss on his wife's head, and bolted for the door. When he reached his car, his stomach heaved its churning contents.

Leo absently wiped his mouth with his handkerchief. He then numbly lowered himself into the driver's seat of the Nash and yielded to the emotions assaulting his body. He slammed his fist into the car's steering wheel repeatedly. Time and time again he yelled at the top of his lungs, "Why, God, why?"

Whether he did this for minutes or hours, Leo had no idea, but he could not bring himself to stop until the last reserve of strength ebbed from his body. When his emotions were finally spent, in a voice barely above a whisper he prayed like he had never prayed before in his life.... for his little girl...for his family...for himself... knowing that none of them could ever be the same again.

CHAPTER ELEVEN

After leaving the DiTrapanis in his office, Dr. Segal and Nurse Catherine met Lenora in the playroom. Their mood appeared cheerful, but that was solely for Lenora's benefit. The child didn't question the doctor when he told her she'd have to stay in the hospital; and she didn't look upset when he said Nurse Catherine would be bringing her upstairs to a special room. Lenora was more concerned about her parents and was informed with the greatest of care by Dr. Segal that her mother "was feeling a little under the weather" and he thought it best under the circumstances that she go home to rest.

"Doctor Segal," Lenora said, "if my mother isn't feeling well, why didn't she stay here with me? After all, it is a hospital and you could take care of both of us in my room."

"I actually entertained that exact idea," he chortled, "but this is a hospital for children and we wouldn't want to break the rules, would we?" Lenora's eyes lighted up and she giggled. She didn't say a word and didn't have to. Dr. Segal could easily read her impish mind.

After Nurse Catherine had settled Lenora in her room and left briefly, Lenora snuck out of bed and headed to the closet, where her dress was hanging. From its pocket, she pulled her small Communion prayer book and pale pink rosary beads. She bounded back in bed, forgetting all about her knee, and was painfully reminded when she landed knees first. She decided not to worry about it. After all, that was God's job. She lovingly hid her book and beads under the pillow.

When Catherine returned to Lenora's room, she was carrying crayons and blank sheets of paper to keep her patient occupied while she waited for her father's return. "Thank you," Lenora said to Nurse Catherine. "It's nice of you to share, so is it okay if I share something with you?"

"Of course," the nurse replied. "We're two peas in a pod, remember?"

Taking her Communion book out from under the pillow, she held it up for Catherine to see.

"It's beautiful and looks like you've been taking very good care it," her companion said.

"Oh, I do," Lenora, replied with the most serious of tones. "My mother told me I read it so much, I'm going to wear it out. That's why I'm very careful."

"She may be right," the nurse responded with a chuckle, but that chuckle soon turned into a frown. "Lenora, I do have some other children to see. Will you be alright if I leave you alone for a while?"

"Of course," Lenora said in a mature voice. "After all, I am eight and a half years old. Now if my six-year-old brother, Leonard, was here, I'd say leaving him alone wouldn't be a good idea."

Nurse Catherine couldn't help laughing. "I have a younger brother, too, and know exactly what you mean!"

CHAPTER TWELVE

Dr. Segal had left word with the staff to track him down the moment Leo returned from taking his wife home. Leo was only in his daughter's room five minutes when the doctor walked through the door. Lenora looked up from her bed and zeroed in on the doctor's hooded eyes.

Before the physician had an opportunity to say anything, she spoke up. "I'm very sick, Dr. Segal, aren't I?" she said as a matter of fact rather than as a question. He sat on the side of the bed and patted her hand. He looked up at Leo then brought his attention back to Lenora.

"You're a very perceptive girl, Lenora. Do you know what that means?"

"Yes, it's what my parents sometimes tell me. They say I may be too smart for my own good."

"I guess that's one way of putting it," he agreed. "Since you're certainly too smart for me, young lady, I'm not going to pretend that we're not facing a difficult road ahead. All the pictures we took tell us it's your leg that's very sick, and we have to do something about that right away. We have to perform a surgical procedure called an amputation, which means we have to take off your right leg."

First she looked at her father then back at the doctor. "You mean, you can just sorta unscrew it, and put in a brand new one that isn't sick?" she asked with rapt curiosity.

"I truly wish it was that simple," he answered with a heavy heart. He gently patted her hand again, knowing full well the amputation at the hip negated the possible use of any prosthesis. It was a subject he had yet to broach with the DiTrapanis.

Dr. Segal swallowed hard. Lenora could see his Adam's apple bob. "Tomorrow morning we're going to take you to a room that is as white as snow and put you into a deep sleep so you won't feel anything at all. You'll be just like Sleeping Beauty. When you wake up, your right leg will be gone, but we don't have another one to put in its place. I promise you, though, you're a very unique case and I intend to do the very best I can." Doctor Segal and Leo were both intently watching Lenora's face, afraid of what her reaction might be. Her response stunned them.

"Does my mother know about this?" she queried in such a challenging manner that both gentlemen were taken aback. She looked from the doctor to her father, who in turn stared at each other.

"I need to call her right now," Lenora demanded, but took pity on the perplexed young doctor and softened her tone. "You don't know my mother, Dr. Segal. She gets very upset and worries about things way too much. But maybe," she continued, "if I tell her myself that you're taking off my leg and you have to do that to make me better and I promise her I won't be afraid because you and God will be there, maybe she'll feel a little better."

Leo looked with utter amazement at his daughter and a lump the size of a boulder lodged in his throat. He tried to speak but she politely cut him off.

"Daddy, this is something I have to do myself, so please take me to a telephone so I can call Mommy." Wisely, neither of the men chose to argue. Dr. Segal went into the hallway and commandeered a wheelchair.

"I don't need that, Dr. Segal," she announced adamantly when the doctor returned with her transport. "I still have both my legs and want to walk on them, even if it's the last time."

"It's hospital rules," the doctor automatically countered, but when he saw the cloud of sadness darkening the little girl's face, his heart could not deny her.

"Okay, let's go, little lady. I won't tell if you won't." A satisfied gleam instantly displaced the gloom and a giggle escaped her lips as she zippered them with one fluid motion of her hand, then turned an imaginary key.

Chapter Thirteen

Vinnie had barely moved an inch since Leo left the house. She was prone on the couch staring at an infinitesimal crack in the ceiling. At first she chose to ignore the intrusive ringing of the phone beside her, but its summoning shrill persisted. When she picked up the black receiver from the end table, she was startled to hear her daughter's voice.

"Mommy, this is Lenora. I know you're not feeling well, but I have something very important to tell you," she said barely pausing to take a breath.

"Dr. Segal said my right leg is very sick and they have to take it off right away. So tomorrow morning they have to put me to sleep, and they're going to take it off. I asked if they had a new leg they could put on but Dr. Segal told me they don't. I know you would be a little happier if they did." Lenora could hear her mother gasp on the other end of the line.

"Mommy, please listen to me carefully. God and Dr. Segal will take care of everything, so I don't have to be afraid and you don't either. I love you, Mommy, and if you feel better tomorrow, please come to see me. But I'm probably not going to look the same without my leg, so promise me not to get upset."

"Oh, my sweet, sweet girl," Vinnie sobbed. "I promise I'll...I'll be there tomorrow. Remember I love you with all my heart."

When the phone line disconnected, Vinnie continued to hold the receiver in her hand. Dropping to her knees, she cradled the phone to her chest. That's how Leo found her when he returned two hours later. He took the phone from her hands and eased her back onto the couch. He then made three important calls. The first one was to Dr. Stevens, the second to Father Bellman, and the third to the Giamontes.

Later, at the hospital, Lenora lapsed into an uneasy sleep as fatigue warred with her desire to remain fully awake. She was restless and kept reaching down to stroke her right leg. It was a movement repeated numerous times, until a handsome figure with the most extraordinary gold-flecked blue eyes appeared in her dreams and clasped her tiny hand within his own.

CHAPTER FOURTEEN

Wednesday, January 5, 1955

Dr. Segal always made a point of seeing a patient's parents before he scrubbed for surgery. When he saw the DiTrapanis, they were speaking to a tall, slender gentleman in clerical clothes. They introduced the doctor to Father Bellman, who accompanied them that morning and would remain at the hospital for the duration of the surgery.

The priest requested a few minutes alone with Lenora before her parents went into her room. When he entered, he could see that the child looked like she had the weight of the world on her shoulders.

He knocked on the opened door. "Would you mind a visitor before your operation?" the clergyman asked.

"Of course not, Father Bellman," she said, sounding like and adult. "I was sitting here thinking about you and hoping you'd drop by. We need to talk."

"Then I'm very glad I came," he said, walking further into the room and pulling a chair next to the bed. "Would you like to talk about what's going to happen today with your leg? You know, I'm not here only as your family priest, but as your friend."

"Thank you, Father, but I don't think talking about my leg will do much good. Dr. Segal says it's really sick and has to come off, but that's not what I wanted to talk you about."

"Okay, Lenora. Then what's on your mind?"

"I was wondering if God is mad at me for asking him so many questions."

The priest was momentarily quiet. He then asked a question of his own. "Do your parents get mad at you for asking questions?"

"Not usually," she replied. "My mom says I'm inquisitive by nature and that's an important part of what makes me Lenora DiTrapani."

"Then what makes you think our Heavenly Father would be upset with you for something your parents readily accept?"

"It's just that He hasn't answered me, Father, and I've been talking and praying an awful lot. Do you think that's because I'm going to Heaven? Today I mean, and He'll talk to me later when I get there?"

"Lenora, there is one thing of which I am certain. God could never be mad at you. You are as important to Him as you are to your family and He will joyously throw open the gates of Heaven when it's time for you to be with Him. But He hasn't confided in me when that time will be. For this morning, I think perhaps we should simply pray together, and as God's humble servant, I will bless you in His name." He proceeded to anoint her with holy water.

"Thank you," she said when he was finished. "I knew I could count on you, but there's one more thing I need you to do."

"I'd be pleased do whatever you ask, Lenora."

"Good," she answered. "I want you to look after my parents while Dr. Segal is taking off my leg."

"You needn't have asked," the priest reassured her. "It was my intention to do that all along."

"I thought you would," she said, "but I had to make sure. Could I see them now?"

"But, of course. I know they're waiting right outside the door and are eager to be with you."

When the priest left the room, Vinnie and Leo only had a few minutes to spend with their daughter, which proved to be a good thing. They were holding on to their emotions by a bare thread. Neither one of them wanted that thread to snap in front of Lenora. They told her how much they loved her and would be at the hospital the entire time. Within a matter of minutes, two staff members came in to take Lenora to the surgical area.

When they wheeled Lenora into the operating room, she felt the sudden drop in temperature. It was considerably cooler here and she blinked at the stark brightness. Despite the funny-looking masks covering their faces, she recognized Dr. Segal and Nurse Catherine right away. They spoke soothingly to their young patient while they deftly hooked her to all kinds of machines.

As the anesthesia was administered, another doctor approached. The vivid blue eyes above his surgical mask instantly captured and held hers. "Lenora," Dr. Segal spoke up. "I'd like you meet Doctor Gabriel. You must have some important connections in some very high places, young lady, for Dr. Gabriel to have flown in this morning to observe."

Suddenly, time stood still for everyone else in the operating room. Each and every individual appeared in suspended animation.

"I'm so glad you're here, Gabriel. I was praying you'd come. I remember you told me in Texas that it's not your usual job to take people to Heaven, but are you here to take me to God?"

"Our Father has told me you've been full of questions, but that's one I can answer right away. When your time comes I will be honored to be your personal escort to Heaven, but today is not that day. In regard to your other questions, God sent me to tell you a story.

"The story starts a very long time ago with a girl named Mary. She loved our Lord with all her heart, in much the same way you do."

Lenora's eyes widened. "You're talking about the Virgin Mary, right Gabriel?"

"Yes, I am. But when God sent me to talk to her, she was but a young lady. I was dressed as an ordinary shepherd when I approached her, but like you, she spotted my wings right off. When I told her why I had come…that God had chosen her to be the mother of His only Son, she said there must be some mistake. She asked how could a simple mortal, one such as herself, be worthy of such an honor. I informed her that God did not make mistakes. He called few and even fewer were chosen. She was his choice.

"Then nine years ago, when God decreed that you would be born, he carefully chose the parents who would give life to you. You already know that God loves all his children, but his Son and you were born to be unique in totally different ways."

There was so much Lenora wanted to say…so many questions to ask, but she couldn't. Her lips, like her eyelids grew heavy. Everything in the bright room turned dark. Her body was wonderfully weightless. She felt like she was floating on a soft fluffy cloud. The only voice she could hear was Gabriel's as he continued speaking to her.

The nurse monitoring Lenora's vital signs noted an increase in blood pressure and pulse rate while her patient's heart pounded with excitement.

CHAPTER FIFTEEN

The January sun shone brightly on the windowsill of Lenora's room, but she was still in recovery, dozing on and off following the removal of her leg. Each time she awoke, she remained lucid for a longer period of time. Perhaps this was all a bad dream. But she was in an unfamiliar place and in a strange bed that had metal railings on each side. She lifted the sheet covering her body and reached for her right leg. The first thing she touched was the bandage covering her hip. When she extended her hand further, there was only empty space where the leg should have been. Her hand recoiled, as if touching a hot flame rather than the coolness of the sheet beneath her. After a few minutes, she decided to try it one more time. She closed her eyes and took a deep breath. Gingerly her fingers retraced their path to nothingness.

No, it was not a dream. Her leg was gone...forever. She allowed herself but a moment to mourn its loss. When her eyes closed, a single tear fell delicately down her cheek as she drifted back to sleep.

Gabriel reappeared at her bedside. He stroked the soft cheek and brushed the lone tear away with his fingertip. "You may not have your wings yet," he told the diminutive sleeping beauty, "but you're every inch an angel."

The next time Lenora awoke, she was back in her hospital room with her parents at her side. Their faces looked so strained, and their eyes displayed a bone-weary tiredness. She knew the missing leg was the source of their distress and she wanted to make everything better.

She smiled as she opened her eyes wide and yawned. "Hi, mommy and daddy. I've been awake a few times and already checked. My leg is gone. It's okay. Really it is. Gabriel told me God will be beside me every step of the way, whether I have two legs or just the one. I think we should be happy that God loves us so much."

Vinnie and Leo looked at one another. They both wanted to cry and wallow in those tears, but for Lenora's sake they did not.

Arrangements had been made for their son to stay at the Giamontes until Saturday. This at least allowed Vinnie the opportunity to lower her guard in the privacy of her home. Her world had spun out of control. She was too upset to contact anyone, including her family. That left the unpleasant task of communicating with family and friends to Mrs. Giamonte, who was barely hanging on to her own sanity.

As Lenora's grandmother, she had visibly aged since the little girl's diagnosis, but she took solace in pray and was determined to keep busy. Having to temporarily care for Leonard helped. The day after the operation, while he was at school, she made a list of names and wrote letters telling of the doctor's findings and Lenora's surgery. The communications resulted in novenas being said on the East and West Coasts and cities in between.

One of the many people she wrote to was Betty Steele. Since the DiTrapanis' move to California, her daughter had kept in close touch with the Steeles in Louisiana. They sent letters back and forth, and cards on notable occasions. In her last letter, Betty had written she was taking pottery classes and joined a thespian group on base. She was working hard on her stage presence and "corralling" her accent before performances.

When an envelope arrived, on Wednesday, January 12, for Betty with the Giamonte return address, she immediately became alarmed. The contents could not be good. The longer she held the white rectangle, the hotter it felt in her hand. With her heart pounding, she ripped it open to find her instincts had been correct. The news inside wasn't only bad, it was earth-shattering.

Betty was still sitting on the couch when Bobby came in from school. He could tell that something was wrong, but when he questioned his mother she said, "Honey, it's not somethin' for you to worry about." She didn't even tell her husband until Bobby was sound asleep and wouldn't be able to overhear their conversation.

Major Steele was equally stunned by the news. He'd been planning his retirement, but decided this was the impetus for them to finalize their plans to move out to California. Looking at the evident pain in Betty's eyes, he made a suggestion.

"I know you'd like to be with Vinnie right now. Why don't we fast-forward our plans and not wait until the summer. Talk to Bobby, and if he doesn't mind changing schools midyear, you two can make the trip out there now. Perhaps you can stay with the Giamontes or rent a furnished apartment. While you're there, you can look at houses and if you see something promising, put a deposit on it while I make permanent arrangements to get out there."

While Betty appeared to be quietly lost in thought, the major continued. "We won't, of course, be able to live in Hollywood with the movie stars, but something close to the DiTrapanis would suit me fine. Once you're out there, I can hire a moving company to do the bulk of the packing, but if you'd like to do a little organizing before you leave, that will make the transition easier."

Betty looked at her husband adoringly. "You always know what's in my heart, Robert," she said as she seated herself on her husband's lap. She deposited a lengthy kiss on his lips. "I'll talk to Bobby tomorrow and see if we can get this ball rolling."

The next morning at breakfast, Betty took her coffee cup and sat across from her son at the kitchen table. When he looked up into her serious eyes, he thought for sure he was in trouble.

"Did I do something wrong, Mom?" asked the eight-year-old, hoping it was only some minor infraction he was unknowingly guilty of. Bobby seldom gave the Steeles any trouble, but on occasions trouble had a way of finding him.

Under other circumstances, Betty would have enjoyed keeping him on the hook a little longer, but today she didn't want to play games. "No, sweetheart. You haven't done anythin' wrong but I do have somethin' important to discuss with you." Betty heard her accent heavily slipping back and took a deep breath.

In the meantime, Bobby had said, "Okay," still feeling an uneasiness in his stomach.

"You've heard your father and me talking about moving out to California to be near Leonard and Lenora?"

"Yeah, sure," he answered although he was far from sure what was coming next.

"Well, how would you feel about leaving in the next few days and finishing out the school year in California? You can pack what you need for now and Daddy will join us once he's taken care of everything here."

"What's the rush, Mom? What's happened? Did the Air Force fire Dad?"

Seeing the look on Bobby's face when he asked the last question, a part of her wanted to smile but couldn't.

"Yes, there is a rush. I'll explain to you why in a second, but please don't go around telling people Daddy got fired! He's retiring... there's a big difference."

Bobby said, "o-k-a-y," this time extending the word. He didn't see what the big deal was.

Now they were at the point Betty dreaded…how to explain what happened to Lenora. As soon as she said, "Lenora is in the hospital," Bobby's face turned deathly pale.

"Did she have an accident, like Leonard did and went to Texas? I had nothing to do with it, Mom, honest."

Betty wore her emotions on her sleeve. "Of course, you had nothin' to do with it, sugar. California is a long ways from here and I think it's about time you stopped feelin' guilty about Leonard's accident three and a half years ago. Whatever happens in our lives and those around us is part of God's plan. We may not understand why God does or doesn't do somethin', but He is the Almighty and we must trust in Him."

"Well then, did God make Lenora have an accident?"

"No, Bobby, there was no accident, but Lenora's right leg was very sick and they had to amputate it."

"What's amputate?" Bobby inquired with widening eyes. It didn't sound like a good thing.

Betty wanted to avoid being too descriptive so she answered in simple terms. "They had to cut off the leg."

"Holy mackerel," her son said. His green eyes were the size of 45 rpm records. "Did they cut it off with a knife?"

"Don't let that imagination of yours run wild," Betty instructed her son. "What happens in real life can be bad enough. But it's important that you understand the situation. Lenora will only have the use of one leg and she's goin' to need our help. So how do you feel about packin' up and headin' all the way to California now?"

"For Lenora I'd walk all the way to China," he replied.

A smile now made its way to Betty's lips and she hugged her son.

CHAPTER SIXTEEN

On Friday Betty placed a call to Mrs. Giamonte. With a two-hour time difference, she waited until her kitchen clock read 11:00 AM before picking up the phone and asking for the long distant operator.

In her acting group, Betty was learning proper diction; but since she was still a true southern gal, she had to allot time for prerequisite social pleasantries when Mrs. Giamonte came on the line. They exchanged "How are yous?" When Mrs. Giamonte replied "We're fine," they both knew that was far from the truth and that it was time to dispense with the small talk.

"Mrs. Giamonte," Betty hesitated "I'm callin' to tell ya I got your letter," she said with a voice filled with emotion. There's nothin' I can say to make the situation better, but there is somethin' I can do. We decided Bobby and I are comin' out to California as soon as we can. Robert will join us later. We're gonna be lookin' for a house and I hate to impose at a time like this, but can Bobby and I stay with you a day or two until we can make other arrangements?"

"Of course," Mrs. Giamonte replied. "Our door is always open to you."

"Now, if you don't mind tellin' me the truth, I'd really like to hear how our Lenora is copin' with all this," Betty asked.

"She hasn't been told the whole story," Mrs. Giamonte admitted, but she is doing remarkably well considering the circumstances. I wish I could say the same for her mother. I think you being here would make a world of difference to my daughter."

"Do they know how much longer she's going to be in the hospital?' Betty asked.

"Probably another ten days, if all continues to go well," was her reply.

"That's perfect," Betty said, making a mental list of things to do before they left. "We'll be out there before Lenora's homecoming," she promised, "and help any way we can."

"Good," Mrs. Giamonte said, sounding relieved. "This is the best news I've heard in a while. Do you want me to tell Vinnie or would you prefer to surprise her?"

"I'm guessin' we should surprise her, but I'll leave that up to you. I'll call you again when we finalize our plans. Talk to you soon."

"Yes, Betty, I'll talk to you soon," Mrs. Giamonte said, ending the conversation. She made the Sign of the Cross before hanging up the phone.

CHAPTER SEVENTEEN

With each new day, Lenora felt a little stronger. Nurse Catherine had brought in a pair of crutches and demonstrated their use. Lenora was told it would be a few more days before they let her up to practice with them. She asked to see them up close and ran her hand along the smooth length of the finished wood.

"Nurse Catherine," Lenora said with a question in her voice, "could you leave them by the bed? I think I have to get used to seeing them and so do my parents."

"I can do that," the nurse replied. "But you mustn't try to use them until you're ready."

"Don't worry," Lenora reassured her. "I won't".

The next morning, before Catherine was on duty, Lenora decided she was ready. She managed to sit up and wiggle her body to the side of the mattress. She positioned the crutches under her arms and pushed lightly off the bed. At first she was convinced she was going to fall, but kept her balance and actually took two tiny steps forward. With some difficulty, she reversed. She took one step toward the bed and slipped. The wooden apparatus fell to the floor, but Lenora landed on the bed. "This isn't going to be as easy as I first thought. Gabriel, please remind God to stay with me every step of the way because next time I might not be so lucky."

Only eight days after the operation, Lenora was proficient at using the crutches. Everyone marveled at the progress she had made, and so another visitor came to call.

Under normal circumstances, he didn't go near hospitals. He visited his brother's office within Children's now and then, but he never ventured beyond the cafeteria. If he traveled passed that boundary, what he referred to as "the hospital smell" assailed his senses and lingered in his nostrils for hours.

It was only because of his brother's constant talk about a particular patient named Lenora that he threw caution to the wind. He wanted to make the acquaintance of this child his brother was so enamored of.

He walked into her room wearing a fawn-colored suit that accentuated his brown hair and topaz eyes. He found her propped up against three pillows, writing on a heart she had cut out from green construction paper. A pair of crutches leaned against the bed.

Lenora looked up from her project when he entered.

"Dr. Segal, you look very handsome," she complimented. "But what happened to your white coat?" She then studied her visitor with increased curiosity. He started to speak but she interrupted with an astute grin. "You're not Dr. Segal! You're his brother, Joe."

"Guilty as charged, little miss, but I have a habit of introducing myself as the better-looking brother."

Lenora giggled. "You both look exactly the same, so how can you be better looking?" she asked, putting him on the spot.

"I'm only joking," he replied under her watchful gaze. "After all the things my brother James has told me about you, I'm not surprised you could tell the difference between us. Our mother is the record holder in that department, but I don't think she'd mind a little competition."

"I'm really glad you came to visit me, Joe," Lenora said earnestly, "but I thought you didn't like hospitals?"

"I don't," he replied, adding, "no way, no how!" with an exaggerated grimace. "Can't you see me turning a little green around the gills?"

"You're funny, just like Dr. Segal," Lenora commented.

"Well, it's easy for him to be funny. He walks around here in those big red shoes wearing a silly stethoscope for a necklace, and I have to wear a suit and tie to work."

"What kind of work do you do?" Lenora inquired.

"I'm a rare breed of lawyer who tries to stay out of courtrooms and hospitals. I work mostly for people in the entertainment business and I'm fortunate enough to have offices here and in New York."

"Well, then," she responded, "you might know my Uncle Victor. He's in show business and works with famous people with very strange names."

"Oh, really," Joe said. "It just so happens I have a few clients with really strange names. What's you uncle's last name? Perhaps I know of him."

Lenora answered, "Giamonte, like my grandparents. His name is Victor Giamonte."

"Who would have thought?" Joe said with genuine surprise. "Your uncle happens to be a client of mine and one of my favorite ones at that. I find this totally amazing. What a small world it is!"

"Yes, it is," Lenora agreed. "I know all about small worlds."

"If you don't mind," he said to Lenora, "may I stay and talk with you for a while?"

"Sure," she said enthusiastically. "I finished my heart so I have lots of time."

Joe pulled his chair closer to the bed. "Yes, I noticed you were working on something when I came through the door. Can I see what it is?"

"Originally, I wanted to make it on red paper," she informed him. "But Nurse Catherine only had green left so I guess that's okay.

I never saw a real heart so I don't know if they're really red. Green is a good color. Here's my heart," she said carefully handing him the piece of art.

He looked at the paper cutout expecting…well, he wasn't sure exactly what he was expecting, but he had to read the words several times. Neatly printed in pencil were the words, *"What shall I give to the Lord for all he has given me?"*

When Joe failed to utter any words, Lenora's brow wrinkled. "It's okay if you don't like it, really it is."

Joe shook his head. "It's not that, Lenora. I was speechless for a moment because it's the most beautiful heart I've ever seen. Did you get the words from somewhere?"

"Yes," Lenora answered. "They were in here." She said pointing to her own physical heart.

"May I ask you a personal question?" Joe inquired, leaning in closer. She nodded with approval for him to go on. "Less than two weeks ago, you had your leg taken off. Most people, whether adult or child, would be mad…very mad at God, but you sound like you want to thank Him."

"Oh, no. I couldn't ever be mad at God. What happens in our lives is all part of his great plan. Gabriel told me that. He's a real angel with wings and all. Do you believe in angels?" she asked, looking deeply into his eyes.

"I can't say that I did when I walked through your door, but if you're telling me they're real," he said not breaking eye contact, "I'm certainly inclined to believe you."

"Good," Lenora responded. "Now, if you're interested, I can tell you what Gabriel did in Texas. It's a really good story."

"I'm very interested," Joe replied without the slightest hesitation. He listened with rapt attention as he learned about her brother's accident, the trip to Texas, and the ever-resourceful Gabriel.

CHAPTER EIGHTEEN

For the DiTrapanis, their worries didn't end with Lenora, but extended to her brother. They were having a difficult time handling Leonard. He was upset because he hadn't seen his sister in almost two weeks. He was still terrified by the feeling in the pit of his stomach that she may not come back at all.

He demanded to know why, if it was a children's hospital, he couldn't visit his sister. "I'm six and a half and that makes me a kid, too. I bet if I prayed really hard to God, he'd send Gabriel to help sneak me in."

"There'll be no sneaking into any hospital," his parents scolded, but then felt sorry for the little guy. They had done their best to explain a situation that defied explanation, but at his tender age, no amount of lip service would suffice. He was mad at the world...his parents, Lenora and God.

He pictured his sister in his mind. He took a mental eraser and wiped away her right leg. He couldn't imagine how she would be able to run after him or play hide and seek. What about swimming in Mary Margaret's pool or Pop's Willow Lake? She had taken dance lessons at Mrs. Newman's, and she loved to dance. How could she dance on one leg?

One weekend afternoon, he had enough. He refused to cry in front of his parents, but stormed into his room and slammed the door. It wasn't acceptable behavior, but Vinnie and Leo decided it was best to let him be. When Vinnie listened at the door, she could hear him crying into his pillow.

The only being he wasn't mad at was Duchess. Every morning when Leonard awoke, he knew he'd find her sleeping in Lenora's bed. Sometimes during the night he would creep out of his room and lay in his sister's bed with his arms wrapped around the dog.

"You miss her, too, girl," he'd say, stroking the canine's head. "I think you're the only one who knows exactly how I feel. We both love her...a whole lot. It's not fair that she left us here to worry." Duchess would woof as if in agreement. If he felt the need to cry, Leonard didn't hesitate to wrap his arms around her and bury his face in her silky coat. He knew Duchess was silently crying with him.

Nearing their wits end, the DiTrapani's came up with an idea. Perhaps if Leonard was able to speak to his sister on the phone, he wouldn't be so miserable. Arrangements were made and a call was placed.

"Hi there, little brother," Lenora said from the phone on the nurse's desk. "I want you to stop giving Mommy and Daddy such a hard time."

At the sound of his sister's voice, he broke into tears of confusion, frustration, and finally relief.

"You have to calm down and be patient," she told him. "There's no need to be so upset."

"Lenora! This is so, so," he had difficulty finding the correct word. "This is so not fair," he finally blurted out. "I haven't seen you in such a long time and I was really worried sick."

"I know you were, but you don't have to be," his sister comforted him. "I'm able to get around on two sticks they call crutches, and if you behave, I'll let you try them out. And when my bandages get taken off, I'll show you where my leg used to be."

"Really?" he said, wiping his snuffles with the sleeve of his shirt.

"Really," she replied with a small smile crossing her lips.

"But when will you be coming home?" he asked, sadness again filling his voice.

"Dr. Segal says another week, maybe less." She heard a faint sigh from the other end of the phone. "I know it seems like a long time, but it's really not, Leonard. While you're waiting for me, you can draw me lots of pictures and I'll hang them in my room when I get there. Some of the kids from school made pictures and cards for me so I'll put everything up on the wall over my bed, alright?"

"Alright," he said, sounding somewhat mollified.

As soon as Leonard got off the phone, he ran into his room to start on the pictures. When the first one was complete, he stood on Lenora's bed and tacked it to the wall. It was a stick figure with only one leg. Underneath it said "LENORA" in block letters.

When Lenora had hung up the phone, Nurse Catherine was waiting for her. Today would be the first radiation treatment. Dr. Segal had explained that the machine was similar to an x-ray machine but much bigger and stronger. But like the x-rays she had previously, he promised her it wouldn't hurt.

Nurse Catherine wheeled Lenora into a room with a cot like bed. A machine extended over the bed like a giant arm and the child's eyes locked onto it.

"It may look a little scary," Catherine admitted, "but there's no need to be afraid. I'll help you up, and after that, it's easy. All you have to do is lie still. But I have to go behind that glass panel," she said pointing to the side of the room. "I'm going to stay there with the person working the machine and make sure they do a great job."

"That sounds like a good idea," Lenora told Catherine. She then closed her eyes tightly and laid as still as she could. Only when she heard his familiar voice did she open her eyes.

Gabriel looked a little different today. He wasn't dressed up like a regular person as he often was when he was around real people. His was beautifully attired all in white and his wings glowed like a rising sun. Today he wasn't a captain or a doctor. He was just the angel Gabriel.

"Is it time for me to go to Heaven now?" she asked him right off the bat. "You look like you're dressed for an assignment."

He laughed at her comment. "No, today is my day off. I was sitting around on a cloud counting sunbeams, but I decided to put my time to better use by coming down to keep you company. And since God didn't send me, the only journey you'll be making on this particular day is back to your room."

"I'm glad to see you, Gabriel. I could use the company, but I have another question."

"Don't you always have questions, Lenora?" he replied, looking more handsome than ever.

"Yes, I do, but I need you to be honest with me. Is this treatment going to help? When my mom and dad thought I was asleep, I heard them whispering about these treatments," she said looking up at the machine. "They said they'd gladly spend every last cent they had to try to make me better. But the truth is, I don't like this at all. It would be stupid to pay real dollars for something, especially if you don't like it, and it's not going to help anyway.

Gabriel couldn't help but grin. "Only you, Lenora, would ask an angel to be honest." She was going to say something, but Gabriel continued talking. "Your honest answer, Lenora, is no. Dr. Segal and your parents have vowed to do everything humanly possible to assist you, but these treatments won't hurt you nor will they help. If you don't want to continue, I know your parents won't insist. It has nothing to do with money, as they're willing to buy the sun, the moon, and the stars so you can stay with them as long as possible. They'll do anything to make you happy."

"Gabriel, you say silly things sometimes. People can't buy what's in the heavens. That all belongs to God and I don't think He'd put them up for sale. But I understand what you're trying to say. I don't want to do this. It doesn't feel right in my heart and my heart tells me not to do it again."

"You're one person in particular, Lenora, who should listen to what's inside of you. There are many times when God will speak to you through your heart rather than your ears." He looked up at the machine. The radioactive waves had been turned off and the machine was silent.

"You're done now, so I'll be on my way. Nurse Catherine will be coming for you in a minute so you won't be alone." He kissed her on the forehead and vanished into a white cloud. "Gabriel," she called after him, "thank you for spending your time off with me."

Nurse Catherine gently patted Lenora's shoulder. "You can open your eyes now," she said smiling down. "I'm glad you were relaxed enough to fall asleep, but I must tell you, you talk in your sleep. That must have been quite a dream you were having."

"Yes, it was," Lenora said beaming. "It certainly was."

CHAPTER NINETEEN

During visiting hours, Lenora did not lack company. There were many adults who loved and admired her, and they made a point of dropping by the hospital. The Sisters from St. Genevieve's came in small groups. Sister Bertrille was the one with the driver's license and thus the designated driver. She thought it lovely that whenever she got beyond the wheel, her fellow nuns took a moment to pray. Lenora, that dear child, she thought, could use all those prayers. But truth be told, the nuns were praying to St. Christopher for a safe round trip to the hospital. Someone in the car had a lead foot and it was none of the passengers.

For the nurses, it took a little getting used to seeing four or five ladies dressed in black habits passing them by. Nurse Catherine commented, "This brings me back to my days in parochial school, but I'm not sure if that's a good or bad thing. Let's suffice it to say I wasn't the quietest kid in class."

Mrs. Newman was also a frequent visitor, but today was Monday and she was paying a visit to Vinnie's mother. When Mrs. Giamonte answered the knock, she looked a little surprised to see Mrs. Newman at her door.

"Connie, if you're looking for Vincenza, I'm sorry, but she's not here. She should be at the house. She may not be answering the door, but feel free to go on in."

"I actually wanted to talk to you before I go over to the house," Mrs. Newman said with slight unease. There was obviously something on her mind.

"Of course, my dear, come in. My husband is out taking his daily walk so you can join me in the kitchen for a cup of tea." Mrs. Giamonte put on the kettle. "You can start whenever you like, Connie. I'm good at fiddling in the kitchen and listening at the same time."

"I have some news for the DiTrapanis, but considering all they've been through lately, I don't want to deliver what they may consider bad news. It's a terrible time to take Mary Margaret away from Lenora."

"What do you mean by take Mary Margaret away?"

"Well, we plan to be moving in the near future. Roger has been given the opportunity of opening an office in Beverly Hills. We plan to put our house on the market and look for something in that area. I don't know how much longer we'll be here."

"Try not to worry about it, Connie. It will be difficult on the girls at first, but they'll adjust like children do. And you really won't be that far away. When we finish our tea, would you like me to go with you to talk to Vincenza?"

"Yes, I'd appreciate that," she answered sounding a bit more relaxed. "But before we go, do you have a minute to tell me how Victor and Lu are doing? I haven't spoken to them since we were all here for the holiday."

"Of course," Mrs. Giamonte replied and chatted happily about her son and daughter-in-law.

Fifteen minutes later they arrived at the DiTrapanis, but no one answered the door, and when she turned the handle, Mrs. Giamonte discovered it was locked.

Inside, Vinnie was on the couch. She had been having difficulty sleeping at night and was resting while Leonard and Duchess played in the other room. "Hey, Mom," her son called, "I think there's someone at the front door." Vinnie sat up. She could now hear her mother's voice. "Vincenza, it's your mother. Why on earth is the door locked?" She didn't want to tell her mother she was trying to lock out the world. "Just give me a minute, Momma."

Vinnie rushed to the bathroom, splashed some cold water on her face and ran a comb through her mussed locks. Even with freshening up, she knew she still looked awful. Her eyes were perpetually red and swollen. She checked herself in the mirror but didn't recognize the person looking back at her.

When Vinnie got to the door, she expected to see her mother standing on the other side, but was startled to see Mrs. Newman there as well. They had talked many times at the hospital, but this was the first time Connie had come to the house since Lenora had been diagnosed.

"I'm sorry," Vinnie said opening the door wider, "I wasn't expecting company."

"Since when did Connie or I become company?" Mrs. Giamonte asked a bit gruffly. She looked at her daughter and instantly regretted the words. She already knew the answer to that question.

"Please excuse my lapse in manners," Vinnie apologized. "Of course you're always welcome. Would you like to have a seat in here or the kitchen?"

"I think here would be fine, dear," Mrs. Giamonte answered more softly, while seeking the comfort of a cushy side chair. Vinnie and Connie shared the couch.

Hearing voices, Leonard and Duchess stuck their heads in the room. "Oh, it's only Grandma and Mrs. Newman," he told the dog, sounding disappointed. They're probably gonna talk lady stuff so we're better off going back in my room." He made a U-turn with the dog on his heels.

There was a moment of awkward silence. Connie leaned toward Vinnie and patted her friend's hand.

"Vinnie, I don't want add to your burden, but I have some news I wanted to tell to you in person. Roger is relocating his business to Beverly Hills. He wants to live there as well, so we'll be putting our house up for sale. It's something he's been wanting and he may not get a second chance. I understand it's a terrible time to be separating the girls. It tears at my heart, but there's no reason their friendship has to end. For as long as Lenora is up to it, they can visit as often as they like."

"What did you tell Mary Margaret?" Vinnie asked, hoping her friend had used discretion.

"I've said little to Mary Margaret about Lenora's illness. She doesn't need to know all the details so I only explained what Mary Margaret would be able to see with her own eyes."

"How did she take it?" Vinnie asked.

"She didn't cry or get visibly upset. She was uncharacteristically subdued so I asked her what she was thinking. She said Lenora was her best friend. If she needed help walking, then she should be the one to help her."

Hearing that brought tears to Vinnie's eyes but a small smile framed her lips. "Well, thankfully this doesn't come as a complete shock. Roger has always had aspirations and worked very hard. I'm happy for you, but sad for us. You've been an important part of our lives since we moved to California. We're certainly going to miss you," Vinnie said with a sigh. "As far as the girls go, we'll just have to wait and see. I can't promise anything right now."

"We'll take it one day at a time," Connie said, putting her arm around Vinnie. "Please call if you need me. I'm still just down the block for now."

The ladies hugged and said their good-byes. When they got outside, Mrs. Giamonte addressed Mrs. Newman with a glint in her eyes. "Connie, I don't think it's going to be necessary to put your house up for sale. I may have the perfect buyer for your property."

CHAPTER TWENTY

Betty and Bobby took a bus from the airport to Children's Hospital on Monday, January 17. The Giamontes had offered to pick them up, but when Betty said they planned to go directly to the hospital, the Giamontes suggested meeting them there. The four of them could then travel back to the house together.

Bobby insisted on carrying the two fully-packed suitcases they had traveled with. He didn't make it far before admitting defeat, and handed one to his mother. Betty had broken the news to Bobby during the trip that hospital rules wouldn't allow him to visit Lenora in her room. He figured it was one of those stupid rules adults made when they didn't know better. Nonetheless, he decided to take a page from Lenora's book. He knew all too well that rules wouldn't stop her and he didn't intend to let them stop him either. He had already gleaned the room number and committed it to memory.

"Oh my goodness," Betty said when they were standing in the hospital lobby. "I should really bring a little gift up for Lenora from the both of us. And I've been so scatterbrained today, I left the bag with our toiletries in the bathroom at home. But I did notice a drug store right down the street. If you can wait here with the luggage, I should only be a few minutes Will you be okay?"

"Sure, Mom. You go ahead. I'm big enough to take care of myself," he told her with an air of confidence.

When Betty had gone, Bobby sat down and scanned the lobby area, planning how he would make his escape to Lenora's room. His first problem would be the luggage. He wouldn't make it unnoticed to the elevator if they saw a kid struggling with two suitcases. If he left the bags unattended, they might be stolen. He wasn't sure how trustworthy the residents of California were, and he didn't want to have to deal with the consequents if someone swiped their stuff.

His brain was working overtime when a young man in a white uniform approached. "Oh, no," Bobby said under his breath. He was sure he had already done something wrong and the jig was up.

"Hi, Bobby," the gentleman said, looking directly into the boy's eyes. Bobby had seen those eyes once before, but his memory wasn't working fast enough to retrieve the information.

"Do I know you, sir?" he asked.

"We did meet briefly four years ago, and it was at a hospital. I won't feel bad if you don't remember me."

"You were a captain then," Bobby said, recalling the scene at Brooke. Lenora had gone off with Gabe to see her brother, and Bobby was so nervous he almost peed himself. "You're the one who made her invisible and snuck her in to see Leonard."

"Well, let's just say I assisted in her quest."

"Lenora said you were an angel. I thought she was only pulling my leg, but if you weren't an angel, you wouldn't be here now, right?"

Gabe's smile warmed the boy to the cockles of his heart. "Let's talk about you," Gabe said, changing the subject. "If I'm not mistaken, you're here to see our mutual friend of whom we speak. Today, you're the one in need of my help. He walked a few steps to where a wheelchair waited and pushed it forward. "Have a seat," Gabe instructed, "and I'll take you up."

Bobby wanted to comply but looked with unease at the suitcases. "I can't leave them here. If my mother comes back and doesn't see me or the suitcases, I'm not gonna be allowed to leave the house until I'm a teenager."

"You don't have to worry, Bobby. I promise you and your luggage will be safe. Hop in."

"Why are we using a wheelchair?" Bobby asked as he sat down.

"Because it makes you look like one of the patients. And since I'm dressed like a staff member, it will be a piece of cake," Gabe replied.

"Okay, but we'd better get going before my mother gets back," Bobby warned. "Believe me, you wouldn't want to see her when she's mad."

With his passenger ready, Gabe pushed the chair ahead. Since no one was watching, he popped a wheelie into the waiting elevator. Bobby thought to himself, I could really get used to this angel stuff. Gabriel suppressed a laugh. Bobby obviously didn't realize angels could read minds.

When the conveyance doors opened, Gabe sedately pushed his new charge down the hall. A nurse looked up before they made the turn into Lenora's room. There was a question in her eyes.

"It's fine," Gabe told her. "Our patient here is leaving and wants to say a few parting words to Lenora."

"Go right ahead," she said pleasantly. It was always the greatest of days when a child got to go home.

Gabe pushed the apparatus into Lenora's room. When she looked up from a book she was reading, he announced, "I have a special delivery for Miss Lenora DiTrapani." To Bobby he whispered, "I'll knock on the door when you have to leave. I've delayed your mom a little bit, but you still don't have a lot of time."

A started Lenora flung the book with her right hand and it knocked over a glass of water. If she or her guest had been focused on the glass, they would have seen that it landed right-side-up and the liquid poured back in. Gabriel shut the door, tittering. He took pleasure in even the simplest things he could orchestrate.

In the room, Lenora and Bobby were focused only on each other. She threw off her bed sheet, grabbed her crutches, and moved toward her friend as though performing a little magic act of her own. They met each other halfway.

"Bobby Steele, what are you doing here?" she asked, her eyes twice their normal size.

"Well, Gabe sorta snuck me in," he replied.

"No, dummy," Lenora responded rolling her eyes. "I meant what are you doing in California? Gabriel didn't fly you all the from Louisiana, did he, cause your mom is going to be mad as Hades if you've gone missing."

"No, so don't have a canary, Lenora. My mom and I flew on an airplane and she's at the drugstore right now."

"How long can you stay?" she asked.

"Gabe said I only have a few minutes," he answered with a frown.

"Bobby Steele," she said wanting to place her hands on her hips, but was unable to. "I mean California! How long are you staying in town?"

"Well, if you're nice to me," he answered with a smirk, "I might stay forever."

At first she thought he was kidding, but read the truth in his eyes. She also saw something else there. He wanted to reach out and touch her, but he viewed the crutches as an obstacle.

Lenora could take care of that. "Wanna see what I can do?" she asked in the impish manner he recalled all too well.

"Sure, why not?" he agreed, thinking Gabe was only a few footsteps away in case this didn't go well.

To Bobby's amazement, Lenora dropped her crutches and pivoted on her left leg. "Ta-da!" she exclaimed.

Even with her bravado, he thought she might fall. It was as good an excuse as any for him to put his arms around her, which he did. Feeling the warmth of her in his arms, his heart skipped a beat. "Lenora, you're as crazy as a bedbug," he stated proudly.

"You've told me that before," she said beaming.

Gabe knocked on the door and came in. "I'm sorry, buddy, your time's up."

Bobby picked up Lenora's crutches and handed them to her. "I guess I have to go. Here's looking at you, kid," he said in a decent Humphrey Bogart impersonation. "I'll see you when you figure a way to break out of this place," he added, trying to keep a straight face.

"Don't worry," Gabe said to him. "She's working on that."

CHAPTER TWENTY-ONE

Lenora was released from the hospital on the late afternoon of Wednesday, January 19. Leo would pick her up at the hospital and bring her home to Vinnie, Leonard, and Duchess. A party was planned.

When they arrived at the house, Leo parked the car as close as he could. Lenora accepted her father's aid as she exited from the vehicle, but when she had her crutches placed securely under her arms, she politely refused his further assistance. "Daddy, thank you for your help, but I have to let Mommy see I can do this on my own. That's the only way she won't have a nervous breakdown."

Leo pushed the front door open for his daughter, then stood behind her as she maneuvered her way through the opening. She was barely over the threshold when her brother rushed to hug her around the waist. He nearly threw her off balance. "Whoa, cowboy, slow down those horses," his father said enjoying, the reunion, but prepared to catch Lenora if she fell. It seemed like a good ten minutes before Leonard released his sister. Duchess made herself next in line and Vinnie had to wait her turn.

The Giamontes came to the house an hour later. They wanted to give their granddaughter some time alone with her parents and a chance to acclimate herself to getting around the house on crutches.

It was a mere five minutes after their arrival that another knock was heard. Leonard, acting as doorman, went to see who it was.

When he saw the two familiar people standing on the porch, his eyes became the size of flying saucers. His mouth tried to form a few words but the only sound that came out was a croak.

Bobby Steele walked in, looking several heads taller than Leonard remembered. He was surprised he had to bend his neck slightly to look up at his old friend.

"You sound like a frog, short stuff. Guess the cat finally got your tongue," Bobby said, gently punching him in the arm. Leonard reciprocated the brotherly gesture. His face brightened with its first genuine smile since Lenora had gone to the hospital.

Betty followed in the path of her son. No one but Leonard showed any surprise at seeing the Steeles enter. Vinnie and Leo had known about the Steeles, but this reunion was bittersweet. They were excited to have the Steeles as their new neighbors on Sandusky, but sad the Newmans would no longer be a few doors away.

Lenora felt a pang in her chest when her mother told her about the Newmans moving. Mary Margaret was her best friend. She had made peace with losing her leg, but she didn't know if she could cope with losing both the leg and her best friend.

Bobby was reading those same thoughts now as she looked up at him. She was temporarily mesmerized when his eyes captured and caressed hers. The intense warmth that radiated from him banished all thoughts of Mary Margaret.

Lenora stood up on her crutches. They pretended it was the first time they'd seen one and another in years, although it had only been two days. They pulled it off so well, Bobby was thinking maybe his mother should take acting lessons from him.

Bobby's parents spoke by phone every few days. It would be another two weeks before Mr. Steele and the moving truck arrived in California. During their long-distance conversations, Bobby's parents debated whether he should attend the public or Catholic school. Arriving at a stalemate, they decided to give Bobby the tie-breaking vote. He took the matter seriously, weighing the pros and cons. Even though Lenora was quite taken with the sisters at St. Genevieve's, Bobby didn't share her enthusiasm for nuns in general. In the end, he made the decision to go to Beachy.

Leonard was in his glory. Every school had its playground bully and Leonard's short stature made him the perfect target. Of course, his occasionally overzealous mouth did get him into hot water, but that changed with Bobby's admittance to the elementary school. Bobby towered over the other boys on the playground, and all he had to do was scowl in their direction to send them scurrying away. Not that there weren't times when Leonard took advantage of his new situation. He would never be mean to another person, but he was mischievous. When he got out of hand, all Bobby had to do was threaten to tell Lenora.

CHAPTER TWENTY-TWO

Within days Lenora was able to get around the house without any significant problems. The next major hurdle for her would be going back to school.

Leo had been collecting Lenora's homework and returning it to St. Genevieve's when it was completed. He was just coming down the front steps of the school when he saw the monsignor approaching. "Mr. DiTrapani, I need to speak to you." Leo assumed the man garbed in black cassock and hat simply wanted to inquire about the well-being of his daughter. He couldn't have been more wrong.

"Mr. DiTrapani, future trips to the school will not be necessary."

"But I don't mind stopping by," Leo said innocently. "It isn't really an inconvenience."

"I'm not concerned about your inconvenience, young man. What I am concerned with is having a cripple at St. Genevieve's, and I will not allow it. Lenora will not be coming back here. I suggest you find a school somewhere that caters to her kind."

Leo stepped back as if fending off a physical blow. "I don't think I heard you correctly, monsignor."

"I think you heard me perfectly fine, Mr. DiTrapani," the older man replied.

It took only one second for Leo's blood pressure to rise above the danger level. His muscles tightened and his face turned crimson. He grabbed the man by his white collar, and lifted him until his heels no longer touched the pavement.

"You sanctimonious monster," Leo bellowed, shaking the clergyman until the old man's dentures rattled. Then suddenly Leo let go. But not out of remorse. He drew his right arm back intending to connect his clinched fist with the man's mouth, but another arm draped in black interceded and grabbed Leo's arm.

"That will be enough, Mr. DiTrapani," Sister Superior, the parish's Reverend Mother, ordered with undisputable authority. With a huff of indignation, the monsignor straightened his robe, regaining some of his composure and arrogance before the good sister's glacial stare froze him in place.

"As for you, Father," she added, dropping his honorary title. "I recommend you make a trip to my office post haste and wait for me there." The clergyman started to say something, but the nun gave him "the look" she had honed to perfection over decades of being a disciplinarian.

"Father, we can do this one of two ways. Either in the privacy of my office, or here in front of Mr. DiTrapani and the others of the parish who seem to be congregating on the sidewalk."

The monsignor looked around taking in the presence of several parishioners and passersby. They were eyeing him as though he were the bogey man. With his ego severely punctured and deflating rapidly, he did an abrupt about-face and marched toward the school's office, muttering under his breath. The Reverend Mother suspected he was not saying a string of Hail Marys.

When the monsignor was out of earshot, the nun addressed Leo in a softened voice. "First of all, Mr. DiTrapani, I want to make it perfectly clear that I do not condone violence in any form, but since I insist on being kept well-informed, I know what you and your family have been going through. Because of that, I will make this one exception for your unfortunate behavior."

Leo grudgingly accepted the chastisement, but would not atone for what he had done. "Reverend Mother, with all due respect, I won't apologize for my actions. If you had not intervened on the monsignor's behalf, I still wouldn't apologize for planting my fist in his face. You have no idea what the 'fine,' he spat the word out, "monsignor said about my daughter."

"I beg to differ, Mr. DiTrapani. I witnessed the entire altercation and heard every word spoken. My intercession was not for the monsignor's benefit, but for your own. You have not, to my knowledge, ever been a man of violence and I did not want you to start now. As for the monsignor, I can make no excuses for him accept to say that even ordained people of faith occasionally stray from the path of righteousness. They, in particular, need our prayers rather than our scorn.

"There is, however, one more thing I want to make perfectly clear to you and your family. While the monsignor may run the church, I alone run the school. My word there is final. I would also like to reiterate an undeniable fact. All of us here at St. Genevieve's have grown very fond of your Lenora. She has always been a dedicated child of God and it will be a privilege to once again have her in our presence. Whenever she is ready, we will welcome her with open arms and joyous hearts.

"Now, with all that being said, young man," the Reverend Mother paused for effect, "you may consider yourself dismissed. I have a matter to attend to in my office."

She turned and strode briskly away, but after traveling a few yards, her pace slowed and she glanced over her shoulder. A rare smile crossed her unadorned lips and reached her wise eyes. "There is one more thing, Mr. DiTrapani. I strongly recommend that neither you nor the monsignor miss confession on Saturday!"

CHAPTER TWENTY-THREE

February to July 1955

The long awaited day finally arrived. So much had changed in her young life in such a short period of time, that returning to St. Genevieve's in February brought Lenora unparalleled joy.

As the Reverend Mother had foretold, Lenora was welcomed back with open arms. There was a small fete and prayer thanking the Lord for bringing her safely back to the bosom of St. Genevieve's.

A few of the children may have looked askance at their returning classmate, but one glance from their teacher reminded them to be kind and understanding. Lenora laughed when Danny McDonald reached from his desk to pull her ponytail. As far a she was concerned, everything was back to normal.

Winter came and went. The flowers bloomed in spring and summer made its entrance on June 21, 1955. School was already closed for the remainder of June and July. Lenora missed being at St. Genevieve's, but this summer held the promise of adventure. She, Leonard and Bobby had dubbed themselves the Three Musketeers and adopted the original trio's motto of, "All for one and one for all." Duchess served as their mascot.

On occasions, Mary Margaret came to play. It was odd for her to visit her old house, which had taken on a definite southern flair now that the Steeles resided there. Betty had turned the dance studio into a pottery room. Her interest in the craft was relatively new and this space was perfect to refine her artistic skills.

Vinnie was terrified to let Lenora go in the pool, but swimming was second nature to the child. "Mommy, the water will hold me up and I'll be very careful until I'm sure of what I can do," Lenora pleaded with her mother. She was persistent in her efforts and it was a daily subject brought up at breakfast, lunch, and dinner. Vinnie's guilt over denying her daughter, what was once a simple pleasure weighed on her heart.

Vinnie conferred with Betty, who promised she'd watch Lenora with the eyes of a hawk and wouldn't tolerate any horsing around from the boys. The boys and their mothers were unnaturally quiet when Lenora made her first foray into the water. She could feel four pairs of eyes watching her every movement, but she had a plan. At the edge of the pool, she let her crutches fall to the side and dove in head first. Vinnie screamed and ran to the end of the pool. It was a shallow dive and Lenora shot to the surface, not giving her mother enough time to jump in after her.

"Mommy, I heard you scream before I even hit the water. You always tell me I'm a very smart girl so there comes a time, like now, when you have to have faith in me." She dove to the bottom of the pool and came up grinning. "See, Mommy, once a mermaid, always a mermaid. My leg may be gone but my gills work just fine."

The summer proved a wonderful time. The Three Musketeers were inseparable. When Lenora was in the water, she felt perfectly normal. Unfortunately, that wasn't exactly the case on dry land. Her friends at school had accepted her without reservation, but when she was in public, people sometimes looked at her strangely. She wondered if it was due to her age, since she had seen soldiers who had lost a limb on crutches or in wheelchairs. She hadn't heroically lost her leg in battle, but it had been a battle she had heroically fought.

In no time at all, Lenora was proficient at using the diving board. She'd put her left knee on the board and push up on her crutches with her arms. When she had her balance, she would let the crutches fall by the wayside, then she'd hop on her left leg to the end of the board. Gracefully, she would dive in.

With Lenora's progress, trips to Pop's Willow Lake were resumed. Although it was difficult to manage the crutches in the sand, Lenora became adept at getting from the beach to the water. After she waded into the water, she would hand off her crutches. The strength in her arms was increasing at a steady rate and she was able to use those appendages as well as her crutches to pull herself up when returning to the shoreline.

On her second trip to the lake, for the first time someone outwardly reacted negatively toward her. The woman, who had a face that could have stopped a clock, hollered as Lenora exited the water, "What in the world happened to your leg?" Rather than exhibiting real concern, the woman looked distastefully horrified.

Bobby had been the keeper of the crutches and automatically reacted. "Hey, look lady," he started to say, but Lenora cut him off. "I've got this, Bobby," she said with a smirk.

Lenora looked the woman straight in the eyes. "I can't believe you didn't see what happened," she said almost breathlessly. "I was doing my best breast stroke when I saw a huge shadow underneath me, but it wasn't simply a shadow, it was a great white shark with huge yellow teeth. I guess it was his lunchtime because he chomped off my right leg. You should have seen all the blood. It was gushing everywhere, making the lake look like the Red Sea.

"If I were you, I wouldn't go into the water above your ankles. My leg was small so I bet he's still hungry, and since your legs are bigger and extra plump, he would probably like them a lot better."

The woman's face contorted, making visible the monster within. She hastily pivoted and ran back to the blanket where her husband was catching some rays. "Harold, get our things. We've leaving this dreadful place and never coming back."

Bobby and Lenora laughed so hard they both fell down onto the sand. He said with great admiration, "I think you must've scared the living daylights out of that old battle axe!"

Bobby finally recovered and managed to get to his feet. He pulled Lenora up with him. "Let's go back in. I've never swam in the Red Sea before or gone shark fishing. Thanks to you, I can do both today." To her surprise, Bobby lifted her from the sand with the greatest of ease. When he was in water chin deep, he dumped her! She went under and didn't come up right away. He started to panic. Maybe dumping a girl with one leg wasn't the smartest idea he'd ever had. But the next thing he knew, something under the water was pulling his legs out from under him and his rump landed heavily on the lake floor. He should have known better. He never had and probably never would get the best of Lenora DiTrapani. He stood up with a swimsuit full of sand and a heart full of admiration.

Chapter Twenty-four

September 1955

Summer vacation came to an end. Lenora had turned nine in July and Leonard was seven. With school starting, it was time to shop for shoes. Vinnie and Leo decided to divide up the task. He would take Leonard and she would take Lenora. It was the first time they had done this since the operation. Her own sadness at the experience was something Vinnie would never forget. Lenora's handling of the situation was something she would always remember.

Vinnie took Lenora to the Buster Brown store. The salesman appeared perplexed and was unsure how to handle a situation that had never arisen before in his career of dealing with children.

An adorable youngster sat in front of him, but only one leg protruded from beneath her frilly dress. He guessed she was eight or nine. He would never ask about the circumstances that resulted in the loss of the leg of one so young, but from all outward appearances she looked healthy, so he feared she must have been the victim of some terrible accident.

Lenora could easily read the questions in his eyes. She was also able to read his name tag. "You don't have to worry about my missing leg, Mr. Curtis. It was very sick and they had to take it off. I can walk just fine with my crutches, but my left leg is getting a workout. We always buy shoes for the new school year, but this is the first time I had to buy only one shoe. Do you sell one shoe for children like me?"

"Well, young lady," the salesman said, taking a moment to think about her question. "I have to admit this the first time I've had anyone as pretty as you as come in needing only one shoe. But I'll measure your foot and find a shoe that's exactly the right size and to your liking."

He brought several boxes out, each containing one left shoe. She picked the one she liked and that fit the best. After the purchase was made, the salesman whispered to Vinnie, "What would you like me to do with the other shoe?" Vinnie wavered a moment too long. Lenora's sharp hearing had picked up the salesman's query, so she answered instead. "I can tell you what you should do, Mr. Curtis. Just put my new shoe in a bag and take the box back so you can put the right shoe in it. This way, if another girl comes in who only needs a right shoe, you can tell her you have the perfect one for her."

He hesitated for only a second. "I'll do exactly that," the salesman said, astounded by the maturity of Lenora's suggestion. Both ladies agreed that future visits to the shoe store would only be made when the kindly Mr. Curtis was on duty.

Chapter Twenty-five

December 1955 to September 1956

Fall quickly turned into winter. It was December 1, 1955, eleven months since Lenora's surgery. To everyone, it seemed like the nine-year old was on the road to recovery. She looked healthy and happiness followed her like a lovesick puppy.

She had been adamant about not continuing the radium treatments after the first, and that left her parents betwixt and between. They wanted what was best for their daughter, but didn't know which course was ultimately better. Anything that would prolong her life would be a godsend, but experimentation, at their daughter's expense, would not. After the operation, they had asked Dr. Stevens if he would do some research on the success rate of radium treatments. He agreed but was devastated to find few positive results.

Leonora persevered and finally both doctors and the DiTrapanis agreed. There was only one stipulation, and that required Lenora to go for x-rays once a month. After the first year, it would go to every other month if all went well. The pictures could be done with little inconvenience at Dr. Stevens' nearby office. That eliminated a trip to Children's Hospital and the results would be on Dr. Segal's desk the next day.

After months of good news, Vinnie and Leo allowed themselves to believe that God had answered their prayers. To them, their daughter was a miracle walking on crutches and about to celebrate another Christmas with them.

Vinnie and Leo had taken the kids to see Santa Claus as they did every year. Lenora decided this year she was too old to sit on Santa's lap. Leonard also had second thoughts. He was only two years younger than his sister, and if she was too old, maybe he was too old, too. Lenora was familiar with her brother's thought process and knew how to handle him. All she had to do was dare him.

There was one specific thing Lenora wanted, but didn't put it on her Christmas list because she knew it was a gift Santa couldn't deliver. The only one who could was God. During her prayers on Christmas Eve, she made up her mind to ask. "God, I'm sure you know what's on my mind because it's your job to know what's in my mind and in my heart. I think Mommy and Daddy should have another baby as soon as possible. A little girl will be perfect.

"Everyone says babies bring joy into the world. Of course, it's important for her to be real good and not cry a lot, otherwise the joy won't be as good. I'm not forgetting about Leonard. He's good at bringing joy when he wants to, but often he can be a handful. He always listens to me, so when I'm in Heaven, you'll need to help him listen to Mommy and Daddy. Plus, when he's a big brother, he'll need to understand it's an even bigger responsibility.

"I've already picked out a name. I hope that's okay with you. Her name will be Denise Jude DiTrapani. Denise is the only name that keeps coming back to my heart. Jude is for the saint my parents have been praying to since my leg got sick. They have a statue of him in their bedroom with a candle so he must be very important. They light the candle and pray to him at night when they think I'm asleep.

"I've asked Father Bellman about St. Jude and he told me he was one of the twelve apostles and may even have been a cousin to Jesus, like Carmine is a cousin to me. I bet St. Jude was a carpenter, too. Since Jesus was a carpenter, they probably had a family business just like the Ciones, but I don't know what their last name would have been. I'll have to ask Father Bellman if he knows."

The first time Vinnie got out the puke bucket, Lenora was thrilled. Not that she wanted to see her mom sick, but she understood what the bucket meant. She had no memory of her mother's pregnancy with Leonard, but she had heard tales about the P.B. Both she and Vinnie were relieved when the morning sickness proved not to be as bad as the earlier pregnancies.

It took six months for Leonard to ask his sister, "Why is mommy's stomach getting so big? She never eats a lot of food." Lenora tried to delicately explain that there was a baby inside, a baby girl, but Leonard couldn't get his head around that idea. His mind was on overload trying to figure out how a baby had gotten in there. Lenora finally said it was a seed growing into a baby and that made some sense to him. He could image his mother swallowing a seed since all kinds of fruits had them. If the seed was smart enough to go to her stomach and grow, that was all well and good.

The only person Lenora confided in about the origin of the baby was Father Bellman. She told him she had asked for the baby and why. He was never surprised by anything Lenora shared with him. It was easy to see, even if a person was blind, that Lenora had a unique relationship with the Almighty. A lesser man may have been jealous, but he was not.

Lenora had told her parents she planned to name the baby Denise Jude. At first they were merely entertained by her presumption, but she was so adamant for so long, they couldn't find a significant reason to name the new arrival anything else...unless, of course, it was a boy.

She and her brother stayed with their grandparents when it was time for the baby to be born. On September 20, 1956, an adorable girl poked her head into the world. When the nurse put her on the scale, the newborn weighed in a smidgen under ten pounds. It took a week before Vinnie and the new baby retuned home. Lenora was thrilled when she got her first look at the not-so-tiny bundle. The baby was so big and so cute, with a ringlet of golden curls. God had made her...she was perfect.

As the big sister, Lenora helped her mother with the baby whenever she wasn't at school, and perfected the art of balancing on her one leg so she could perform diaper duty. She would hold the two large diaper pins between her lips and could change the baby's cloth diapers in record time.

Leonard didn't mind holding the baby, but he didn't want any part of dirty diapers. He reasoned it was girl's work and so he had no responsibility to attend to the mess. No matter how cute he found his new little sister, he wouldn't admit that the smell of her diapers made him gag.

He took turns holding the baby in the rocking chair, but whenever Bobby showed up, he handed Denise off to Lenora and was out the door as quick as his television hero Flash Gordon. He was happy when the trio was together, but felt a bit more grown up when it was only the two boys traveling light years from 1956 to 3032. Often they donned costumes to make them look more like real members of Flash's Galactic Bureau of Investigation. Usually a discarded box served as their futuristic Skyflash craft. Bobby, being the elder of the two, was generally the pilot, but since his mother had taught him the golden rule of sharing, he did give his copilot, Leonard, turns at the imaginary controls.

CHAPTER TWENTY-SIX

September 1957

The earth quickly rotated and in what seemed like a blink of an eye, the calendar read September 1957. When it was time to go back to school again, Vinnie and Lenora made another trip to the Buster Brown store when Mr. Craig was on duty. This time, she needed shoes for school and for Sundays, and sneakers for play. He measured her foot, commenting that its growth was right on target. He again brought out only the left shoe. The new shoes went into a paper sack and Mr. Craig put their mates back in the boxes. He didn't have the heart to throw them away, so he stored them inconspicuously in the backroom.

Danny McDonald was again able to snag a seat assignment behind Lenora, and he managed to affectionately pull her ponytail at least once a day.

One day during lunch recess, they were side by side on the swings. Danny was industriously pumping his legs to soar as high as he could. Lenora used her upper-arm strength and left leg to gain momentum. "Hey, Lenora," he called to her as his swing flew back and forth. "There's a movie playing this Saturday at the Panorama Theater. It's my birthday, but I don't want any kid party. My Mom said I can take a friend to the movies and then to Hody's to get something to eat afterward. You wanna come with me?"

"Sure, I'd love to come," Lenora said, trying to contain her excitement, "but I'd have to get my parents' permission."

"Well," Danny said, "since our moms know each other, how about I have my mom ask your mom?"

"That sounds appropriate," Lenora agreed in a ladylike fashion. She took a sideways glance at the crutches leaning again the swing frame. She smiled all the way from the bottom of her left toes to the top of her of her golden head. Nothing had stopped her so far from living a normal life; and if she had her way, nothing ever would.

When Saturday came, Mrs. McDonald chauffeured the young couple. She was amazed at the maneuverability Lenora had on the crutches.

The movie was *Old Yeller*. The ending brought Lenora to tears. When she looked at Danny, she saw his eyes looked a little watery, but he was quick to wipe them with the back of his hand.

His mother drove them to the restaurant on Lankershim Boulevard in North Hollywood. Danny asked for a table instead of a booth. He thought a table might be easier for Lenora. She was surprised when Danny pulled her chair out for her. She had only seen that done in romantic movies. He also took the liberty of ordering cocktails…ginger ale with double cherries. Dinner was a gastronomic delight of fried chicken and all the accoutrements.

After dinner, Mrs. McDonald dropped Lenora at her house and Danny walked her to the door. When they said good-bye, a little awkwardness snuck in between them. Instinctively, Danny wanted to kiss Lenora on the cheek, but if his friends saw him, there would be no living it down. So he did what he had seen adults often do, and instead shook her hand. It was a vigorous shake which made Lenora laugh. "Are you trying to take my arm off? I already have just one leg. I'd be in a lot of trouble if I only had one arm, too."

Danny's face turned red and he promptly apologized, but Lenora didn't let him dangle in the wind. "It's okay, Danny. I was only teasing, but I want you to know I had a great time."

"Me, too," Danny admitted, while looking at his feet rather than at Lenora. "Well, I guess I'd better go," he said, glancing at his mother waiting in the car. When he started to walk away, Lenora called to him. "Danny, thank you. I'll never forget today. And the next time you want to kiss me, ask instead of nearly breaking my arm."

His smile was the size of a full moon. His feet may have walked but his heart skipped all the way to the car.

When Lenora went to bed that night, she wrote about her day's adventure in her diary. She was eleven years old and had had her first date. She felt all grown up when the realization sunk in. Even girls with two legs weren't going out with boys at her age. She fell asleep grinning ear to ear.

The other two Musketeers, however, challenged her euphoria the next day. Bobby was furious and Leonard didn't understand why his sister would go anywhere with anyone aside from him or Bobby.

"Why did you do a crazy thing like go to the movies with Danny McDonald?" Bobby demanded to know. "If I knew you wanted to go on a stupid date, I'd have taken you on one. You're my girl, Lenora, and I don't want you going out with anyone else."

Lenora looked like she was going to crown him with one of her crutches. This wasn't what he had expected, but in reality she was quite pleased. "First of all, Bobby Steele," she said, "I am my own girl and I'll do whatever I please. And if you keep acting like the rear end of donkey, I might even marry Danny McDonald when I'm older."

Bobby's face turned violet and it looked like steam was about to blow out of his ears. "Okay, Miss Smarty Pants. Have it your way. You never listened to me when we were kids and you don't listen to me now; but I'm telling you one thing, the only boy you'll be marrying is me!"

Thinking he had finally gotten the last word with Lenora, Bobby stormed off in a huff and Leonard quickly followed in his friend's wake.

"He'll get over it," Lenora yelled after her brother, but Lenora's stomach was doing its own little happy dance. She had not one but two young men vying for her affection. She had to be the luckiest girl in the world.

CHAPTER TWENTY-SEVEN

December 1957

With ten-year-old Lenora doing so well, the DiTrapanis were looking forward to a happy holiday season for their family of five.

The visits to Dr. Stevens' were still made every other month. He had allowed himself to be lulled into a false sense of optimism, until he saw the December x-rays. The cunning disease had reasserted itself and claimed Lenora's right lung.

Lenora could read Dr. Stevens like a book. "It's not good news this time, right, Dr. Stevens?"

"No, Lenora," he answered. He couldn't lie into those penetrating orbs, which appeared to be looking right through him like an x-ray machine. Betty had volunteered for the last few months to take Lenora to her appointment so Vinnie didn't have to take the baby out. "Since Mrs. Steele is here with you today, let's not say anything to upset her. I'm going to give Dr. Segal a call the minute you leave and see what we're going to do next. I'll ask him to phone your parents."

When he went into his office, Dr. Stevens felt like giving himself a swift kick in the rear. "There's no fool like an old fool," he lamented aloud. "Maybe it's time for me to retire." He was so absorbed in his thoughts, he hadn't heard his wife come into the office.

"Aloysius, dear," she said and he looked up from his desk. "You may be getting on in years, but no one in their right mind could ever accuse you of being a fool. The Good Lord will advise you when it's time to retire, but there may be some things He wants you to see through to the end."

He smiled up at her. "You're right, as usual, my dearest. I wouldn't have made it so far in my career without your vast wisdom and loving support. And those are exactly the two things I'm going to need an extra dose of today. After I get Dr. Segal on the line, I'm calling it a day. I'll be in shortly."

"Good," his wife replied. "I'll be waiting inside."

Dr. Stevens picked up the phone and dialed Dr. Segal. "James, it's Aloysius, he said with a tremor in his voice. "Today was Lenora's appointment."

"Yes, Elizabeth makes a practice of reminding me when the x-rays are being done. I was expecting to see the results on my desk tomorrow morning, but it sounds like you're about to tell me something I don't want to hear."

"Well, as you well know, next month marks two years since the amputation, and Lenora has been doing miraculously well. Considering the aggressive nature of the carcinoma, I expected to see something well before now, and allowed myself to entertain the possibility of remission."

"It wasn't only you, Aloysius," Dr. Segal empathized. "We've known the odds all along, and the staff here has been as optimistic as you. But let's get down to brass tacks. Where is the cancer now?"

"Centered in the right lung," Dr. Stevens answered, sounding even older than his years. "The DiTrapanis weren't with Lenora today, so I'm going to take advantage of our friendship and ask you to do the dirty work. Please call them and set up a time to talk to them. If you'd like, I can make myself available at the hospital during their appointment."

"That's not necessary, but I do appreciate the offer. What I think would be a better option would be for you to make a house call right after I see them."

"Of course. That's the least I can do," Dr. Stevens answered. "Our Lenora has already surmised the news isn't good. With Christmas right around the corner, this couldn't have come at a worse time."

"I'll take care of whatever I can, Aloysius," Dr. Segal replied with a soft sigh. "As men of medicine, we do what we can but God made us as human, too, and that gives us the ability to hope when our training tells us otherwise. As you can attest, it never gets any easier."

"No, it doesn't," Dr. Stevens agreed, "but I sincerely hope that by the time you're my age the only place cancer will be found is in medical journals listed as a disease that was conquered and obliterated from the earth"

"From your mouth, Aloysius, to God's ears." There was nothing left to say.

As promised, he made the phone call to the DiTrapanis. He tried not to alarm them, remembering full well Vinnie's breakdown on their first visit. He suggested they come in the next few days and said he'd be in office late if they wanted to wait until Leo's workday had ended.

Two days later, he had Vinnie and Leo wait in his office, and instructed Elizabeth to offer the couple refreshments and try to temporarily distract them while he examined Lenora.

As soon as he walked into the examination room, Lenora asked, "What's the bad news that Dr. Stevens saw on the x-ray? You're not wearing your red shoes so I don't know if that makes the bad news worse."

He hadn't given the shoes a second thought until she mentioned it. When he looked from his shoes to her, she could read the distress in his eyes.

"Dr. Segal," she said, "just spit it out. My friend Bobby says that's the best thing to do when you don't know how to say something. It sounds like a boy thing so it's fine with me if you really have to spit to do it."

"Okay, in this case, since I have your permission, I think I'll take your friend's advice." Lenora found herself slightly disappointed when he didn't actually spit, but he did get right to the point.

"The disease that was in your leg rested for a time after the amputation, but now it's wide awake and set up housekeeping in your right lung." He showed her a picture of the interior human anatomy and pointed to the colored lung area. "The next step won't be easy. You and your parents have to decide whether to leave the lung as is or remove it."

"I'm not a doctor like you and Dr. Stevens," she admitted, "but even I know you can't cut off a lung, because it's inside my body. How do you remove it and how will I breathe? God gave us two lungs for a reason…unless," she said thinking, "unless the reason is that one can be used as a spare, like the extra tire in the trunk of a car."

"Lenora, you never fail to amaze me. Are you sure you're only eleven?"

"I was born in July 1946 and it's December 1957 so the answer is I'm really eleven and a half."

"That explains it," he acknowledged, "but let's get back to the subject at hand." He pointed to an area on the diagram. "We'd would have to go into your chest here to make an opening to get to the lung. When we go into the chest cavity, we'd separate the lung from all the places it's attached, then sew everything up. God in his wisdom made it possible to live with just one lung. It has to work harder being the only one, but it can do the job."

"I sort of get the idea, but I have one big problem," Lenora informed the doctor. "You see, Mommy had the new baby last year in September and Denise is only going to be fifteen months old. I know God has plans for me, but I asked Him for the baby and He sent her to my family. I don't think he would give me the baby then take me to Heaven so soon."

"Unfortunately, I'm not privy to what plans God has for you… or any of us. If the sick lung stays in, the disease will grow faster. If we take it out, perhaps God will give you more time."

"I need more time," Lenora stated matter-of-factly. "I guess the next thing we have to do is tell Mommy and Daddy that my lung has to come out. It won't be easy."

"Lenora, I'm going to send you off with Nurse Catherine while I explain the situation to your parents. I'll let them know how you'd like to handle this."

"Are you sure you want to do it alone, Dr. Segal?" she asked worriedly. "I can guarantee my mother is going to be very upset and maybe I can help to calm her down."

"I certainly appreciate your offer, Lenora, but I think it's best if I do this alone. However, she's going to need your help when you go home, and I'm counting on you."

"You can depend on me," Lenora reassured him.

The surgery two days later was text-book perfect. Gabriel put in an appearance as an observing doctor as he had during the first operation. He and Dr. Segal shook hands before they scrubbed and entered the operating theater together.

Lenora smiled when she saw two of her favorite men beside her. Both looked handsome, even with the surgical masks, but Gabriel's eyes were riveting. "Don't fret, little one. I'm only here to keep an eye on you. Our Father understands you need more time."

CHAPTER TWENTY-EIGHT

When she awoke, she was in her room with her parents by her side. They looked as though they were the ones who had undergone surgery rather than her. Both appeared haggard and worry was etched all over their faces.

Lenora felt like a truck was parked on her chest, but didn't complain. "Hi," she whispered through dry lips. She sat up and reached for the water glass left by the bed. After several swallows, she found her voice. "Please don't look so upset. The lung is gone but I have more time. That's the important thing to me. I promise, I'll be up and around in no time. It's almost Christmas and it's time to think of Jesus, not ourselves."

Lenora was in the hospital for only ten days this time, but that didn't ease her brother's distress. Leonard stuck to Bobby like glue, and he was only appeased after the two of them were taken to the hospital and allowed to wait in the parking lot outside of Lenora's window. When the shade was pulled up, Lenora came in sight. She waved enthusiastically and threw a single kiss. Leonard was certain the kiss was for him. Bobby was hoping it wasn't.

With the holidays approaching rapidly, Betty and Bobby went Christmas shopping together. Their store of choice was F.W. Woolworth, where they could shop and have lunch at the store's soda fountain. Bobby made sure he pointed out the punching bag he wanted from Santa. The undefeated Rocky Marciano had replaced

Flash Gordon as his hero and he imagined having a heavyweight title of his own one day. Buying a gift for Leonard was easy since he was currently enamored with trains and baseball. He used an old mitt that was too small for Bobby so a new leather mitt would be the perfect gift. For Denise, they bought a yellow rattle in the shape of a bunny.

Betty was a little surprised when Bobby mentioned he had his own idea for Lenora's gift and he'd pay for it out of the money his grandparents in Boston had sent him. After lunch they went across the street to Quade's Jewelry Store. Artfully placed in the window display was a delicate cross attached to a gold chain. "This is what I picked out for Lenora," he said with great pride. "She's always sticking her rosary beads in her pocket so I wanted her to have a cross she can wear."

They walked into the store. Betty stayed in the background, allowing Bobby to make the transaction on his own. He told the saleslady what he wanted and his face flushed slightly when she said, "This must be for someone very important. Would you like me to wrap it for you?'

"Yes, please," he answered in the most grown-up voice he could muster. He pulled out nine one-dollar bills from his pocket and handed them to the lady. It took her only a few minutes to wrap the tiny box, which she put in a Quade's Christmas bag and handed to Bobby.

Lenora's surgery had left Vinnie and Leo with little desire to celebrate the holiday, but they decorated solely for the sake of the children. Jolly old St. Nick did make his annual stop at the house on Sandusky on Christmas Eve. Under the tree he left a fashionable poodle skirt and blouse for Lenora and several new cars for Leonard's Lionel train set. For the new baby there was a dress and matching bib.

The holiday was spent more sedately than previous ones. Lenora sat in the living room chair for a few hours while people came and went. For most of that time, she held the baby on her lap. Duchess laid by the side of the chair, content to be near Lenora.

Denise gave a slight yawn. "Mommy," Lenora said, "I think Denise needs a nap so I'll rest with her."

"You haven't eaten much today," Vinnie mentioned with concern, "and I'm sure the Steeles will be stopping by soon."

As if on cue, the Steeles knocked once and opened the door. Duchess remained by Lenora's side, but her tail was wagging to beat the band. Lenora liked to tease Bobby that Duchess had the biggest crush on him.

The Steeles brought a carved ham and placed it on the dining room table among a variety of delectable dishes. Vinnie took Denise from Lenora's arms and there was no further discussion of her resting with the baby.

Leonard opened his present and was thrilled. He put on the mitt and started pounding his fist into the leather to break it in. He was so busy he didn't see Bobby slip the box behind Lenora on the chair. "Open it later," he told her softly, not to be overheard. She tucked the gift into her dress pocket and sprinted with her crutches to her room the moment the Steeles were out the door.

Lenora's eager fingers made short work of the wrapping paper. When she lifted the cover, the cross sparkled on the black velvet like the magi in a midnight sky. Looking in the mirror, Lenora fastened the gold chain around her neck. Wherever it touched her skin, there was a gentle warmth that made her tingle. She vowed never to take it off.

When the Christmas break was over, Lenora returned to school. She looked no different on the outside when she came back to St. Genevieve's. The scar was well hidden under her uniform blouse. This time around, she wouldn't share her new scar with anyone but Mary Margaret, and when summer came, she wore a tee shirt under her bathing suit to hide the ugly marks left by the surgery.

Summer was the best season of all for Lenora. With the Steeles' pool and trips to Pop's Willow Lake, her days and her weekends were full. The Three Musketeers were usually found together, unless Mary Margaret came to visit. At least the boys were smart enough to go off on their own and leave the girls to do whatever girly stuff females did.

CHAPTER TWENTY-NINE

December 1958

For the DiTrapanis, time had taken flight landing them again in December. It was a month they had come to dread since in recent years, it had been the harbinger of bad news. December of 1958, was no different. It was then Lenora's headaches started, and at times the pain was excruciating.

Vinnie and Leo had taken one day at a time since the lung surgery last December, but hope sprang eternal. They wanted to believe the headaches were caused by eye strain since Lenora continuously had her head in a book.

The December x-rays showed cancer activity in the brain. Immediately Dr. Stevens made the agonizing call to Dr. Segal. "James, it's our Lenora," he said in a voice laden with defeat. "The headaches she's been having are a direct result of the cancer. It's metastasized to the cerebral hemispheres. There will be no reprieve this time. I fear there's not much time left."

Dr. Segal, replied with a heavy heart. "When we did the lung surgery, she asked me if it would give her more time because that was paramount to her. The last twelve months have gone by inordinately fast, but we should consider them a gift. We have to keep in mind that three years ago, when she first came to us, we had our doubts she'd make it to age nine, no less twelve.

"I'll look over the x-rays tomorrow," Dr. Segal went on, "but at this point, I'm sure your assessment is correct. Let's put her on something for the headaches, and we'll increase the pain medication as we go along. Does she know?" he asked, already surmising the answer.

"James, she knows a lot more than we do at this point. She asked me not tell anyone, but you and the family's priest until after Christmas. I'm not comfortable with that. She could very easily die at any time."

"Under normal circumstances," Dr. Segal said, "I'd agree with you wholeheartedly; but there's nothing normal about our Lenora. She and God have a very interesting relationship and if she wants us to wait until after Christmas, I think it should be her call. In her particular case, she really does know more than we mere mortals do. Let the family get through Christmas. I'll pay a visit to them on the twenty-sixth. There's no need for them to come to the hospital. Each of their visits to my office has put them through the ringer and I'd rather have this discussion with them in the privacy of their own home."

"I agree, but I'd like to be there," Dr. Stevens added.

"That was going to be my next suggestion," the young man confessed. "After all, the DiTrapanis are your patients, and I'm going to need all the help I can get. If you don't mind phoning them on Thursday to tell them you'll be stopping by around 7:00 PM, they won't be totally caught off guard. I'll park across the street and wait in my car until you get there."

"That's the least I can do, James. In the past, I've left the more unpleasant tasks to you, but now it's my turn.

Christmas was a good day for Lenora and her family. There were no headaches and no need for medication.

The morning after, Vinnie was, in fact, glad to hear Dr. Stevens's voice on the other end of her phone line. When Lenora got up for breakfast, she had some difficulty keeping her balance. He advised her to keep her daughter quiet for the remainder of the day and he would be by in the evening.

Lenora anticipated what was coming. Her temporary reprieve was over.

She asked Bobby to keep her brother occupied when the doctors came and she kept Denise in the bedroom with her. Father Bellman arrived soon after the doctors left. Vinnie had been sedated, but Leo refused any medicinal support. "I need my wits about me," he told Dr. Stevens with despair in his eyes. Only after everyone left did he allow himself time to surrender to his overwhelming despair.

That night, Lenora slept with both Leonard and Denise in her bed. Bobby and Duchess camped out on the floor. The kids thought it was some kind of party. Only Lenora and Duchess were the wiser.

CHAPTER THIRTY

January 1958

Since the doctors' visit to the house, twelve-year-old Lenora seldom left her bed. The disease had rapidly taken control over her body, but even with the headaches, she still possessed clarity of thought. The day after the New Year holiday Lenora had asked her brother to bring Bobby into her room. After her visit with Bobby, she would reluctantly remove his cross before the swelling of her body caused it to become imbedded in her skin.

Leonard did as his big sister asked, but his feelings got a little hurt when she asked him if she could have some time alone with Bobby.

Bobby was relieved to see her. "Lenora, I've missed you. It's not fun being the Three Musketeers when there's only the two of us," he complained.

"Well, that's what I wanted to talk to you about. From now on, it's only going to be the two of you," Lenora stated.

"No way," Bobby said. "It's all for one and one for all! When you're better, we'll be back together."

"Bobby, I'm not going to get better...not this time." Bobby wanted to get a word in but Lenora's stern expression froze him in place. "Please listen to me," she said, her eyes locking onto his. "This is very important and I'm counting on you." Bobby didn't move a muscle.

"I'm not sure how much time I have left, but I need you to take care of Leonard for me. He doesn't need to know how sick I really am, and I don't want him to find out. I need you to keep him occupied or at least make sure he's busy with some of the kids his own age. You have to keep his life as normal as possible, and that doesn't include worrying about me. And after I've gone to Heaven, he's going to need you even more."

"Lenora, you're completely off your rocker. You're not going anywhere," Bobby said, hoping that saying so would make it true.

She smiled at her friend. "Bobby, its God's plan."

Tears came to his eyes. He knew she was telling the truth and he could feel his heart starting to break.

"No!" Bobby shouted. "We're supposed to grow up together. When we're old enough, we're going to get married. I love you, Lenora. I always have."

"I love you, too, Bobby, but today is the last day I want you to come visit. My body is starting to change on the outside as well as the inside. I don't want you to see me when I'm really sick. I need you to remember me like I am, not what I'll be."

"You'll always be beautiful to me. I'll visit every day," Bobby promised.

"No, you won't!" she stated in a voice that sounded foreign to him. "I've never been more serious about anything in my entire life. Your job is to see to Leonard. The only people I'll let visit me besides my parents and grandparents will be Father Bellman and my doctors."

"Then I'll sneak in," Bobby challenged.

"Sorry, but Duchess has been told not to let you in my room. Right, girl?" The dog barked what sounded like a yes.

"But Duchess won't hurt me," Bobby said with an air of confidence. "She has a crush on me, remember?"

"Show him, girl," Lenora instructed the dog. Duchess jumped on all fours and growled at Bobby. It was the first time he noticed what big teeth the dog had, and Duchess's body language made her intentions perfectly clear.

"Okay, okay. Call her off. I get the message."

"Duchess, you can lie down now," Lenora said gently. The dog leaped on the bed and rested her head on Lenora.

"How can you do this to me, Lenora?" he questioned in a voice choked with a sob.

"I'm doing it because you're the best friend I've ever had and if I was going to grow up, I would definitely marry you...not Danny McDonald."

With that, Bobby almost smiled.

"Bobby, I'm sorry, but I'm very tired and need to rest for a while. But before you go, there's one last thing I need you to do. I've never had a real kiss from a boy. I'd like my first and only kiss to be from you."

He leaned over the bed and kissed Lenora on the lips. When she kissed him back it sent little shockwaves through his lanky body. She had felt it, too, and it caused both their hearts to skip a beat. "Thank you," she said and closed her eyes. A womanly smile spread across her face. Within a minute, she was sound asleep, but the smile lingered.

"Duchess, can I stay a little while longer?" he pleaded with the dog, who was no longer just a pet but Lenora's guardian. He was surprised when she woofed a yes. Letting the tears flow, he laid on the bed and held Lenora in his arms. Only once before had he momentarily embraced her when Gabriel snuck him into her hospital room. This would be the second and very last time he would hold the girl he had been in love with since he was five years old.

CHAPTER THIRTY-ONE

Father Bellman came to the house on January 3. He asked about the cross which was missing from her neck. He could easily see the filigree outline where it had been. "I took it off yesterday after Bobby left," she told him. "My neck got a little too big for it, but I found another perfect spot," she added triumphantly. She held up her left wrist, where she had twisted the chain in several circles to make it into a bracelet. "It's the only time I've taken it off, but it was just to move it. Do you think that counts?"

He knew of her promise never to take it off. "No," he replied with a reassuring smile. "I think you're good."

By the middle of January, the priest was coming to the house every day before Mass. It was often still dark and the home's occupants asleep when he arrived. A small lamp was kept on in the kitchen to provide a warm welcome as he came in through the unlocked door. His predilection for early morning coffee was a poorly kept secret so the percolator was on the stove ready to go. All he had to do was turn on the gas and strike a match. A china cup and sugar bowl were left on the counter for him. He preferred his coffee black, but Vinnie had told him the milk was in the refrigerator should he want a change of pace.

Lenora knew she had little time left and didn't want to waste it sleeping, so he usually found her awake. But if she felt the bone-tiredness setting in, she would write him a note about the topics she wanted to discuss at length and tuck it under the corner of her pillow. With that done, she would allow her eyes to close and succumb to the weariness.

Often during the night when she lay awake talking to God, he'd talk back. She was among the handful of people, since the beginning of time, that God had entrusted with his secrets, and her heart swelled with pride. Some of these discussions she would never divulge to another living soul. Others, He encouraged her to share with Father Bellman. At first the priest just listened carefully to whatever she had to say, but soon realized the growing depth of her knowledge. He began to take meticulous notes on every word emanating from her swollen lips. What he was learning from this child was more potent than his classes at seminary.

They talked about what God had planned for her. She said it was His surprise. The only hint given her was that it had do with children. Father Bellman said, "I believe with all my heart that it would be totally befitting if God made you the patron saint of sick children throughout the world."

Lenora smiled and touched the priest's hand. "Father, you know as well as I do that God doesn't canonize people for sainthood. It's something humans do for extra special people after they've gone to Heaven, and they are remembered forever. But sainthood is not given by God. It's only an earthly title given to people by other people."

"Well, Lenora, I think you're one of those extra special people and once you're in Heaven you should be remembered."

"Oh, but I will, Father. I will live on in the hearts of those who knew me, and many years from now, hundreds who didn't. God has that planned, too. And when I'm in Heaven, if people pray to me, I will listen to every word they say. If God gives me the power to help them, I promise to do just that."

"I know you will, Lenora. Of that, I am one hundred percent certain."

CHAPTER THIRTY-TWO

Each day it grew harder. A licensed practical nurse (LPN) was hired to come in two times daily to administer morphine injections, but they were no match against the disease. Weeks ago, Lenora had stopped looking in the mirror because she didn't recognize the person staring back at her. She looked pasty and there's wasn't a part of her that wasn't swollen.

Her two joys were her brother and sister. Leonard make a point of sticking his head in the door before school and after. Vinnie allowed Denise to play on the floor in Lenora's room. Considering she was a toddler, she was very well behaved. Each visit ended with Denise in the bed with Lenora and Duchess. With what little strength Lenora had left, she would manage to get her sister on the bed. On bad days, Duchess assisted by pushing the two-year old's rump up with her nose.

It had become more difficult to breathe. She was aware of the fact that her left lung had been doing double duty and was wearing out. Each breath was physically and mentally draining. She was waiting for God. He would be sending for her soon, but now she prayed he would hurry.

Duchess was her constant companion, and only left her bedside vigil when nature demanded. The canine would whine at the door to be let out, hurriedly take care of business, then return to Lenora's side. Vinnie and Leo tried coaxing the dog into the kitchen for meals. When that proved futile, Leo, as gently as possible, pulled the dog from the room, not releasing her until they were in front of her dish. Rather than looking at her food, Duchess turned her head in the direction of Lenora's room and howled.

"I give up," Leo said, raising his arms in defeat. He consulted with Dr. Stevens during one of his daily house calls. Although the doctor was not a veterinarian, Leo valued his opinion.

"It's obvious the dog sees herself as Lenora's protector and as such doesn't want to leave her side. Try making it easier for her," he advised. "Put the food and water dishes on the floor in the child's room where the dog can eat when she's hungry enough and still keep an eye on Lenora at the same time."

Duchess had demonstrated a protective posture on the LPN's first visit and barked at the woman in an unfriendly fashion. Lenora instructed the dog to sit, but Duchess chose to be disobedient. When Lenora explained to the canine that the nurse was only there to help, the dog visibly relaxed.

The little girl was especially pleased to see the nurse in the evenings. Since it was the last stop on her schedule, she made a habit of spending extra time at the DiTrapanis. She always arrived with the biggest of smiles and told Lenora interesting stories about her childhood in Alabama. She never let her patient see the tears that formed in her eyes when she was leaving.

Lenora waited patiently for Gabriel. He visited late each night since the morphine only induced a temporary state of sleep. The pain running helter-skelter throughout her body would soon awaken her. Often she'd lie there with her eyes closed because it took too much effort to open them. In the stillness of her room, the sound of Duchess's rapidly wagging tail announced his nocturnal arrival and she would open her eyes to the beauty that was Gabriel. He would take her hand in his and the pain would finally ease, enabling her to rest. Duchess would inch as close to Lenora as possible, until their bodies were touching, but the canine was careful not to put any weight on her mistress's frail body. Only when the dog heard the softened breath of Lenora in sleep would she allow herself the same luxury.

On the evening of Saturday, March 7, Lenora was wide awake and waiting for Gabriel. When he appeared at midnight, she felt a sense of relief tempered with sadness. "Gabriel, is tonight the night?" she asked hopefully.

"Yes, Lenora," he answered. "Tonight our Heavenly Father will bathe you in His Glory and welcome you home. Give me your hand."

Lenora took hold of Gabriel's outstretched hand and she rose from the infirm body on the bed. She stood before him healthy and whole. "Gabriel," she shouted, "my leg...my leg is back."

"Indeed, it is, my dear, so you can do this." Gabriel held her arm aloft and twirled her in a pirouette. Duchess softly woofed and stood on her hind legs, turning in circles mimicking Lenora. "Gabriel, I feel so... wonderful...so very happy. I can't even begin to explain it."

"I think I remember the feeling," he replied with a wide grin. "It's time for us to go, Lenora. They're waiting for us. There's to be a grand celebration tonight in your honor and then your job begins.

"What exactly is my job?" Lenora asked, jumping up and down on two legs, her pain-free eyes shining with excitement. The only thing you told me before is that it has to do with children."

"Yes, it certainly does," he confirmed. Looking directly at the shell of the child on the bed, he explained, "This terrible disease, this plague on earth they call cancer, is only in its beginning stages and will destroy countless lives. It will take mercy on no one, affecting adults and children alike. In His infinite wisdom, God has designated you to be His emissary for the children. You will be their shepherd and they your flock. He wants you to comfort them and reassure them that they have not been forsaken. If the time comes for them to leave this world, you will take their hands and escort them to Heaven, just like you and I will be doing tonight."

"But how can I possibly do that?" Lenora asked incredulously.

"Look in the mirror," Gabriel instructed. Lenora gasped as she took in the sight of the most delicate and beautiful wings, their edges dipped in gold that matched the color of her hair. "These are for me?" she asked in awe. Her hazel eyes sparkled to match the brilliance of her wings.

"Yep," he said, "special order from our Heavenly Father." He looked at her radiant face and asked, "Are you ready?"

"I think I was born ready, Gabriel." Lenora kneeled on the floor and hugged Duchess to her. "I love you, girl. You're the best dog in the whole world." Then she walked over to the bed and said good-bye to the physical remains of the child who had once been her. She stroked the pale limp hair and kissed the forehead that was still warm to the touch.

A beam of light appeared, illuminating the room. "Let's go," Gabriel said, his hand clasping Lenora's. Duchess excitedly tried to follow.

"I'm sorry, girl," Lenora said. "I really need you to stay here and take care of Mommy, Daddy, Leonard, and Denise. They're going to need you more now than ever." Duchess woofed what sounded like a sigh of resignation. The dog looked longingly as the brilliant light faded, then realized she still had a job to do. She jumped on the bed and took her place beside the silent body. She rested her head on the spot where Lenora's heart had pumped for the very last time.

In the other bedrooms, beams of light spread their rays over the sleeping occupants, delivering a gentle but lingering kiss of farewell. The beams were Lenora's first act as an angel. It would be the first of many.

CHAPTER THIRTY-THREE

The DiTrapani's phone rang Sunday morning at 6:00 AM. It was Father Bellman calling from the hospital. Vinnie had been up with the baby so she answered the phone.

"I'm sorry to call you so early on the weekend, Mrs. DiTrapani. Normally, at this hour, I've already been to your house and back. But a few hours ago the monsignor was taken to the hospital.

"Oh, my goodness," Vinnie said. "I hope he's alright."

"Thank you, yes. He's going to be okay. He suffered a mild heart attack and will be out of commission for a while. As soon as I finish things up here, I'll be around to see Lenora. Would you please apologize to her for my tardiness? She's probably worried because I'm so late."

"Of course, Father, but I have one question. Who will be saying Mass this morning?"

"Father Strickland has volunteered to fill in wherever needed so we're all set."

"That's good news," Vinnie said. "We'll see you later on." After hanging up the phone, she walked back to her bedroom with the baby.

"Who was that at this hour?" Leo asked his wife.

"It was Father Bellman. It seems the monsignor had a heart attack and is in the hospital."

"Couldn't have happened to a more deserving person," Leo remarked while turning his head into his pillow.

Vinnie couldn't make out his muffled words. "What did you say, honey?"

Leo lifted his head. "It was nothing worth repeating, sweetheart. Do you want me to check on Lenora?"

"Please, the baby is out of sorts this morning and I have yet to calm her down."

When Leo entered the room, Duchess didn't move. The first thing he noticed was the sorrow in the dog's eyes. His heart began to race. His daughter looked as though she were still sleeping, but there was an unusual sereneness about her face. Leo lightly shook her arm. There was no response. He tried again. Duchess whined, nudging his hand as if to say, "It's too late. She's already gone." Leo leaned over and kissed Lenora's forehead, but the warmth had left her body hours ago. Leo kissed her again and ran a trembling hand along her tranquil face. He then reverently kneeled on the floor beside the bed. With his head in his heads, he let the floodgates open. The grief flowed from the inner most parts of his being.

It was fifteen minutes before Vinnie was able to put the baby back in her crib. Then she went to see what was taking Leo so long. He looked up. When she saw his face, she knew the worst day of her life had arrived. She ran to the other side of the bed screaming. She raised her daughter from the bed trying to wake her.

"No, no," Vinnie kept saying as sobs emanating from deep within her body broke free. She grasped her little girl even tighter repeatedly kissing the golden hair.

If Leo had a choice, he would have preferred to simply lay down and die himself, but Vinnie needed him. He went around the bed and his arms encircled both his wife and daughter. He rocked them back and forth letting his own tears flow.

Duchess, with ears suddenly standing rigid, bounded from the bed, making a mad dash out the door. Coming down the hallway was Leonard, vigorously yawning. She barked at him with urgency, using her teeth to tug at his pajama sleeve. She physically pulled him toward the kitchen, almost ripping the sleeve in the process. "Boy, you must really have to pee bad, Duchess," he joked. "I'll put my bathrobe on and go out with you."

Leo, hearing the commotion, released the girls from his arms. He commanded his brain to work and was grateful when its wheels began turning. He went into the living room and picked up the phone to call the Steeles. When Mrs. Steele answered, he said, "Betty, I need you to come get Leonard right now. He's in the backyard with the dog and still in his pajamas. Please keep him at your house for the rest of the day and possibly overnight. I'll send some of his clothes over when I can."

No further words were needed. Betty's hands shook as she replaced the receiver.

Leo's next call was to Dr. Stevens. The doctor made it there in ten minutes. It was the first time the DiTrapanis had seen him with his hair uncombed or his mustache askew. He had hurriedly dressed, grabbing whatever clothes his hand touched, so he was almost unrecognizable except for his crop of white hair and the little black bag at his side.

His heart broke when he saw Vinnie sitting on the bed still holding her daughter. The first thing he took out of his doctor's bag was a sedative. Vinnie didn't even flinch when he injected the fluid into her body. He waited a minute then spoke to her softly.

"Vinnie, I'm so, so sorry. I can't help Lenora now, but I can help you. Please let me do that."

She looked at the doctor with vacant eyes. He gently pried Lenora from her arms and laid the little girl to rest. He then took Vinnie's arm and with Leo's help led her back to their room.

Dr. Stephens tucked her in and waited there until her eyes closed. He asked Leo to stay with her. He then returned to Lenora.

"Well, my child," he said, delicately taking her hand in his, "we're all going to miss your smiling face. In all my years, I have never had the privilege of meeting someone quite like you. God graced us with your presence for a very brief time on earth and now He will fulfill His eternal plans for you in Heaven. I look forward to seeing you again when it's my turn at the Pearly Gates. It wouldn't hurt if you put in a good word for me with the Almighty. Mere humans like me need all the help we can get." He wiped the tears away before he called Wagner's Funeral Home.

Father Bellman arrived after Wagner's had picked up Lenora. He walked in the door and was instantly assaulted by the gloom. He saw no one, and the hairs on the back of his neck stood on end. His heart told him that Lenora had taken her last breath. He raced to her room to find it empty. "Where is she?" he asked Leo gruffly when he returned to the kitchen and found Leo numbly sitting at the table.

"Where do you think she is?" Leo answered angrily. "Do you think she's running around outside on the two legs and lungs she was born with? No, of course, not. Thanks to our divine deity, she's at Wagner's." He spat out the words, venting some of his anger. Leo dropped his head onto the table and sobbed openly.

"I'm, sorry, Leo. I didn't mean for my question to come out like that." The priest walked over and put his hand on Leo's shoulder. "I think you and I should have a little talk about Lenora, and then I'll look in on your wife."

Vinnie was awake and rocking on her bed with Denise in her arms when Father Bellman knocked on the door. She didn't answer, so he knocked again and walked in.

"We knew this day was coming, but it doesn't make it any easier, does it?" he asked the woman whose face was ravaged by grief.

Vinnie simply shook her head no in response. She used one hand to push away the tears but they were rapidly replaced with new ones.

"Do you trust me, Vinnie?" the priest asked. Again she nodded, but this time in the affirmative. "I've already spoken to Leo. I'd like to attend to all the details concerning Lenora and I want to have her removed from the funeral parlor. She has been a rare child of God's since birth and she doesn't belong there."

Vinnie looked at him questioningly. "Then where?" she whimpered.

"God wants her in His house. I'm going to have her taken to the church tomorrow. With the monsignor's temporary incapacity, the Lord has opened new doors. Mary Immaculate will do something that it, or any other church, to my knowledge, has never done for a parishioner. Our Lenora will be laid in state. It's an honor reserved for dignitaries; but in Lenora's case, the honor will be all ours."

Chapter Thirty-four

Father Bellman stopped at the Giamontes on his way back to the church. He thought it best if he was the one to break the news to them. As soon as Mrs. Giamonte saw the priest on her doorstep, she knew her granddaughter was gone. He consoled them the best he could under the circumstances then took his leave.

When he arrived at the church, he called a meeting of all members of the parish council. In the interim, he had asked for Sister Superior. He had work for the sisters to do. He also made a long distance telephone call to a friend in Rome.

The men of the council arrived within the half hour. The priest had not called them together to ask for their permission. Instead, he was simply extending them the courtesy of knowing, beforehand, what his intensions were concerning Lenora. When several asked him, on whose authority he was doing this, he pointed to the ceiling. "The Big Man upstairs," he said with finality. "If you have any questions, take them up with Him. Our meeting is adjourned."

The sisters got a list of names from the Giamontes. With the help of other volunteers, phone calls were made and telegrams flew out of the Western Union office. An extra evening edition of the local newspaper went to press to inform citizens of Mary Immaculate's plans for Monday and Tuesday. For the first time anyone could remember, the doors of the church would be locked in preparation for a person of importance being laid in state. The funeral itself would take place on Tuesday at 11:00 AM. All the Masses scheduled for that morning were cancelled.

Aside from the newspaper notice and a special announcement on the radio, a sign was posted on the large oak doors of the church informing parishioners that after the 6:00 AM Mass Monday, the doors would be locked and would reopen at 10:00 AM for those wishing to pray their last respects.

*   *   *   *

While Vinnie and the baby dozed on and off, Leo went to talk to his son. Bobby and Leonard were in the Steeles' backyard making a Flash Gordon outpost where they could spend the night if they chose. Leonard ran to his father when he entered the yard. He knew something was terribly wrong, but Bobby had warned him not to let his imagination get the best of him.

Betty called Bobby into the house. If Leo was going to tell Leonard, now was the time for her to break the news to Bobby. She would have rather cut off her own finger than be the one to tell her son that his beloved Lenora had died.

Leo grabbed two milk boxes the boys were using and asked Leonard to have a seat next to him. The boy sat nervously on the edge of the crate. His stomach had been doing flip flops since Betty came to get him.

"I'm sorry we had to have Mrs. Steele come and get you this morning, but it was necessary," Leo informed his son. "When I went to Lenora's room this morning... she was gone."

"Gone? As in missing?" Leonard responded, his eyes narrowing with bewilderment as his heart forcefully resisted the news. Leo reached out and put his hand on Leonard's shoulder.

"I'm sorry son, but..."

Before Leo could finish, Leonard pulled away from his father's reach. With his voice growing more intense, Leonard probed further. "She was sick, where could she have gone?"

Leo titled his head downward, closed his eyes, and exhaled. He took one more deep breath, then looked up, locking eyes with Leonard, "Lenora died this morning."

Heated anger replaced bewilderment as the child's fists clinched and he abruptly stood. He stomped his foot and sent the crate behind him flying with swift kick.

"No!" Leonard screeched. Tears began to roll down his cheeks as he struggled to regain composure. "You're wrong! The nun at Sunday school told me that if I prayed for my sister, she'd get better. I prayed real hard every day waiting for her to get up and play with Bobby and me again."

Leonard stopped. He looked to his father, anticipating some sort of confirmation, but the expression in Leo's eyes communicated nothing of the sort.

"Look," the boy continued, "She's probably just sound asleep. Sometimes the medicine does that to her. I'm going now and proving you wrong." But before he could even take a step, Leo grabbed him by the left arm and pulled him back.

With his free right hand, Leonard took repeated swings at his father, smacking him against the chest. With each punch, Leonard shouted, "Let me go, Lenora needs me!"

Leo pulled Leonard in closer and wrapped his arms tightly around the boy until some of the fight went out of him. When it did, he desperately clung to his father and let the dam inside him break.

CHAPTER THIRTY-FIVE

Monday, before having the doors of Mary Immaculate opened to the public, Father Bellman thanked the Holy Father for moving heaven and earth to accomplish the impossible. The white casket from Wagner's was discreetly rolled in the side entrance and placed near the altar with room for passage on one side. A rope of burgundy velvet outlined the pathway. Two honor guards were present, watching over their charge. They would switch off with other volunteers during the next twenty-four hour period. Flowers seemed to sprout from the church floor and walls, transforming it into a Garden of Eden. There were white roses on the closed bottom portion of the casket. The top section was opened, revealing an angel clad in pink. Wagner's had done an amazing job.

The clergyman smiled when he saw the pink and white flower-halo placed around Lenora's head. It wasn't his doing, but he appreciated the thoughtfulness of another. Her small hands held her worn rosary beads. On her arm, a chain with a cross was hidden from view under the sleeve of her dress. Everything was perfect.

Word had spread like wildfire and a line starting forming as early as 8:00 AM. Once the doors were opened, hundreds of people walked along the burgundy rope and passed the child, who laid in graceful repose. Some reached out, wanting to simply touch her. Family members were told not to stand in line. They would be afforded private time whenever they chose.

Uncle Victor had fortuitously been in Los Angeles on business. He received word of his niece's passing during a rehearsal. Without a moment's hesitation, he made his apologies to his fellow entertainers and raced out the door. He mentally scolded himself for waiting. He should have made time to see her earlier and say a final good-bye before the light that was Lenora had dimmed.

Victor took one of the shifts at the altar on Monday. He was stunned when some of his friends from rehearsal and other entertainment people made their way along the rope. Lenora would have been so pleased that a lot of the people "with funny names" who her uncle worked with had made a special trip to see and honor her. People recognized the celebrities, but had the good sense not to ask for autographs.

On the way out, people were asked if they'd like to sign the Visitor's Book. The celebrities were pleased to add their names to the growing list. Wagner's had provided several books, but more were needed.

The inside traffic tapered now and again but the vigil continued through the night and wee hours of the morning.

At 10:00 AM Tuesday the viewing line and church were closed in preparation for the funeral service at 11:00. The church would reopen in forty-five minutes. The first four rows of seats were reserved for the family. It was impossible for any of the relatives from New York to get across country in such a short period of time, so they asked the priests in their local parishes to pray with them.

Adele didn't give two hoots about the time factor. She packed up the car with the kids and intended to make the trip across country despite all of Mike's sensible warnings to the contrary. In order to stop her from leaving, he had to physically position himself in front of the idling car. He stood there with his arms spread out and eyes closed, praying his wife would come to her senses, otherwise his fate was sealed. She finally relented and turned off the engine. She leaned against the steering wheel and wept. Mike took the kids into the house then came back outside. He took his wife in his arms and cried with her.

Chapter Thirty-six

At 10:55 AM Tuesday, Mary Immaculate was filled beyond capacity. People were standing in the aisles and doorways. Some had even taken seats in the confessionals, pulling the dark curtains open.

Vinnie and Leo were seated in the first row. Vinnie was moderately sedated or she wouldn't have been able to function at all. The families agreed it was best for Leonard and Bobby to remain at the Steeles. Leonard was having an awfully difficult time. Bobby was solemn but the younger boy was mad.

"I prayed like Sister said," he yelled at Bobby, "and look what happened." For both boys the pain was raw and deep. Bobby wanted to put his fist in that nun's mouth. He was twelve years old and had learned from Lenora that praying helped people in many circumstances, but it was up to God if and when those prayers were answered. No human being had the authority to make promises to others on the Lord's behalf. Bobby set up his punching bag in the yard and he and Leonard took turns pounding out their frustration and sorrow.

Mrs. Newman drove the short distance from Beverly Hills with her family. She asked to sing before and during the service. She was accompanied on the organ by Uncle Victor. Three choir members stood behind Connie as her chorus. The sound of people crying could be heard throughout the church. Some were relatively quiet in their grief while others' sobs echoed off the walls, but the strangest phenomena happened during the service. The four voices picked up by the microphone were multiplied tenfold. A melodious harp resonated within the church walls. People turned their heads to see where the other choir members were stationed, but not a soul was visible. Neither was a harp.

Father Bellman looked up. He was the only one looking in the right direction. "Thank you, God," he said with a heart bursting with joy. "I promise I'll remember this moment to my dying day. I will serve as your most humble servant with eternal gratitude for the gift of Lenora."

The priest had a lot of things to say to this congregation before him…none of which was written down on paper. His words were not merely a eulogy from the heart, but a celebration of Lenora's life on earth and her new eternal life in Heaven.

When the service was coming to its conclusion, he again looked up from his pulpit, taking in the sea of faces before him. "In my many years of conducting funerals, I normally ask for those in attendance to pray for the soul of the dearly departed. Today I cannot do that." Murmurs were heard throughout the pews.

The priest put up his hand and continued. "The little girl whose earthly body lies before us does not need you to pray for her because she is already seated at the right hand of God. Instead, we must pray to her, for she is the saint who walked among us on this earth and she is now the angel who will lovingly look down on us from the heavens. I ask you all to rejoice in God's name. Our Lenora is home."

CHAPTER THIRTY-SEVEN

Father Bellman's words had a profound effect on the community. Following the poignant service, people clamored for any object belonging to Lenora. If there was anything she had even touched, they wanted it. The police had escorted family members and their closest friends to the cemetery in Mission Hills, and dissuaded others from following. The interment was a private affair. Then again in the days following, many people made their own pilgrimage to Lenora's final resting place.

A week after Lenora's service, Mrs. Steele came in and helped pack up the child's belongings. Items of sentimental value were given to relatives, but her clothes were anonymously donated to avoid a frenzy. Other personal items, such as her Communion book, Bible, diary, and the green construction paper heart, were carefully packed with tissue paper and put in a box. The box was hidden away.

Despite the beautiful service delivered by Father Bellman, Vinnie's faith in God had been shaken to the core. With her daughter's death, she no longer saw God as a friend but as the enemy. She gathered all her treasured religious items, even the rosary blessed by the pope, and threw them in the trash with a "good riddance."

Leo faired only slightly better. He had written in his journal for the last time on that Sunday. He never wanted to open its pages again. Part of his heart didn't believe in God anymore… his faith ended with his daughter's last breath.

It was a day that was branded into their souls. Over a long period of time, the sorrow and pain would ebb, but like Lenora, it would never be forgotten.

October 2000 Las Vegas

As Vinnie sat in her chair, she felt what seemed to be a kiss on her forehead. She opened her eyes and was totally disoriented. She had been back in 1959 and the pain felt raw. She put her hands to her face and brushed away the tears. Through blurred vision she looked at her surroundings and realized it was not 1959 and she was not in California. It was the year 2000 and she was in her little house in Nevada, and both Lenora and Leo were gone.

She reached for a tissue and dabbed at her eyes. In her mind's eye she could see the hidden box with Lenora's remaining earthly possessions. She had put it safely in the car when she and her husband had moved to Nevada. It was the first thing she brought into their new house and she had tucked it securely away. Never had she opened it.

When she looked up, she physically jumped an inch off her seat and her heart pounded as if it might take flight out of her chest. Standing only inches in front of her, was a young girl. The girl's hair was the color of spun gold and her wings were the most extraordinary things Vinnie had ever seen. "Lenora?" Vinnie questioned with a quivering voice.

"Yes, Mommy, it's me," the angel in white said. "I can't stay long, but there are a few things you need to hear. I have tried to come to you in your dreams but it's difficult to get past the pain and guilt in your heart. It's been way too long. It's time to let the pain heal, and you must stop feeling guilty. You and Daddy did everything humanly possible to make me better, but my getting well was not part of God's plan. You may have wanted me here but God needed me in Heaven. He chose me and He doesn't make mistakes."

There was so much Vinnie wanted to say. So much she wanted to ask.

Lenora could easily read her mother's mind. She didn't have to be an angel to accomplish that feat.

"You want to ask me about Daddy," she said with the grin Vinnie so well remembered. "He's fine and misses you. I wish I could explain to you how Heaven really is. It's so far beyond anything an earthly person could comprehend or ever imagine. Someday, when you join us, you'll get to see it for yourself and understand exactly what I mean."

"When?" was the only word able to escape Vinnie's lips.

"Not for a long time yet," Lenora said with a smile. "You still have some work to do here. But when your time comes, Daddy and I will both come for you. It will be a day of great celebration. I can also share another little secret. Gabriel asked to be the gatekeeper when you arrive. He did the same thing for Daddy and that's a really big compliment. He says he has 'a soft spot' for all of us DiTrapanis.

"But there's something else you need to know. There's someone coming into your life. She is going to take a significant interest in our family, particularly in my life. I want you to take my box out of its hiding place and let her see and touch everything that's in it. My heart will speak to hers, and she has my permission to write my story and share it with the world."

Lenora kissed her mother for the second time that day. Vinnie reached out. Every day for the last forty-one years she had said, "If I could only hold my daughter just one more time, I'd never ask for anything else in my life." Today her wish came true. She was able to feel the pleasure and warmth of her daughter's solid embrace.

"Thank you, God," Vinnie said with tears of joy streaming down her face. "Thank you so very much."

"You're very welcome, Vincenza," a masculine voice resounded from the heavens. "But it's I who should be thanking you."

About the Author

The author is originally from Long Island, NY. From the age of eleven, writing was a hobby. Once in six grade, she did a book report on one of her own stories. But when she grew up and joined the corporate world, there was little time for writing.

When her children were born, she retired from business life to concentrate on raising her two sons. In 1994 seeking the therapeutic desert environment of Las Vegas, the family of four moved out west. It was there she meet a very special woman and was captivated by the story of this lady's family. It was a story she felt compelled to write and share with the world.

It took twelve years to complete this book. During that time, several serious detours took her from the project for extended periods of time, but her heart always led her back. A widow with grown sons, the author divides her time between Florida and Nevada. She lives with a very interesting feline, named Mr. Mitts, who has a few tales of his own to tell and plans on putting them in print.